THE DARKER THE NIGHT

A Note on the Author

Martin Patience was a BBC foreign correspondent for more than fifteen years with postings in Jerusalem, Kabul, Beijing, Lagos and Beirut. He covered wars and insurgencies in many countries as well as producing award-winning investigations into issues such as babies being sold online in China. He studied history at Glasgow University while working at several Scottish newspapers and, later, journalism at Columbia University in New York City. Martin currently lives in Washington, D.C. with his wife and son. He is a senior producer at NPR on the *Weekend Edition Show*. *The Darker the Night* is his first book.

THE DARKER THE NIGHT

Martin Patience

Polygon

First published in 2023 by Polygon,
an imprint of Birlinn Ltd.

Birlinn Ltd
West Newington House
10 Newington Road
Edinburgh
EH9 1QS

www.polygonbooks.co.uk

1

ISBN 978 1 84697 633 9

A catalogue record for this book is available on request
from the British Library.

Typeset by Initial Typesetting Services, Edinburgh

For Arpan and Ayan

A world without facts means a world without truth and trust.

— Maria Ressa, Nobel Peace Laureate (2021)

Chapter 1

It was well past dark but still an hour to midnight. The rain was hammering down. Yet the man remained standing under the soft glow of the streetlight as if he were an actor in a play. He was handsome, in his late fifties, the right side of six foot, with short, cropped black hair, greying at the temples. But there was an emptiness in his pale blue eyes that hinted at a loss that would never be reconciled.

He pulled up his sleeve to glance at his watch. It was almost time. He checked the small plastic bag in his pocket again, straightened the sprig of juniper that was pinned to the lapel of his black raincoat, and rocked on his heels until he heard the low thrum of a vehicle approaching. Surely, this was it. He steeled himself. But then a black taxi swung by, leaving only spray in its wake. He relaxed momentarily. 'The truth will never out,' he whispered under his breath. 'The darker the night, the brighter the stars, the deeper the grief . . .'

He bowed his head. He retained his faith that it would come and, in the end, it came quickly enough. The motorbike's roar cut through the howling wind before pulling up on the pavement opposite him. There were two men on the bike and they both looked over at him. He held up the plastic bag – it twisted furiously in the wind. The passenger swung his leg over the bike. He was dressed in black leathers, helmet on, visor down. He strode across the road, not bothering to check for approaching cars, and stopped in front of the man. He took the plastic bag. Without a word, he opened it, saw what he'd come for and stuffed it into his pocket.

The biker then took a step back and slowly unzipped his leather jacket. He pulled out a revolver, carefully wiped the rain off the barrel with his glove, and raised it with both hands until the gun was pointing squarely at the man's head.

The man flinched, his face contorted with fear. Three shots rang out.

Chapter 2

Fulton McKenzie ducked as the dirty, fat pigeon dive-bombed straight at his face only to suddenly swoop up over his head and away past the sullen sea of commuters spilling out of the train onto the platform behind him. He glanced right and was irritated to see a young boy, dressed in shorts and the fancy blazer of a well-known private school, stifling his giggles. Smug little prick, thought Fulton, trying to tear a strip off the boy with his stare. But as he looked away even Fulton couldn't suppress a wicked smile. What better way to brighten up Monday morning's march of misery than the thought of a pigeon smashing into someone's face?

Fulton ran his fingers through his black hair, so thick it consumed combs. His swarthy face was dominated by a nose that had been mashed by one too many punches. As he strode though the Central Station concourse in his smart linen jacket, fresh white shirt, black jeans and red Converse trainers, he tried to shake off the effects of a restless night. No change there: he hadn't slept well in years.

Outside the station, Fulton saw a row of black cabs on the rank. The drivers were all peering out from their windscreens scanning the crowd for their next fare. Diesel fumes scented the air. Should he head straight to the office? Or take a brief detour? As he ran through the choices in his head, Fulton watched as political activists – young enough to still believe in hope – ambushed commuters bursting out of the station. The volunteers were all brandishing leaflets – 'A Brighter Future: An Independent Scotland'. The big referendum that would decide the nation's fate was less than two weeks away. It was shaping up to be a real nail-biter. One of the activists caught Fulton's eye and approached him with the certainty of his cause.

'Just wondering if you could spare a minute to talk about independence?'

Fulton gave him the look – *I'm really not interested, pal, so don't piss me off* – and brushed past him as he marched away from the station in the direction of Bath Lane. He'd decided to check out last night's murder scene after all. Probably nothing to see, but you never know. He'd filed a short news story about it at midnight. A trusted police source had phoned to say a guy had got his brains blown out in the city centre.

Blue-and-white police tape was stretched across the entrance to Bath Lane. About ten metres away, Fulton could see a white tent close to an overflowing rubbish bin used by the nearby shops and restaurants. A couple of forensic officers, wearing white suits and paper shoes, were down on their knees taking samples. Fulton knew that the victim's body would have been removed in the early hours of the morning and the police would spend most of the day gathering evidence. Shootings weren't uncommon in Glasgow, but a fatal hit in the city centre was rare. The cops would likely be under a bit more scrutiny than usual.

A policeman standing just inside the tape gave Fulton a very bored once over. He was gangly and looked like he'd barely finished high school. The radio clipped to his chest was gabbling away.

'Morning, officer,' said Fulton, hoping to initiate a quick conversation that might glean a bit of information. Young cops with time to kill could be astonishingly indiscreet. Fulton was careful never to be duplicitous in his dealings, but it was advisable not to advertise the fact you were a journalist up front. It was guaranteed to shut someone up quicker than a smack to the face.

'Busy night?'

'Aye, you could say that.' The man yawned.

'What happened?'

'Some bloke got properly done over,' said the policeman, matter-of-factly, but warming to the attention. They really couldn't help themselves once you respected their uniformed status.

'Poor bugger. I'm guessing it was gang-related?'

'Aye, well, it's funny you say that. That's what we thought. Turns out it's different this time.'

Fulton felt a tiny shiver, the sensation he always got at the sniff of a story. He covered his mouth with his hand and stroked his stubble to buy himself a few seconds. For now, the cop had him pegged as a concerned member of the public. Fulton knew the next question would almost certainly blow his cover, unless the policeman proved to be particularly thick, but he had nothing to lose. 'How do you mean? If it's not gang-related, what is it then?'

The young cop's demeanour changed instantly. Fulton knew the oh-crap-my-job-might-be-at-stake look well.

'Too many questions. You a reporter?'

'Aye,' replied Fulton emphatically. 'Investigative reporter for the *Siren*.'

The cop gave him a dirty look. 'I shouldn't be talking to you,' he said. He unclipped his radio and held it up to his mouth as if he was going to bark an order. But, realising Fulton wouldn't buy the charade, he fired back. 'Why is your rag so against independence?'

'What's that got to do with anything? And it's not anti-independence,' said Fulton, riding a familiar riff but then thinking better of having an argument in public. 'Look, mate, I'll just be here for another minute or so and then I'll be on my way.'

'Aye, all right then,' said the policeman. 'But don't take too long.' He turned his back on Fulton and mumbled something into his radio. Typical polis, thought Fulton, always need to have the final word. He was about to remind the jumped-up copper that he was well within his rights to stay as long as he wanted so long as he was behind the police tape. But he took the charitable view; he had turned him over and got what he wanted. *It's different this time.* If that didn't smell like a story, thought Fulton, then what did? He looked up the lane and saw one of the forensic officers holding what appeared to be a bullet casing pinched between his fingers. He hollered to his colleague. They were too far away for Fulton to hear what they were saying, so there wasn't much point hanging about. He started walking away from the lane but in the end baiting the polis was just too much fun to let the chance pass by.

'Keep up the good work, officer,' said Fulton, with a nod in the cop's direction.

'Bugger off,' came the reply.

The *Scottish Siren*'s office was located on the second floor of a modern glass-fronted building in the heart of Glasgow. The bosses liked to say the architecture reflected the paper's commitment to transparency. It was this type of mumbo-jumbo that made Fulton despise the place even more. He'd spent almost two decades working his way to the top of an industry that was now crumbing beneath his feet. In the office there was an archipelago of desks, each cluster dedicated to a different section of the newspaper, no, the 'multi-media company', as the head honchos now insisted on calling it. A few of the crustier staff were waging a low-level insurgency against the new open-plan environment by piling newspapers, magazines and books on their desks like castle ramparts.

When Fulton entered the newsroom, he saw the editor standing with one hand on his hip and the other on the door-frame of his corner cubicle. He looked like a model posing as a deckhand on a yacht for some cheap catalogue. Christopher Bellington was tall, a good three inches taller than Fulton, and had floppy brown hair. He had been the editor for four years and, as far as Fulton was concerned, had sharply accelerated the newspaper's decline. Constant cuts meant fewer journalists and Chris was running an ever-tighter ship. He required his dwindling pool of reporters to rewrite press releases and provide colour and analysis – cheap and cheerful copy that filled up the newspaper and which they could slap on the insatiable website.

'You all right, Fulton?' Chris asked, a flash of concern sweeping across his face. 'You're looking a bit peely-wally.'

Peely-wally. It sounded patently absurd coming out of the mouth of an Englishman whose accent purred upper-middle class. Fulton didn't have a problem with English people, unlike a couple of his colleagues, but, if he was honest, posh *and* English tipped him over the edge. It was Chris's beige chinos, his gold pinky ring, the way he appropriated Scots words in a futile attempt to ingratiate himself. Bellington was a public-school boy and Oxbridge graduate whose path to Fleet Street had only been stymied by the fact that his Scottish wife refused to live in London. Everything about him made Fulton bristle.

'It's hard to switch off when you work till midnight.'

'Ah, yes, thank you for filing last night. It gave us a good splash for the morning but we need a follow-up. Do we have the name of the murder victim? Do we think this was run-of-the-mill stuff? Crooks knocking each other off? Or the start of a more worrying trend?'

Fulton stared blankly at the man for a few seconds. It was the usual editor's talk, he thought, all questions and no answers.

'I swung by the murder scene on the way to the office. It's why I'm late.'

'Okay.'

'And there's something unusual about the case. But you're going to need to give me a couple of hours to find out more. That all right?'

'Sure. But let us know if you've got anything to post for lunchtime. We need to drive a lot more traffic to the site and blood and guts make for good copy. People are sick to death of all the referendum stuff. Let me know if you need anything.'

Bellington ducked back into his office. Fulton wandered over to his own desk, his head throbbing with the editor's demands. He said a cursory good morning to a few of his colleagues. Mostly they were still waking up, or traumatised by the fact they might be pulled into the editor's office and sacked on the spot at any minute such was the state of Scottish journalism.

Fulton removed his rucksack and let it slide gently to the floor. He opened it up and pulled out a plastic container with rocket salad, Gorgonzola and walnuts that he'd prepared the night before. He placed it on the edge of his desk so he wouldn't forget to stick it in the office fridge. Below his computer monitor were a couple of photos: a school picture of his daughter, Alana, and one of his dad with a ciggie hanging out of his mouth at Shawfield Greyhound Stadium. Fulton reached across his desk to turn on the screen. But no matter how hard he pushed the button nothing happened. He was about to give the monitor an admonishing slap when he felt his phone vibrating in his pocket.

'Davy . . . How are you doing? Just give us a minute.'

Fulton tried to avoid speaking about anything remotely sensitive on the phone in front of colleagues. They may have looked comatose but any hack worth their salt would be eavesdropping. It would be a silly way to lose a scoop. Fulton made his way through the desks to the fire exit, pushed open the heavy door, and sat down at the top of the cold, concrete stairs.

'Sorry about that,' said Fulton. 'By the way, thanks a million for last night. Even Lord Snooty was pleased.'

Fulton knew it was immature but Chris was the closest thing he'd ever met to the top-hatted aristocrat who blessed the pages of the *Beano*.

'Well, you can tell his lordship there is even more,' replied Davy.

'What's that?'

'It's big – huge in fact. The guy shot dead last night wasn't a gangster.'

'Okey dokey,' said Fulton slowly, teasing out the delight of a revelation. 'If he wasn't a gangster, who was he, then?'

'Well – and you won't bloody believe this – we think he was actually a top civil servant.'

'Really?' said Fulton, letting out a low whistle that echoed round the stairwell. 'But who the hell knocks off an Edinburgh civil servant over here? Have you got the victim's name yet?'

'Aye, but look here, it's a wee bit sensitive. I'm in the office and can't talk at the moment – the gaffer's about. Why don't we meet at the usual place in a couple of hours?'

Chapter 3

The Empire Bar was the ideal pub for a discreet meeting as it was the kind of place most folk wouldn't be seen dead in. It boasted the cheapest pint in the city and for that reason it was the preserve of hardcore, heart attack-prone drinkers, alcoholic gargoyles who could be found sitting at or slumping over the bar depending on the time of day.

When Fulton walked in, a handful of regulars were busy lapping up the first pints of their daily session. He noticed the options on the specials' chalkboard hadn't changed since his last visit: 'Soup of the Day' or 'Lasagne' or 'Onion Rings'. Not that any of the regulars were interested in the food. They looked up at Fulton with yellow eyes, their tobacco-stained fingers grasping their drinks. One of them, a man with a burst sausage for a face, gave Fulton a brief nod of recognition. Fulton moved to the empty end of the bar and pulled out a stool. He kept a respectable distance from the cluster of regulars, although one of them didn't get the message. Sensing an opportunity, he broke away, hustling up to Fulton. The guy must have been in his late twenties – slicked-back hair, cheeks scarred by hideous acne. His denim jacket was bulging.

'How's it goin', big man?'

'Aye, fine. What you after?'

'I was wondering if I could interest you in a wee present for yer missus.'

He pulled out a handful of Swatch watches from the inside pocket of his jacket.

'It's all right, mate, I'm not interested,' said Fulton, pulling one of the tabloids lying on the bar towards him and flipping it over to read the back pages.

The guy wouldn't take no for an answer. He laid five of the watches on the bar and then with a salesman-like flourish draped one over his fist. The face was dotted with artificial crystals.

'Beautiful. In the same way I'm sure yer missus is beautiful.'

Fulton tapped his silver Celtic wedding band on the bar's wooden top.

'And imagine how happy she'll be when she sees this – a token of yer love.' The hustler grinned, revealing his badly stained teeth. 'It's normally about a hundred quid, but for a gent like yer good self, I can dae it for twenty.'

'Oi, Billy, whit have I told you!'

Both men looked up, startled, to see the barmaid storming out of the storeroom. Denise's normally pretty face was scrunched up in fury. She lifted up her hand as if she was about to either slap Billy or sweep his watches off the bar. He hurriedly grabbed his stash, stuffing it into his jacket.

'If you try and sell your knocked-off goods in here again, I'm going to have to call the polis. Have I made myself clear? I'm fed up with yer nonsense.'

'Sorry, doll,' mumbled Billy. He shuffled back to the other end of the bar, downed the remainder of his pint, and sloped out of the pub like a chastened schoolboy. Not one of the regulars looked up during the commotion.

'For God's sake,' said Denise, turning to Fulton. 'Every time I look away one of them is trying to flog something.'

She swept back a loose strand of auburn hair that had fallen over her brow and smiled at Fulton.

'How are you doing anyway, hon'? I've not seen you in a long time.'

'Been busy, very busy.'

'And how's that pal of yours, Davy?'

'You know . . . the same old Davy. He should be here in a few minutes.'

Denise's eyes lit up. 'What can I get you?'

'Just make it a Diet Coke.'

'A Diet Coke?' Denise's eyes widened with surprise. 'Oh, that's right, you're one of the rare yins in here that doesnae have a drink problem. Ice and lemon?'

'Please.'

Fulton watched as she scooped the ice out of a bucket and then wielded the soda gun to fill up the glass. She dropped a slice of lemon that had seen better days into the drink. Fulton pretended not to notice it.

'Here we go,' said Denise, planting the glass in front of him. She gave him a quick wink and nodded towards the regulars. 'You'll be safe. They'll think it's a whisky and Coke.'

Fulton gave her a wry smile and pulled a few coins from his pocket. Denise rang it up on the till and returned to the storeroom where she was working on the stock count. Fulton took a swig of his Coke. The ice clinked against his teeth and the bubbles fizzed up his nose. The sensation almost made him sneeze. The problem with not drinking alcohol while in the Empire was that you then experienced everything in real time. Fulton watched a chubby mechanic excavate his nose and then wipe the snot off onto his oil-streaked overalls. Another punter drank a couple of inches of his pint and then marched outside for a menthol cigarette. He did this three times, by which time he'd drained his pint and then, of course, ordered another one. The Empire was truly Glasgow's answer

13

to a euthanasia clinic. Fulton really didn't want to have to sit there much longer. Where the hell was Davy? Late as usual. Fulton had first met him on one of the city's brutal red ash pitches, where a slide tackle was enough to put you in hospital. Big Davy Bryant was the coach, pushing the teenagers to their absolute limits, especially if he suspected they'd been out on the bevvies the night before.

When Davy finally arrived at the Empire, the regulars, who normally only had eyes for their drinks, all looked up and gave him the nod. He possessed the swagger of an Oscar-winning movie star – the only difference being that he thought supermarket suits counted as designer and that strong, cheap aftershave was somehow sophisticated. Denise – who seconds before had been nowhere to be seen – emerged from the storeroom like an actor afraid of missing her stage call. Davy walked up to Fulton, slapped him on the back, apologised for being late, and then immediately turned to Denise who was cocking her head and gently stroking her hair.

'Hello, Denise. How's my darling today?'

'Just fine, Davy. All the better for seeing you.'

'If I had my way, I'd see that beautiful face of yours every day. How's that new fella of yours? I hope he's treating you like a princess. He's a lucky lad.'

'There's always room for improvement,' she said, with a giggle.

'Well, if you need me to speak to him, just give me the nod.'

She smiled demurely. 'I'll keep that in mind, Davy. Now, what can I get you?'

'Make it two pints of lager.'

'Eh, hang on a minute, Davy,' said Fulton, nursing his glass of Diet Coke. 'I'm fine for now.'

'What? You're not going to join me? C'mon, just the one.'

'All right,' said Fulton reluctantly. 'But any chance you could make it a gin and tonic?'

Davy pulled a face of mock disgust. 'Do you think they serve cocktails in here? Denise, just make it two pints of lager, will you – this one's forgetting where he is.'

Fulton didn't bother protesting further; it wasn't worth the aggro. When Coach wanted to drink – you drank. That was the time-honoured tradition.

'Keep the change, darling,' said Davy to Denise after she'd finished pulling the pints.

'Thanks, hon', and gie us a shout if you need anything.' She turned her back and started loading glasses into a dishwasher.

'She's a lovely lassie. I just wish I was twenty years younger,' whispered Davy to Fulton as they carried their pints to a corner table.

Fulton took a quick gulp of his lager. It set off a series of small explosions in his head like one of these cheap sherbet dips he'd loved as a kid, the ones that crackled over your tongue. By the second slug his head began to settle.

'Sweet Jesus, have I got something for you,' said Davy gleefully, before all of a sudden catching himself. He took a sip of his lager. It was almost if the alcohol tightened rather than loosened his tongue. He had on his serious face now. 'But we're going to need to be careful, very, very careful.'

Fulton was taken aback by Davy's cautious tone. His polis pal was normally boisterous about business – he was like a kid at the sweetie shop, he just couldn't help himself.

'C'mon, Davy, you know you can trust me. I've been more loyal than most of your wives.'

'All right, no need to get personal,' replied Davy, with half a smile, which quickly disappeared. Fulton gave him a few seconds before offering another gentle prod.

'So, what have you got for me? You've not pulled me out here to talk about your football team losing again at the weekend.'

'All guns blazing, I see. It's just—'

'Just what?'

'It's just this could blow up big style and I cannae have it coming back to me.'

'And since when did Detective Sergeant Bryant start giving a toss? Or do I need to record today's date for posterity?'

Davy gave him a dirty look and took another gulp of his lager. He made a show of straightening his shirt collar. Fulton realised the gentle ribbing was getting him nowhere.

'All right, Davy, I get it. I'll run everything by you before it goes to print. If I use anything it doesn't need to be a police source – just a source. I can live with that and get it by the boss. And if you change your mind, I'll ditch it. Does that work?'

'Aye, okay. Sorry, it's just … Ah, never mind.' He watched as Fulton pulled a black Moleskine notebook and a Bic pen out of his jacket pocket and laid them on the table. Old-school, as ever.

'So, what's the name of the guy who was killed?' asked Fulton. 'Who was he?'

'His name is John Millar.'

'Is that spelt with an *e* or an *a*?'

'A for Alpha.'

Fulton wrote the name in his notebook and underlined it. His handwriting was neat and tidy.

'He was fifty-nine,' said Davy. 'Worked for the Scottish Government in the department that deals with overseas investments. He was head of one of the sections, so pretty senior. As far as we can tell – and we're trying to get more info on this – he worked there for five years or so.'

Davy knew to pause while Fulton caught up with his note taking.

'Do you know what exactly he was doing? Was he a paper pusher, a bean counter?'

'A bit more interesting than that. We think he was doing some kind of oversight: background checks on firms wanting to invest in Scotland. He'd check to see if the money was clean, that sort of thing.'

Fulton licked his fingertips and flipped over the page in his notebook. He used his palm to smooth out a crease on the page. 'And any idea what he was doing before he was a civil servant?'

'Foreign Office. The boys are asking questions about what he was doing there but we've got nothing back. Feck, it's frustrating.' Davy picked up his pint and took another glug. 'I tell you, even when someone is shot dead in the city centre, you still need to jump through all these bureaucratic hoops – no sense of urgency – it drives me up the wall.'

'So, who do you think killed him? And why would anyone shoot dead a civil servant? It makes no sense.'

'We're checking the CCTV footage to see if we can get anything on the killers. But as for the motive . . .' Davy held up his hands and then slapped them on his thighs for dramatic effect. 'You tell me. Your guess is as good as mine. To be honest, we're all scratching our heads. I mean this is so out of the ordinary. Perhaps, he owed someone money. Maybe someone wanted him dead to pick up an inheritance. A family thing. I'm sure once we start digging around it will become clear. But at the moment, we've got nada.'

'Anything else I need to know?' asked Fulton. He looked

up at Davy who was draining his pint. Davy placed the empty glass back down on the table and stared vacantly out the window at passing cars.

'Davy,' said Fulton sharply. 'Is there anything else I need to know?'

Davy looked at him. He tapped his empty glass. 'Get me another pint first – it's your round.'

Fulton couldn't remember a time when Davy had acted so cagily. He caught Denise's eye, stuck up a finger and mouthed: 'One lager.' She pulled the pint and brought it over to their table. The pint foamed over the glass as she put it down, forcing Fulton to whip up his notebook before it was drenched. Denise ran to the bar, grabbed a rag, and cleaned up the mess.

'Sorry about that, guys.'

'Don't worry about it,' said Davy, with a wink. 'Happens to the best of us.' He took a sip from his lager and watched Denise sashay off. Davy lowered his voice. 'Look, Fulton, I've got to trust you on this one. It's actually way bigger than what I've just told you.'

'Davy, I've got your back. How long have you known me?'

Davy sighed. He glanced over both his shoulders to make sure nobody was within earshot. Apart from the usual crew, the Empire was empty. Davy pulled his chair closer to Fulton, leaned forward, and whispered into his ear.

'The victim had a number in his back pocket. It was written on a piece of paper – a mobile phone number.'

'And?' asked Fulton quietly.

'And I dialled it.'

'And who picked up?'

Davy pulled away from Fulton. His leg was jogging up and down. He took another slug of his pint before wiping his mouth with the back of his hand.

'C'mon, Davy, tell me who picked up,' said Fulton, a bit too loudly, drawing a filthy look from Davy.

'Jesus, mate, if you ever tell a soul I told you this, I'll break you in half,' said Davy, under his breath. 'This is career-ending stuff for me.'

'Davy, who picked up? Just tell me. Who picked up the call?'

'Ah, Jesus.'

'Davy?'

Davy picked up his pint and put it to his lips. But this time he didn't take a swig, instead putting it back down on the table. He glanced over his shoulders again, then leaned forward, cupping his hands round Fulton's ear.

'You're never going to believe this. It was the First Minister.'

Chapter 4

With two police outriders clearing the way, the maroon Toyota Prius was kicking up a jet of spray as it swept through the outskirts of Glasgow. In the back, sat the First Minister, Susan Ward, alongside her top advisor, Brian Mulvey. Susan's fair hair had been coiffed that morning by one of Edinburgh's top stylists, for a small king's ransom. He'd been sworn to secrecy that he'd ever set foot inside Bute House, as it would blow Susan's socialist credentials to smithereens. She flicked listlessly through a ten-page speech resting on her knee. The last few months of campaigning had been intense but in the final days her side was gaining momentum. Independence was now a real possibility and that piled yet more pressure on Susan. She knew the vote was hers to lose.

Susan sniffled and reached forward to pull a tissue from the seat pocket. Her immune system was shot and she was running a constant cold. She'd put on a bit of weight – no more than a couple of kilos – but some of the crueller magazines deemed it worthy of comment. She batted it off but no one likes being called fat in public. She'd lost her slim figure after the birth of her second child but knew she wouldn't win any favours pointing out the sexist hypocrisy. The subtext of the follow-up pieces would be: 'There goes that uppity First Minister, again.' Those dead set against breaking up the Union would beat her with any stick they could find.

'For God's sake, this pissing rain,' groaned Brian, using his sleeve to wipe away the condensation building on the window. 'You can't give one of your final speeches looking like a drowned rat. Whatever you do, make sure you don't get your hair wet. I checked with the Met Office yesterday and they said there was a twenty per cent chance of rain – this is like a tropical storm. How the hell could they have missed it?'

Susan had come up with the idea for the 'Countdown to Independence'. Every week in the final two months of campaigning she was to deliver a speech against a cinematic backdrop. Critics likened it to a tourist marketing campaign but that was the whole bloody point, thought Susan; people will take pride in the beauty of their country. The backdrop of Stirling Castle, located in the heart of Scotland, would serve as a fitting finale. It was close to the site of the Battle of Bannockburn, where the Scots had delivered a crushing defeat to the auld enemy in 1314, leading to independence from the English state. Brian at first complained that the campaign was complete and utter crap but after seeing that it was being hailed as a masterstroke by some in the media, he seamlessly swung behind it as if it had been his own idea all along.

'You got any questions about the speech?' he asked.

'No, I'm happy,' replied Susan, staring out the window.

'Good, because we can't afford any cock-ups.'

Susan shot him a look, eyes narrowed, lips pursed like she'd brushed up against a nettle.

'What, like the one on page eight when you confuse Gross National Product with Gross Domestic Product?'

'Must be a typo,' Brian mumbled defensively.

'Funny that, because you confuse those figures with

remarkable consistency – someone less charitable may conclude you don't know the difference.'

She turned away from him with a childish sense of satisfaction. Both of them were getting on each other's nerves more than ever before but in such an atmosphere it was to be expected. They both knew what was at stake – this was a once-in-a-lifetime opportunity. It wasn't a normal election where you could come back swinging five years later if you lost. This was a referendum where the rules were different. Any misstep would be magnified tenfold. A grim expression could be enough to swing a vote or two: the difference between success and failure; an independent Scotland versus a nation still shackled to the Union. Susan knew that a No vote this time would kill the independence question stonedead for a generation, perhaps longer. And as she looked out the window, field after field flashing by, she knew that yesterday's phone call could change the course of history.

It was just after eight in the morning. Susan Ward was sitting alone in a leather wingback chair in the drawing room of her official residence in Edinburgh glancing through the latest polls. Above her was the massive French chandelier that she always feared might come crashing down at any moment. She scolded her two girls when they threw paper airplanes at it. On the wall was a full-length portrait of John Stuart, the 3rd Earl of Bute and the first Scotsman to be British Prime Minister.

Her mobile started ringing: a withheld number. Only a handful of people had this number – her husband, her mother, the kids and a few senior politicians, including the Prime Minister. Perhaps it was him, she thought, although he normally scheduled a call.

'Good morning.'

'Good morning, this is Detective Sergeant David Bryant from Police Scotland. Who am I speaking to?'

Susan paused. What was this all about? 'This is the First Minister, Susan Ward. Good to hear from you, officer. But just wondering if you've got a wrong number? Were you after me or someone else?'

Davy's turn to hesitate. What the hell? Is this a wind-up? But it definitely sounded like her. How do you address the First Minister? He switched to what he thought was a posher telephone voice.

'Eh, well, you see, ma'am, I've been given a number and told to dial it and, well, you see . . .'

'Can you please explain what this is all about,' asked Susan curtly. 'As I'm sure you're aware, I'm pretty busy at the moment. And, please, there's no need to call me ma'am.'

'Yes, ma'am,' said Davy. 'I'll get to the point: do you know a John Millar by any chance?'

'Yes, I know a John Millar.'

'I don't know how to say this . . . I'm sorry, but he's dead.'

She was confused. John? Dead? 'Sorry, officer, there's surely some mistake. Which John Millar are you talking about? The one who worked in my office?'

'Yes.'

'And you're saying he's dead?'

'Yes.'

Susan almost dropped her mobile. She felt as if she'd been hit by a car and then run over by a truck.

'First Minister,' said Davy, anxiously, after a few seconds of silence. 'I'm really sorry to have to break the news. Sorry, First Minister, are you still there?'

'Yes, I'm here. It's just, it's just . . . How did he die? What happened? Was it a heart attack?'

23

Davy knew from experience that he couldn't prevaricate. 'He was shot dead in Glasgow.'

Susan felt sick. This wasn't happening. It couldn't be true, could it, that John had been murdered?

'First Minister?'

'Yes, yes . . . Are you sure?' asked Susan. 'Are you absolutely sure there isn't some mistake?'

'I wish I could tell you otherwise, First Minister, believe me, but it was John Millar. His body's been positively identified.'

More silence.

'But why are you calling me?' asked Susan finally. 'Shouldn't you be in touch with his family?'

'We've already done that, First Minister. But the reason I called was that your number was in his back pocket. Look, there is no suggestion . . .'

'My number, this number, was in his back pocket?' said Susan, in astonishment. 'Why was my number in his back pocket?'

'That's what we're trying to establish. We're just trying to find out who might have wanted Mr Millar dead, and in order to do that, First Minister, I'll need to ask you a few questions. You can be guaranteed this will all be done in the strictest confidence. Is that okay?'

'Yes,' said Susan. Her voice was cracking.

'How well did you know Mr Millar?'

A chasm of silence. Davy suppressed his urge to speak. He would have hung on for as long as it took.

'Eh, I knew John very well,' said Susan, before breaking down.

Back in the car, Brian undid his seatbelt and reached over to the front seat to grab a plastic bag.

'Don't say I'm not good to you. Think of it as an early Christmas present.'

He pulled a pair of wellies out of the bag. Susan shot him a look of disdain.

'I chose blue because you look good in it. If I'd gone for red, you'd look like Paddington Bear.'

'I'm not wearing them.' Susan turned away. She didn't need to see Brian's face getting redder to know what was about to happen.

'Aye, you are. You can't go marching through the field in your high heels. I don't give a damn how your calves look. All I care about is you not going flat on your face. Do you hear me?'

Susan traced a streak of rain on the window with her finger. She knew Brian would be infuriated by her act of defiance. She was the sort of woman men generally loathed and other women respected but did not necessarily like. She was tough, opinionated, and she didn't finesse the truth. Didn't have time for it. As far as Susan was concerned being nice got you nowhere. She knew the system was rigged and by her reckoning the only way to bring about change was by starting a brawl – fisticuffs at least gave you a fighting chance even when you're completely outmatched. She didn't like herself for it. The constant confrontation wore her down.

'Remember, if the hacks ask about the wellies tell them you're an all-weather leader. It's supposed to be a joke, so try and make it sound as natural as possible; there's nothing worse than a cardboard cut-out politician parroting their advisor's lines.'

Susan squeezed her fist. She had never wanted to hit Brian so much in her life – the patronising bastard. As she dug her nails into her palm the impulse subsided. He may have been a total prick but he happened to be a prick with superb political instincts. Susan could see a smeary Stirling Castle off in the distance. She knew she wasn't a dazzling speaker, more a middle-of-the-road orator, which fitted with her gradualist approach to independence – gently coaxing people to the point where they're more than ready to make the jump. She noticed a break in the clouds. She relaxed: it wasn't going to be a total washout after all.

The car pulled up to the edge of a field that was fast resembling a bog. A couple of police officers in high-vis vests directed the driver to park close to a couple of hay bales, which was designated the VIP zone. The car slithered and snaked in the mud for a few seconds before regaining traction. Susan saw a crowd of supporters carrying saltires and chanting: 'Scotland, Scotland, Scotland.' It buoyed her spirits. Nearby a young boy was kicking a fluorescent ball high into the air. His mother hared after him when an errant kick came down on a thicket of black umbrellas sheltering a group of journalists. Off in the distance the tops of the trees were licking up against the steep cliff, and on top of it, Stirling Castle and its solitary turret loomed against the bruising grey sky. The scene was set. Brian gently touched her arm in the back of the car. 'Show-time,' he said as the car came to a stop. Susan opened the door, and as her blue wellies squelched on the soggy ground, cheering broke out.

Forty miles away, Fulton was silently cursing himself as he hurried back up his street. He'd been standing in front of the ticket machine at Clarkston train station when the only thing he fished out of his pocket was an old cinema ticket. He'd realised his wallet was still on the bedside table. The school run was now in full swing, and cars were backing out onto the road with the children inside bouncing around with energy. Living in Clarkston had not been Fulton's choice. He found the place stultifying: full of middle-class folk who fretted over the make and model of their car and spent a small fortune trying to remove moss from their front gardens. But his wife Clare wanted to be closer to her parents. They'd helped with the deposit on their semi-detached home. And, as her parents repeatedly pointed out, the state schools in the area were excellent. The son-in-law with no means hadn't stood a chance.

Fulton opened his glass-frosted front door and noticed a pair of large black leather shoes beside the stairs. They weren't his: they were at least three sizes too big. He inhaled and exhaled deeply a couple of times. The day had arrived, he thought to himself, and he really didn't want to deal with it now.

'Alana,' he shouted. No response. He gave it a few seconds. 'Alana.' This time louder and angrier. Still no response. But a few seconds later, he heard murmurs and the muffled sounds of movement from Alana's bedroom. He heard her door creak open. There were heavy footsteps on the landing. Fulton waited at the bottom of the stairs, not sure how he would react. All he knew was that he needed to keep his cool even if his instincts were to the lamp the guy who was upstairs with his daughter.

Alana appeared first. She glared at her father in a silent rage as she slowly descended the stars. She had long dirty-blonde hair that reached almost to her waist, unusual greenish eyes and the high cheekbones that marked her out as Clare's daughter. She was beautiful and sassy and she knew it. One swish of her hair and she could attract more than a few admiring glances. She was wearing her black blazer, a stubby red tie tucked inside her shirt, a pleated skirt and black knee socks. Behind her on the stairs was a teenage boy. His head was lowered. He was handsome, built like a sprinter. When he looked up, Fulton detected an impression of innocence that clearly couldn't be the case. But if Fulton took any comfort from the whole situation, it was that the boy, too, was wearing a school uniform.

'What?' barked Alana. She stopped on the bottom stair, so she was eye-level with her dad. 'What are you doing here?'

'What the hell is *he* doing here?' cried Fulton, pointing at the boy who was leaning up against the wall like a prisoner who was about to be shot. His eyes could barely have grown any bigger.

'Sorry, Mr McKenzie,' he said hesitantly. 'We were just going over homework. I think it might be best—'

'Aye, I think it might be best if you buggered off and let me speak to my daughter.'

The teenager could hardly believe his luck that he'd got off so lightly. He squeezed past Alana on the stairs. Fulton moved out of the way so the lad could reach down and grab his school shoes. He quickly slipped them on, not bothering to tie the laces. But as he went for the door handle, Alana made a sudden move. She pushed past her dad and grabbed the boy's shoulder, pulling him around and kissing him squarely on the lips, making sure it lingered. The boy was trapped and squirming to get away.

'I'll see you in a few minutes,' said Alana, stroking his cheek with the back of her hand while she gave her dad a defiant look.

The boy couldn't have got out of the house quick enough. He jogged along the paving slabs in the garden with his shoes slapping about like slippers and threw open the front gate without looking back.

'Who was that?' demanded Fulton, after the boy disappeared from view.

'None of your business.'

'It is my business, I'm your dad. Now, who the hell was that?'

'I need my privacy.'

'You're a sixteen-year-old girl for God's sake.'

'Old enough to get married. Now I need to get going. I'll be late for school.'

'Since when has that ever bothered you?'

'Screw you, Dad,' said Alana, marching out of the front door with her leather rucksack slung over her shoulder. Fulton felt his anger spike: who the hell did she think she was, casting him aside like a toy she'd outgrown?

'Don't ever speak to me like that,' he shouted. He could feel his body tensing. 'How dare you. Come back here.'

Fulton knew that Alana was not coming back. She was more pig-headed than him and almost at the gate. He opened his mouth. He regretted the words the instant they left his lips.

'Do you think your mother would have let you get away with this?'

Alana stopped dead. Fulton watched as her rucksack slipped off her shoulder as she dropped it to the ground. It was like slow-motion ballet. Her accusatory index finger swung round first followed by the rest of her body. 'Mum's dead, Dad, she's been dead for years. And you need to stop using her to guilt-trip me. Just leave me alone.'

She picked up her rucksack, turned and stormed off, slamming the front gate so hard that it banjoed back open again. Fulton stood for a few seconds in the hallway before running out into the garden.

'Alana, Alana,' he cried. 'Alana.' But his voice trailed off. He knew it was futile. She was already halfway up the street chasing after her boyfriend. Fulton ran his hands through his hair. I don't know how to get through to her, he thought. Clare would have handled it so much better. But Clare was long gone.

Fulton went back into the house and closed the front door. There were dirty plates lying in the kitchen sink. Alana was meant to have washed them before going to school. Fulton lifted one of the plates smeared green with the residue of last night's Thai green curry and dropped it, cracking a glass. He bit his lip. He would deal with it later. He opened a cupboard beside the back door and lifted out his red and white boxing gloves. The leather was scuffed slightly but other than that they were in pretty good nick. Fulton pulled open the backdoor. He stepped out into the garden, which sloped away steeply down to a shed badly in need of a lick of paint. There was a path running down the middle of the grass. On one side were a couple of iron poles that in the past were used to hang a drying line. On the other side was a hulking object about seven foot tall covered by a black sheet of tarpaulin, which birds frequently used for target practice.

Fulton lay the boxing gloves on the backdoor steps. He started undoing the buttons of his shirt as he walked over to the drying line. The poles had hooks and Fulton ran a finger along one of them to make sure it wasn't dirty. He then pulled off his shirt and hung it up. He looked down at his stomach and pinched the roll of fat around his waist. It was about the thickness of a hotdog. Fulton shook his head: he had let himself go. He reached down and pulled off his trainers, and after stuffing his black woollen socks inside, he placed them by the steps. The grass tickled his toes. He pulled off the tarpaulin, revealing a metal stand with a steel hook from which hung a black punching bag with a yellow trim. The stand was weighed down by a couple of concrete paving slabs. Fulton folded up the tarpaulin peppered in bird crap and laid it neatly beside the garden fence. He pulled on one of the gloves, picked up the other and used his teeth to pull it up his wrist and then secure the Velcro strap. He banged the gloves together. One-two. One-two. He heard the satisfying snapping sound on the punch bag as he made contact with quick jabs. He danced to the movement of the bag. Another flurry of quick punches. One-two-three. One-two-three. His head bobbing and weaving. Fights are fought in combinations. When he got the rhythm of the punches right, it felt sublime.

A neighbour had once asked him why he didn't train in a gym. The simple answer was that when Alana was younger Fulton couldn't leave her alone in the house. She'd sit on the step with a dishcloth draped over her knees. When she saw the sweat running into her dad's eyes, she'd jump up, run over, dab it off, and return to the steps. But if Fulton was honest, it always felt rawer, more elemental in the back garden – stripped down to the waist, it felt like he was not only fighting himself, but taking on the world. He loved how in the winter months the freezing rain lashed his back. He never felt more alive. For Fulton the punches helped pulverise the pain.

Fulton's mother had left him when he was two years old. She visited a few years later. Fulton felt like she was with them for months but later realised it couldn't have been more than a fortnight. He remembered the thick, braided hair that fell over her shoulders and the sparkly eyes that could bring a dark room to life. He remembered her soft black skin. He remembered how gentle her voice was and yet how it sounded strange. After that visit, Fulton and his dad never talked about her again.

One-two-three. One-two-three. Don't look down. Don't fall into the bag. Keep the eyes up. Focus on the duct tape used as a mark. One-two. One-two. Give it all you've got. Smash in someone's cheekbones.

And so it was just the two of them – Fulton and his dad. They'd roam for miles and miles looking for anything useful they could find. As a young boy Fulton became adept at spotting glass bottles in long grass. He learned to carry them so they wouldn't clink and then crack. Whenever they had enough for a crate his father would lug it to the newsagents and collect the money. They would never pass a skip without scouring it for electronics or metals or anything they could sell on. There was always something.

Deep breaths. Keep moving. One-two-three. If only Fulton could keep it up for ever. But after a few minutes, his fists, his arms, his shoulders would start aching with tiredness – and the world that he'd left behind in those ferocious moments would slowly come back into focus. Fulton bent over, resting his gloves on his thighs, and sucked in air with the intensity of an industrial ventilation system. Off in the distance, he could see the tower blocks they'd moved to when he was about twelve. It provided him and his dad with their first home in years; before that it had been bedsits, squats and caravans. It was then he started playing football, regularly attending school, and after he turned fifteen, helping out at a nearby kennels. Fulton's main job was to feed the greyhounds. The flies would hover around the lumps of meat coagulating in big metal containers. The dogs were all housed in small fenced-off cages – two or three in each – where they rolled around on mats and in the sawdust. One night the owner asked Fulton if he wanted to make a bit more cash.

'Sure.'

'Come at eleven tonight then.'

One-two-three. One-two-three.

'Start digging over there . . . see them bushes . . . dig as close as you can to them.'

'What for?' asked Fulton.

'Whit did I tell you, son, no questions. Just do as you're bloody told.'

Fulton's head torch created a soft circle of light on the ground. He felt the spade slicing through the soft turf with ease. He dug for half an hour. His body tensed when he heard the first blast of the shotgun triggering a cacophony of yelps and howls. But the sound that stayed with Fulton was the sickening thud of the greyhound's carcass being dropped at his feet.

'An injured dug just costs me money,' said the owner. 'Get him in that hole.'

Fulton looked down at the lifeless dog. It had been shot through its shoulder leaving a huge gaping wound. Fulton knew the animal from its distinctive black and white patches: Renton. Fulton had encouraged him to chase after a squeaky toy when he was just a pup. In the darkness, he pushed the carcass into the freshly dug grave, covering the greyhound's limp, bloodied body with soil. Fulton heard another seven shots that night.

When the First Minister wrapped up her speech, supporters broke out with chants of 'Freedom, freedom, freedom!' Ward was elated. She had delivered the speech without a hiccup.

She went over to the hundred or so supporters and shook hands and thanked people for coming out in the rain. Susan had an uncanny knack for remembering the names and details of people she hadn't seen in years. 'Lovely to see you again, Margaret.' 'David, how's that boy of yours? He must be big now.' 'And, Janice, please give your dad my best.' The moment didn't last long, though. One guy at the back of the crowd started singing 'God Save the Queen'. He was thrown dirty looks and told to shut it by a ruddy young farmer wearing a Scotland rugby top.

Brian was watching all this out of the corner of his eye. The last thing he wanted was the First Minister being associated with any nastiness. He moved up behind her and whispered that it was time to move on.

As Susan walked back to the car, her blue wellies squelching in the mud, the journalists pursued her. One of them called out a question that stopped Susan dead in her tracks. She heard the words – John Millar – as if they were being mushed in a dodgy, old video recorder. She turned and faced the TV cameras.

'John Millar was a good man who worked for a better Scotland. My thoughts are with his family at this extremely difficult time. Thank you.'

Susan started walking again but the hacks were not letting her off that lightly. Brian put his hand on Susan's back and gently pushed her forward, trying to keep things moving along.

'Is there any sign of a motive?' cried another of the journalists jostling behind them. 'Any suggestion that John Millar's murder was connected to the referendum?'

'Bloody hell,' said Brian, under his breath. He felt his chest tighten and his heart pound. This is spinning out of control, he thought. Say nothing now and it looks like we've got something to hide.

Ever the professional, Susan knew instinctively what to do. She stopped, addressing the journalists. 'I have the utmost confidence that the police will investigate this matter fully and bring Mr Millar's killers to justice. As I've said before, this is a terrible tragedy and my thoughts are with his family. There is nothing more I can say on this matter. Thank you for your time.'

She started moving decisively towards the car, sensing the danger of yet more follow-up questions. Brian scrambled ahead of her to open the car door. As she climbed inside, the journalists were still throwing questions. Brian gave them a strained smile as he closed the door. He ran to the other side of the vehicle and jumped in. The car immediately pulled away.

'What a vile wee prick,' cried Brian, as they bumped across the field. 'That was a real cheap shot asking if John's death had anything to do with the campaign. We're living in a world of conspiracy where any old crap can take hold.'

Susan sat in silence. Brian saw her fidgeting with her watch. It was a tell-tale sign that something was wrong. Brian knew almost everything about Susan. It wasn't that there was a black book of sins, but when he first started working for her, Brian had been clear: 'I need to know everything.' He knew what age she was when she first got laid; the names of ex-boyfriends; the drugs she'd taken – cannabis at university (fine) and cocaine twice as a young biochemist (definitely not fine); but thankfully this had been in the days before smartphones and social media. There was no mortgage scandal, no offshore accounts, no dodgy inheritances, and all her shares were in a blind trust. As far as Brian was concerned, there was nothing that might come out in the final days to blow up the campaign. But Susan knew differently: there had been one bridge that she couldn't bring herself to cross.

'Brian,' she said, turning to him, 'there's something I need to tell you. It's about John and me.'

Chapter 5

Fulton loved chasing a good story but he loathed doorsteps. It wasn't just the fact that you have ten seconds before they slam the door in your face – although that was nerve-wracking enough. Some of his colleagues thought there was nothing better than rattling on people's doors to ask them about their dead relatives: a great way to get a scoop that earns you brownie points in the office. For Fulton, though, doorsteps were always personal. He felt sick when the front door swung open and he glimpsed a mother who had lost everything. But this was a massive story and one doorstep that he couldn't palm off on a junior reporter.

Fulton marched up the wheelchair ramp to the front door of the dreary-looking bungalow. He rang the bell. No response. He had come all this way and she wasn't even in. He then knocked gently on the door. Nothing. A bit harder: still no response. He took the third approach: pushing open the letterbox and shouting, 'Hello, is anyone there?'

'Who is it?' came a startled cry.

'Fulton McKenzie.'

'Are you with the police?'

'No, I'm a journalist.'

There was a long silence. This really could be a wasted trip, thought Fulton.

'Oh, hang on a minute, I'll get the key.'

Squatting on his haunches, Fulton could see a woman with purple slippers heading to the kitchen. The brown shagpile carpet was so thick that you could lose a penny in it. She staggered as she walked. He wondered if she was pissed. When Fulton saw her lurching back towards the door, he gently closed the letterbox and stood back up. He heard her scratching to get the key in the lock. It took three attempts. She pulled the door ajar six inches or so, the brass safety chain still on. Fulton saw a woman who had clearly been a stunner in her day – the outlines of her natural beauty were still there but life had ground her down. Her greying hair was held in place by kirby grips that kept it from falling over her pale eyes.

'I'm really sorry to bother you. Are you Elaine Millar?'
She nodded.

'I was very sorry to hear what happened to your brother.'
She bowed her head. 'Thank you. It was a real shock. Did you know him?'

'Actually, I didn't, but that's why I'm here – to find out more about him.'

Elaine let out a sigh. She was in two minds. But she was obviously a polite woman and her manners got the better of her.

'Well, you better come in then, I suppose. You'll catch your death standing out there in the rain.'

Elaine tried to unhook the safety chain, fingers jerking. After a few attempts she pulled open the door. She was wearing a thick woollen jersey under a purple dressing gown. She showed Fulton through into the living room. He sank into a green sofa patterned with yellow embroidered whirls. There was an unlit gas fire beneath the mantelpiece. Hanging on the white, wood-chipped wall, Fulton spotted a framed photo of what looked like Elaine's family on a rocky beach. There was a young boy, with a towel over his shoulders, shivering in his swimming trunks.

'Is that John?' asked Fulton, pointing at the boy.

'Yes, that's him. And that's my mum and dad and me.'

'Where was it taken? It looks beautiful.'

'Millport. We went every summer. Those were happy days, really great days, probably the best of my life.' Elaine looked away from the picture and smiled wanly at Fulton. 'But then my mum died just after. She was hit by a drunk driver coming back from the shop with the messages.'

'I'm sorry to hear that.'

'What are you to do?' said Elaine, holding up her hands. 'Some families have no luck.'

'I'm sorry.'

'The police were here yesterday. A man called David Bryant? He was very kind.'

'Eh, yes, we've crossed paths,' said Fulton, keeping it deliberately vague, as he wasn't sure where the conversation was heading.

'It was just that he told me not to speak to any journalists about John. He said it wouldn't help the investigation.'

Fulton squeezed his fist tightly. He knew Davy's advice was sound – speaking to journalists about anything sensitive, never mind a murder case, rarely helps matters for the police. But he was pissed off that Davy hadn't at least flagged this up before he dished out her address.

'Look, Elaine, let me be straight with you. I'm really sorry to turn up like this. It's not normally how I do things. I just wanted to hear more about your brother. I don't know if you read the *Siren* at all, but I'm the newspaper's investigative reporter and the one thing we don't do, like the tabloids, is hatchet jobs. I know this must be a deeply upsetting time for you and I genuinely don't want to add to your grief – that's not why I'm here, it's really not what I'm about.'

Elaine was standing resolutely in the middle of the living room. As she was thinking over what Fulton had said, her hand started trembling. It began gently enough, you could have almost mistaken it for a shiver, but then the hand started shaking violently.

'Sorry, but you'll have to excuse me for a minute,' she said, visibly embarrassed. 'I need to take my pills.'

'Please ... please take your time,' replied Fulton. He watched as Elaine staggered out of the living room almost tripping over one of her feet. He winced when he saw it. He listened as she moved about in the kitchen, opening and closing cupboards. Then he heard the gush of water from the tap. It ran for a long time – too long.

'You okay? Do you need a hand?' shouted Fulton.

'I'm fine,' she replied. She returned a minute later, carrying a glass of water, half of which she spilled on the carpet. Fulton looked the other way, pretending not to notice.

'Sorry, I didn't get you anything,' said Elaine, after taking a couple of sips of water. 'That's very rude of me. Would you like a cup of tea?'

'Honestly, I'm fine.'

'Are you sure?'

'Absolutely, I just had one.'

'I won't force you then. As you can probably tell, simple things are no longer easy for me. I've got motor neurone disease. I lose track of how many pills I need to take every day. The doctors told me they can't really do much for me, other than try and manage it, but it's a horrible, horrible disease. I was forced to give up my job a year ago, which was a serious blow.'

'And what did you do?'

'I was a nurse. It became way too physical for me.'

'You've not had it easy.'

'That's one way of putting it.'

Elaine placed her glass of water down on a small mahogany table beside an armchair. Fulton watched in horror as she bent her knees and collapsed into the chair. He was forced to look away as she squirmed to sit up straight.

'You seem like a nice man,' said Elaine, when she'd found a position she was comfortable in. 'It's just the police – I really don't want to upset them. What with all that's going on, that's the last thing I need.'

'Why don't we talk,' said Fulton, a tinge of desperation in his voice, 'and I'll guarantee you that not a word of it will appear in print until you're happy. I know this isn't easy but would that work for you?'

'How do I know I can trust you? You know what they say about journalists.'

'Elaine, I can only give you my word. It's your call. If you don't want to speak about John, I understand, I really do.'

She glanced at the picture on the wall and then looked back at Fulton. 'He was such a handsome boy. All my friends used to fancy him. Because he didn't say much they all thought he was moody and mysterious. You know what teenage girls are like: daft.' She gently bent back a couple of her fingers, trying to relieve the pain. 'Let's do it,' she said, at last. 'But you have to give me your word that it won't appear in the paper until I say so. I'll want to check with that David Bryant first.'

'Whatever makes you happy.'

'Okay, what do you want to talk about then?'

Fulton opened his rucksack and pulled out his notebook and pen. He flicked open the cover and found a fresh page.

He wrote the date and then asked Elaine for the correct spelling of her name. She watched as he scribbled it down and underlined it.

'What was he like?' asked Fulton. 'As a boy growing up and as a young man?' He always wanted to get a sense of a person before he established the facts. And he found it best to warm up people before hitting them with the hard stuff.

'Ah, he was a great brother,' replied Elaine, a small smile briefly catching on her lips. 'The best a girl could have hoped for. We're four years apart but he was always looking out for his wee sister. John was always bright – using them big words that none of us knew the meaning of. We'd tease him about that. The teachers used to say to me, "Why are you not as smart as your brother?"'

Fulton was writing fast. It was all great colour. He didn't interrupt. When people are talking – and you're not right up against a deadline – there's nothing to be gained from disrupting the flow.

'Some folk are blessed with talents and John was one of them. But everything changed when Mum died. It hit us all hard, of course, but I think it hit John the hardest.'

'Why was that?' asked Fulton, turning over a fresh page and putting a star at the top of the page to denote its importance.

Elaine sighed. She gently stroked her hand, which was resting on her knee. 'He and Mum were very close; he was always her favourite and she would dote on him. But after she died, he kind of withdrew into himself – we all deal with these things differently, I suppose. You'd always find him in his room reading, not really wanting to talk to anyone.'

For a few seconds, Fulton wondered whether to ask a follow-up question but decided it wasn't relevant to the bigger story. 'Where did he study?'

'He was at Oxford.'

'I can't imagine they get a lot of students from Falkirk.'

'Yes, you're right about that. One of the teachers, Mr Mitchell, I think, helped John out after class – giving him extra tuition, which made the difference. Most of the boys from around here got a trade or would go down the pits but John was always marked out for a different path. I think he did Russian Studies. It was during Reagan and all that, and I guess he thought learning Russian would land him a good job. But Oxford was a long way from Falkirk in every way.'

'How so?' asked Fulton, knowing the answer but wanting an example.

'Well, I remember one time he came home with one of his girlfriends – she was a beautiful-looking lassie, the type you see in those glossy magazines – and she spoke like she was a member of the Royal Family. I think her dad was a lord or something like that. I mean, it was unbelievable having such a posh girl in our wee house. Well, I tell you, Falkirk was a real eye-opener for her. I don't think she ever quite recovered from it,' said Elaine, laughing at the memory.

'But it never worked out between them. That was always the way with John – the women came and went. He had no problem getting them but hanging onto them was a different matter. He never really settled did our Johnnie.'

'And how long was he with the Foreign Office?'

'Let me think now, gosh, it must have been about twenty-five years. We didn't see him much for a long time. My poor old dad used to get very upset about that. Don't get me wrong, he was very proud; he worked all his life as a joiner and now his son was a diplomat. But whenever John came they'd argue about politics. Falkirk was broken by Maggie Thatcher but John used to defend her. My dad would get so angry I'd think he was going to have a heart attack. They'd properly scream at each other. I hated it, just hated it.'

'Sorry,' said Fulton. 'My pen's run out.'

'When I get talking there's no stopping me.'

'No, no, it's great,' replied Fulton with a grin. He dug about in his rucksack until he found another pen. 'And when did you last see him?'

'About a month ago, he came to Falkirk. We saw a bit more of each other after he took the job in Edinburgh but he really wasn't himself that day.'

'How so?' asked Fulton, looking up from his pad. He drew another star.

'Well, and this definitely isn't for the papers, he was angry about some woman. He kept saying she had ruined his life. I'd never seen him so upset but he wouldn't tell me who she was or what she had done.'

Fulton could sense Elaine was on the verge of getting upset but he fought the urge to say anything.

'Until that day, I had never really worried about John,' said Elaine finally. 'He was a man who could make his own way in the world but seeing him in such a state scared me. It made me worry that he might do something stupid. I tried not to think about it, I thought maybe I was being silly, but then the police came and told me he had been murdered.'

She looked up at the family picture on the wall and then out of the living-room window. She stroked her hand on her lap.

Fulton gave her a moment to reflect. He went through the page filling in some of the missing words until he felt she was ready for the last, brutal question. 'I'm really, really sorry to have to ask you this but do you have any idea who might have wanted John dead?'

Elaine stared through him. 'No, I don't. But whoever killed him, I want to know. I wouldn't wish this upon my worst enemy. If there's any blessing, it's that my parents weren't around for it.'

'And is there anything else you want to say?'

She was silent for a few seconds, looking down at her lap. Fulton recognised the sorrow stirring inside her. 'Do you know what makes me really sad?' she said. 'John never had any children. He'd have made a wonderful father. He just loved kids and they adored him.'

Fulton watched as this brave woman began to cry. He reached over and pulled a tissue out of a box on the coffee table. He stood up and handed it to her. She dabbed her cheeks and started apologising. Fulton reassured her there was absolutely nothing to be sorry about. 'It gets easier, I promise you that,' he said.

'You lost someone, didn't you?'

'Yes,' said Fulton uncomfortably. He flipped over the cover of the notebook and reached down to grab his rucksack. 'But it was a long time ago.'

'God bless you.'

'No, thank you, Elaine, and sorry for intruding. I know this can't have been easy.'

'It was nice to meet you but please, please, remember our agreement.'

'Absolutely, and I'll be in touch. You can trust me.' Fulton hesitated before conducting the casual act of professional sabotage. 'And by the way, Elaine, Officer Bryant was right. Probably best if you don't make a habit of speaking to the media. They can really make your life a misery.'

Elaine gave him a tight smile before insisting on show-ing him out. She cut a forlorn figure on the doorstep as he rounded the street corner. The rain had stopped and Fulton decided to walk to the train station so he'd have the time to mull over the interview. Clearly, one of John's relationships had turned sour but who on earth was the woman? The chances of getting a name were remote, and even then it was unlikely to explain the killing. And what exactly had John done at the Foreign Office? Why had he never risen up the ranks and become an ambassador? Surely, he was smart enough. But wasn't Oxbridge where a lot them got recruited for the intelligence services? Maybe John Millar had been a spy, thought Fulton, but he knew he didn't have much chance of standing that up. And, even so, while it might make for sexy copy – SCOTS SPY SLAIN IN CITY CENTRE HIT! – what would be the motive for the killing? Fulton knew that the only realistic way to get the inside track would be through Davy. He checked his watch – it was almost five. He knew he needed to speak to the editor and that it wasn't going to be an easy call.

'Fulton, how are things? We're just finalising the front page. What have you got for me?'

'At the moment, nothing.'

'It was a bust?'

'Not exactly.'

'So, did you speak to the sister?'

'Yes.'

'And she didn't say anything?'

'She gave me a lot of background on John, good colour. But I've got a problem.'

'*You've* got a problem? I've got a problem. I've got a newspaper to fill for tomorrow and not enough copy.'

'She didn't want to go on the record. Not for now, anyway, and I agreed.'

'And why did you agree to that, Fulton? Correct me if I'm

wrong but you're our star investigative reporter and not the work-experience boy.'

'She's just lost her brother for Christ's sake! I didn't want to push her.'

'And what about professionalism and putting a newspaper to bed?'

Fulton knew the editor had a point: it was an exclusive after all. 'Look, Chris, we have to finesse the situation. I'm pretty sure she's got more to give. So why go with it now when we can get better stuff if we wait a day or two? We do a big splash for the weekend, front page and the magazine – I'm sure she'll come round. But if we publish now she's never going to speak to me again.'

Another long pause, so long that Fulton checked his screen to see whether Chris had hung up.

'All right, but let us be clear about one thing: if another newspaper gets the interview, I'll be furious, and I'll expect us to go to print immediately. I'll give you the benefit of the doubt on this one, but I expect results.'

Chapter 6

You never know when it's going to hit you. It's not like you see it off in the distance slowly approaching and you can prepare yourself. It's more like a car bomb going off on the street you've walked down every day of your life. Everything you held true is gone and you're plunged into a world from which you suddenly fear you cannot escape.

Fulton was returning home after buying eggs from the local shop. A tall, lanky teenager was approaching him on the pavement. His black hoodie was pulled up, his earphones were in, and his head was down, bobbing along to the music. He was staring at the ground so intently it was as if he was tracing ants. If it had stayed that way, nothing would have happened. But a few steps away from Fulton the teenager looked up from the pavement and stared directly at him. It was barely a second but in that moment Fulton's world was shattered by the furious, rushing return of the past. In that face he saw his beautiful young son, Daniel – the boy who would never grow old. He'd be a teenager now; he would have the same lithe limbs, the same light stubble, and the same smattering of spots on his face. The boy passed by, completely oblivious, as Fulton felt the box of eggs slip from his hand, its lid springing open and the eggs smashing on the pavement, their yellow yolks streaking the tarmac.

It had been seven years since that night. They were on the

road to Kilmarnock that rises out of Glasgow onto the bleak, soggy, unforgiving moors. A place where a misstep means you can be up to your neck in a peaty bog. That was Fulton's recurring nightmare. That was what he woke up from more nights than he cared to count – the collar of sweat on his neck like a cordon of water that he was about to slip under. The waking up Fulton took as a sign that, deep down, he never wanted to put an end to it all. He'd even recce'd a bridge where he could quickly finish it. One small step and it would be over. But Fulton would be jolted by thoughts of his daughter. He would see the dimples that appeared on either side of Alana's mouth whenever she smiled. The way she said 'Dad' like no other word. It came from the heart rather than the lips. And Fulton knew then he would never do it. Instead he was left living, wrestling with the truth of what had happened that night. Throughout the years only a few shards of memory had revealed themselves.

He remembered his son kicking the back of his seat. It was in three-kick bursts and Dan would laugh and shout, 'Too slow, you can't catch me.' Fulton remembered taking his hand off the wheel and awkwardly reaching back and tickling under his son's knee. Dan started squealing and twisting in his car seat. And then he would promise he wouldn't kick any more, only to repeat it a couple of minutes later. But that wasn't what caused the crash.

Fulton remembered Clare's stony expression. They had had a massive argument. But what was the cause of the fight? Money? Family? Or something else? No matter how many times Fulton cast his mind back he could never find the truth. It was like a bleeding sore that he constantly picked at and that never healed. Other than telling Fulton to keep his eyes on the road, Clare had said nothing. It was already dark. The rain was drilling down. The windscreen wipers weren't working fast enough. It was as if they were in rough seas and were being swamped by the waves. The sweep of car headlights over the undulating road were like search lights on rescue boats arcing skywards only to dazzle you when they came to rest on a flat stretch of the road again.

Fulton remembered thinking he should pull over. But the weather would have only got worse and, anyway, he was used to the conditions. He was a good driver. Even Clare said so. He had driven the road numerous times and knew the black spots. And they needed to get to Clare's mother's house for dinner. His mother-in-law scolded them whenever they were late. As the shadows of the moors kept slipping by, Alana, who had been silent up until then, demanded to know if they were there yet.

They approached the brow of the hill. Just beyond it was a dangerous bend. Fulton prepared himself. He dropped a gear, slowing slightly, his fingers tightening on the steering wheel. He remembered seeing the lights of a truck casting into the night sky. Then the truck's full beam began levelling out on the road. Fulton remembered the flash of white light as intense as burning magnesium. It blinded him for a second or two, and he remembered feeling the car shudder as a curtain of water washed over them. But the truck passed. They were fine. Fulton relaxed his grip on the wheel. And then he remembered the bend.

Chapter 7

It was an ominous sound that always set Davy on edge. The click of highly buffed black leather shoes on the white marble floor, which signalled the imminent arrival of the acting Chief Constable of Police Scotland. Ian Larbert's craggy face appeared at the door. His thick grey hair was swept into a side-parting, not a strand out of place. He looked like the severe church elder he was: the type of man who would disapprove of people laughing in a comedy club.

'You got anything for us yet?' said Larbert, tapping his fingers rhythmically on the doorframe. He'd long ago dispensed with pleasantries at work, regarding them as a time-wasting indulgence.

'Nothing solid as of yet.'

'Well, keep pushing. We need answers, Davy, the right answers and as quickly as possible. I shouldn't need to remind you of that.'

'Understood.'

Larbert gave Davy a withering look.

'Understood, sir.'

'I'll be in my office if anything comes up.'

Larbert executed a military about-turn. Davy relaxed as the clicking slowly receded up the corridor. 'Arsehole,' he said, under his breath. He rubbed his chest. It was probably only indigestion caused by the cheese-and-coleslaw baguette he'd just wolfed down. But more likely it was the stress of the investigation. The bosses were coming down hard. Davy knew that if it had been a gangland shooting, they wouldn't have given a monkey's. But this was different, this was political – and that always made the chiefs nervous, very nervous indeed. Especially Larbert who was gunning for the top job after the previous Chief Constable was forced to step down a couple of months ago after a sex scandal. He was constantly at Davy in a way that he'd never experienced in thirty years on the job. Larbert kept phoning him or popping by his office or sending underlings down with messages. Davy was struggling to think, never mind get anything done. Part of the reason he was drinking so much coffee was just to get out of the damn building for a few minutes.

He took a sip from his third latte of the day. Two sugars: you need to get your money's worth. It wasn't even mid-morning yet. He got up and locked his door. No more interruptions. He then pulled down the blinds to stop the sun striking his computer screen. He sat down and stared at the monitor. He'd spent hours trawling through all the available CCTV footage connected to John Millar's murder. In the last hour, he'd finished pulling together a timeline.

Davy knew the assassination had occurred at approximately 11:00 p.m. on Sunday night. Footage showed that John Millar had arrived in the area around 10:30 p.m. A motorbike carrying two men appeared at 10:59 p.m. Frustratingly, there was no actual footage of the murder itself. Bath Lane was one of the few blind spots in the city. But at 11:00 p.m. a man wearing a dark helmet, his visor still pulled down, casually walked into the lane. Then he must have shot John Millar. Thirty seconds later he appeared again. He was of average height and build. Davy guessed he was probably twenty to thirty years old. But that didn't narrow things down at all.

The footage then showed the murderer climbing onto the back of the motorbike being ridden by the getaway man. The registration plate was covered with masking tape. These guys were the real deal, thought Davy, they'd done this before. That did narrow it down. But it still left him with potentially dozens of suspects.

The weather had been awful that night and the city centre quiet. Davy had spotted two potential witnesses approximately fifty metres from the murder scene but neither of them had reacted to the sound of the three gunshots. It almost certainly meant they'd heard nothing. Davy decided it wasn't worth wasting the time on tracking them down. He watched as the video, jump-cutting between the footage he'd spliced together from various cameras, showed the killer's motorbike speeding up a deserted Bath Street past several bars, whose names Davy could never remember, then the King's Theatre, and over the motorway to the Mitchell Library. The pair had been travelling fast, around 70 mph, but the roads were empty. Luck was also on their side. Every time they'd approached a traffic light, it tripped from red to green. It was almost as if they'd programmed the lights themselves.

Within a minute they were on Maryhill Road and by that time they were truly flying. The bike's red brake light momentarily broke the gloom as they turned right onto Firhill Street, up to the football stadium, and then the bike vanished from view. It was yet another blind spot.

'What the hell am I missing?' Davy muttered to himself. It was likely, he thought, that they'd either parked the motorbike in a nearby garage and it was still there or, perhaps, given the intense media interest, they'd decided to dump it in one of the canals. There was always a slim chance, of course, that they'd taken a back road and then slipped onto the motorway heading towards Edinburgh. But Davy decided to ditch that line of inquiry for now. If the bosses heard he was pursuing that angle they would know he was pissing in the wind.

He would do anything for a breakthrough. Back to basics: he knew the decisive clues are normally at the start and the end of a journey. Since there was no end, he flicked through the first fifteen seconds, this time frame-by-frame. He magnified the moment the murderer climbed onto the motorbike. He scrolled back and forth – and then his chest eased noticeably. He had spotted something.

As the hitman climbed onto the bike his black leather jacket briefly rode up. Davy freeze-framed the footage, then enhanced a screen grab, which revealed the man's white shirt: it had a distinctive bunny rabbit pattern. Interesting fashion choice, thought Davy, very interesting. Who do I know with a flamboyant dress sense? He reclined on his seat to the point where he almost tipped over. He only righted himself after frantically flapping his hands. And then with the revelation that dawns when you realise you've won the jackpot on a scratch card, Davy exclaimed, 'You daft bastard . . . if you'd worn a black T-shirt you might just have got away with it.' He pumped his fists in joy. 'Ya dancer,' he repeated over and over again. He knew that an item of clothing alone wasn't enough to bring the suspect to the station. But it was more than enough to warrant a casual chat. And he knew exactly where to find the Glaswegian most likely to have a bunny shirt in his wardrobe.

In Glasgow, bookies are largely the preserve of the desperate and the dangerous. One such establishment could be found just off Partick Road, wedged between a Greggs and a gastro pub that had just gone out of business. This was a corner of the city where gentrification was running into stubborn resistance, a place where people preferred to eat food they could actually pronounce.

When Davy entered the bookies, he immediately spotted Charlie Easter hunched over a circular table close to a bank of TV screens. The horses were lining up for one of the final races of the day. Charlie was wearing a bright yellow shirt that wouldn't have looked out of place on one of the jockeys. What is it with this boy and fashion? thought Davy. Is he colour blind? With a pencil stub, Charlie was crossing off his white betting slip in a manner that suggested he was either anxious for a winner or was coming down from a chemical high or perhaps both. Sidling up beside him, Davy whispered into his ear, 'Which one are you goin' fir?'

'Tender Surprise,' replied Charlie, without even bothering to look up. He was a regular here and other customers frequently hit him up for tips, which he dispensed with generosity.

'Well, I've got a tender wee surprise for you,' said Davy, beginning to massage Charlie's shoulders. 'It's your old pal, Davy Bryant here. How are you doin'? It's been a while, son.'

Charlie froze. He had the look of a man whose fight or flight instinct had been temporarily disabled. Davy always had a certain sympathy for poor wee Charlie and his chib-marked face. It wasn't that he was born a criminal but he had been marked out for the job at an early age. When he was sixteen, someone took the liberty of smashing a pint glass into his cheek. With the best will in the world, Charlie would always struggle to find gainful employment with a face that made people cross the street.

'Where were you on Sunday night, Charlie?' asked Davy,

slapping him on the back. 'We can make this quick or long and painful – c'mon, which would you prefer? I know which I'd prefer.'

Charlie said nothing. Davy slapped him on the back again, like he was a remote control that needed a jiggle.

'C'mon, Charlie, I don't want to spoil your night and take you down to the station. Let's be reasonable here. Where were you on Sunday night?'

Charlie shifted on his stool. He looked down at his pristine white trainers. 'At hame with the burd,' he mumbled.

'Oh, really! Since when have you had a burd with a face like that?' Davy took hold of Charlie's chin like he was a young boy. 'She's either fat or blind, son, more likely both. And this beautiful burd of yours, Charlie, does she have a name?'

'Aye.'

'And what is it then?'

Davy shuffled forward. His groin was now inches from Charlie's face. Charlie didn't know where to look or what to say.

'Chantelle.'

'Nice name. You got a picture of her,' said Davy, looking down at Charlie's greasy hair, which was speckled with dandruff.

'Naw.'

'And why would that be, Charlie? Is that because she doesn't exist? That this *Chantelle* is a figment of your imagination? Is that not the case, son?'

Charlie hunched over further on the stool. His knee started jogging up and down like a guy who was about to bolt.

'You see, Charlie, I've been speaking to some of the boys and they tell me you were up on Bath Street on Sunday night.

And, as you may have heard, someone got murdered up there. Now, Charlie, they're spreading the rumour that you were behind the killing. And I said to myself that can't be right, that's not the Charlie I know and love. So, I thought I'd swing round here and do you a favour by trying to settle the issue.'

Still Charlie said nothing. Davy gave him a push with such force that he almost knocked him off his stool.

'What's wrong, Charlie? You lost your tongue?'

Davy rubbed his face. He knew Charlie was far from being the sharpest but even he wasn't falling for the old-time pals' routine.

'How's big Tam doing? He still running that pub of his?'

On hearing Tam's name, Charlie twitched like a dog when a stick is thrown for him to chase. He looked up at Davy.

'Or is he still in the tanning business? Turning the lassies orange before they head out to Tenerife? Or is it taxis now? He must be taking quite the hit what with the old Ubers everywhere. Quite the entrepreneur is our Tam. Someone more cynical than my good self would think he makes his money from crime – perhaps even drugs. But not me, Charlie. How could a man with a box at Ibrox ever be a criminal?

'But here's the thing, Charlie. I've got the bosses screaming – and I mean screaming – in my ear to solve this case. Now get this through your thick heid: they don't like it when a civvy winds up deid in the city centre. So why don't you do me a favour? Tell Tam his old friend Davy wants to have a wee chat with him. He knows how to contact me. Could you do that for me, Quasimodo?'

Davy patted Charlie on the cheek. In that instant, even he realised he'd gone too far. There are only so many humiliations a man can take even when they're cornered. Charlie shot to his feet like a firework going off.

'Fuck you,' he said, spraying spittle over Davy's face. Davy was secretly impressed by the burst of bravado. But he held the menacing stare as Charlie marched to the counter and slapped down his betting slip.

Chapter 8

Fulton pushed up his eye mask. He'd been woken by the crows squawking in the back garden again; they didn't half make a racket. The morning light, streaming in through the thin curtains, was making him blink. He rolled over, sandwiching his head between two pillows in a vain attempt to block out the light and the noise. As his drowsiness wore off, he was gripped by a growing sensation that something was wrong. He threw off his duvet in a panic. Where the hell was Alana? Normally, her music would be blaring as she got ready for school. His heart was pounding. And then he remembered that she had texted the night before to say she was staying at her aunt's house. It wasn't the first time. He lay back down on the bed, the stress slowly receding.

Fulton checked his phone. It was almost 8:00 a.m. He had an important meeting in the city that he couldn't be late for. He rolled out of bed in his black boxer shorts and white T-shirt. He had a habit of showering last thing, to keep the bed sheets as clean as possible. He pulled off his T-shirt, neatly folded it, and placed it under one of his pillows. He made the bed, smoothing out the creases in the duvet with the palm of his hand. He grabbed the deodorant on top of the chest of drawers and sprayed under his armpits. He glanced in the mirror, stroked his chin. The texture was like sandpaper but the stubble wasn't too heavy. He could skip the shave. He pulled open the double doors of the wardrobe. He glanced down at his shoe rack: three pairs of Converse. But it felt like a smart casual day. He pulled out a pair of brown leather shoes, then dark blue jeans and a belt. Ten identical white shirts hung from the rack. When Fulton reached for one, it slipped the hanger, falling down the back of the wardrobe. As he bent over to retrieve it, Fulton heard a rustling sound. He felt a plastic bag, before realising what was inside.

He hadn't worn his hiking boots in years. The first time had been on a trek up Ben Lomond after joining a mountaineering club. Fulton had resolved never to go again. He felt like an outsider, a bit rougher, a bit more Glaswegian than most of the others, who were university graduates. But one of them had made a point of making Fulton feel welcome, of walking along-side him on the path, of saying I really hope you come again as they climbed out of the minibus. Clare had always assumed the best of everyone and everything. It was what Fulton found so beguiling about her. Six months later she was pregnant.

Fulton bit his lip.

The sun was out and the mood in Kelvingrove Park was like that of a mini music festival. It was a real freakshow of flesh: various shades of grey and pink. Stretched dolphin and lopsided star tattoos were visible on girls' hips and plenty of piercings were getting an outing. Amid all the lazy revelry, an elderly man wearing his signature trilby was shuffling through the crowd. In spite of the heat, he was wearing an ill-fitting Italian wool suit. To the uninitiated eye, Trilby Tam was a wealthy gent who was a touch eccentric – the grandpa figure who had liked to give kids sweeties until parents started flipping out about that sort of thing. And that impression of Tam wouldn't be entirely wrong. He really did love children.

It was just that a decade later his boys would be flogging them smack, coke, meth or whatever else took their fancy.

Davy was sitting on a bench a stone's throw from the bandstand watching it all unfold. He couldn't help marvelling at the strangeness of the scene. For years, he had been obsessed about putting Trilby Tam away. But he was a wily old bastard who knew exactly how to the play the game. One time, Tam suggested to Davy that they come to a gentleman's understanding, as he put it. Tam was offering generous payments for a heads-up on big drugs busts. He must have known Davy was at a low ebb, struggling through his first divorce. Davy declined but did so in a fashion that Tam found sufficiently respectful – it was the only reason he was turning up today.

As he approached, Davy stood up and waved to him. He moved forward to take Tam by the arm but was pushed away. Davy watched as he sat down on the bench and leaned his walking stick up against it. Tam readjusted his hat – a little red and yellow feather was tucked into its band.

'Beautiful day, Tam, it's been a while since we last crossed paths,' said Davy, sitting beside him.

'Aye, a few years by my reckoning.'

'How are things? How's that boy of yours doing?'

Tam shot him a look of displeasure. 'He died of a heart attack last year.'

'I'm really sorry to hear that, Tam. My condolences. Can't have been an easy year for you.'

Tam shrugged his shoulders more in annoyance than anything else. 'If I wanted a fucking counselling session, I would have phoned the doctor. So, tell me, what's Strathclyde's finest after? I'm guessing this isn't a social call to catch up on family stuff. Charlie mentioned you wanted to see me about something.'

'Did he say what it was about?'

'Gie me a break. That boy is so daft he can barely string a sentence together. Tell me what you're after. I've not got all day.'

'All right then, Tam,' said Davy. 'I'll get straight to the point. Why did one of your boys whack that civil servant in the city centre? I may be wrong but it doesn't strike me as your usual line of work.'

Tam didn't even look offended by the question. He took a cream-coloured silk handkerchief from his top pocket and dabbed at the sweat forming on his forehead.

Davy tried again. 'I know Charlie did it.'

'Well, if you know he did it, why are you talking to me, and why don't you charge him?' Tam was now glaring at Davy. His mouth curled up into a crooked half smile. 'Oh, that's right, you've got nothing on him. Last time I checked, a hunch wasn't enough to put away someone for life. Shame, isn't it? Otherwise, I would've been put in the big hoose a long time ago. I hope the polis haven't pulled me out here expecting me to do their job for them. I know you boys are struggling with cuts but this would be a first.'

'It's only a matter of time, Tam, you know that as well as I do. We can do this the easy way or go round the houses. But in the end, the result will be the same.'

'Is that so, Davy? So, you're really telling me that you've got me out here on nothing more than a wing and a prayer. If I'm honest, I'm a wee bit disappointed, Davy. I thought you were better than that.'

Tam gripped the armrest, his knuckles whitening as he prepared to stand up. Part of Davy panicked; he needed to get something out of the meeting. Normally, he would have laid it on heavy but Tam was a man who had survived two assassination attempts, including one outside his bungalow in Lenzie when he was taking his daughter to school. Men with lead in their bodies weren't moved by mere words.

'Okay, Tam, let's quit the bullshit. What you need to understand is this case is far bigger than us. Pretty soon I won't be the one running the show. Already there are some boys up from London and I don't think they're polis. It's worth bearing that in mind.'

Tam released the armrest.

'After all your hard work, Tam, it would be a shame to see it all unravel, just when you're at the age when you should be enjoying your retirement. You don't need all this hassle now. And I know that you wouldn't have sanctioned this hit, Tam. So, why should you end up paying the price for it when one of your boys got greedy?'

Tam couldn't help smiling at Davy's performance. There's nothing quite like a cop feigning that he's got your best interests at heart. It's like a man holding a gun to your temple and apologising for having to pull the trigger.

'Okay, Davy, I can see you're a wee bit worked up. How can I help you?'

'I want Charlie down at the station spilling his guts.'

'You know that ain't going to happen.'

'And why's that?'

'Davy, will you stop being such a dense, fat bastard. You're doing yourself a disservice here if you think I'm going to grass on my own guys. I may be getting older, Davy, but it's still all here.' He tapped a finger on the side of his head.

'I've got him on the CCTV, Tam. He was wearing one of those stupid shirts of his. I could bring him in now but I would really appreciate your help on this. Think of it as a strategic move.'

63

'A strategic move, you say,' said Tam, with a chuckle. 'I've heard a lot of shite in my time but that's one of the best yet. But if I was to make a strategic decision, what would be in it for me? I'm not minded to charity, especially when it comes to the polis.'

Davy stared up at the rare blue sky. Tam had him in a position he always vowed never to be in.

'I can't promise anything, Tam, you know that. But if you help me, I'll see what I can do to repay the favour.'

Tam patted Davy's knee, a broad smile on his face.

'Nothing's for free, son, you know that. But let me think it over and I'll get back to you.'

A few hundred metres away, the magnificent, four-storey townhouses of Park Circus sat on the crown of the hill like snooty aunts looking down on relatives who hadn't done so well. It was the rarefied heart of Glasgow, where the rougher elements rarely trod, home to those with burgeoning bank accounts and organisations after a coveted postcode. Inside the basement meeting room of one of them, Fulton sat scrolling through his phone. He was waiting for the boss of the Freedom Foundation. The door opened and in walked a woman with fiery red hair, the shoulder-length curls tumbling over her black top. Her zebra-skin stilettos made her tower over most men.

'Chief executive . . . well, well,' said Fulton standing up from his seat, a grin spreading across his face. 'Some of us have certainly moved up in the world. Janet Rae, how the hell are you?'

She gave him a big hug and a peck on both cheeks.

'You still smell good,' she said. 'So, how is the best-looking man in Scottish journalism?'

'Not too bad, although to be fair, the competition's not a worry.'

'I certainly wouldn't disagree with you there. What's it been now, seven or eight years since I last saw you?'

They were interrupted by a young secretary, wearing a black-and-white striped dress and kooky, big-framed glasses, who was hovering nervously at the door.

'Excuse me, Mrs Rae, do you want tea or coffee?'

Janet gestured at Fulton.

'I'm fine, honestly.'

'We're all good, thanks, Naomi.'

Fulton watched as the secretary closed the door as carefully as if she was handling a sheet of glass.

'She's feart of you.'

'Not scared, Fulton, just respectful.'

'So, it's still Rottweiler Rae?'

Janet smiled coyly. She'd first met Fulton when he started as a copyboy at the paper. She had been a senior reporter and barked at him on his first day.

'Hard as you may find it to believe, even the cut-throat corporate world doesn't always appreciate my silky diplomatic skills. Anyway, how are things at the paper?

'*Titanic*, *Lusitania*, take your pick.'

Fulton felt his phone vibrating in his pocket. It was on silent, so he ignored it.

'I certainly don't regret taking redundo,' said Janet. 'How's Chris doing as editor?'

'Pissing his pants as usual; with all the cuts, he's no longer allowed to employ a nanny.'

'And they call me the Rottweiler,' said Janet with a smirk. 'I can see the years haven't softened you one jot. You're still doing great stuff – the Crestwell kids' home reporting was superb.'

A worker at a children's home had been jailed for life following Fulton's 3,000-word exposé on decades of sexual abuse at the institution. It had been one of his more satisfying jobs.

'Aye, that bastard had it coming to him for decades,' said Fulton.

'You knew him?'

'Not directly but he assaulted a couple of boys I knew. One's dead – threw himself off the Kingston Bridge; the other's an alky. When I last saw him, he was so pissed he could barely stand up. That was all his doing. The man can burn in hell for all I care.'

'The world can be a grim place. But look, take a seat, Fulton, I've got something I need to talk to you about.'

They both sat down on opposite sides of the long glass-topped table, which had a bottle of sparkling mineral water and two glasses placed on top of paper doilies in the centre. There was a small bowl of mints beside them.

'What do you know about the Freedom Foundation?' asked Janet.

'Bugger all, except they've got a lot of money,' replied Fulton, his eyes scanning the room and landing on three very expensive-looking Scottish landscapes. 'Who's paying for all of this?'

'Charles McGowan, heard of him?'

'Nope.'

'He's an American billionaire with Scottish roots hence our office in Glasgow. He made his money in hedge funds.'

'So, a geriatric billionaire who sucked the system dry has now become a bleeding-heart liberal who wants to save the world.'

'Exactly,' said Janet. 'And Charles believes journalism is an essential pillar of democracy. You know the Yanks, Fulton, they take themselves very seriously. But, anyway, that's where you come in.'

'Okay.'

'The organisation's pumping money into investigative journalism and we're on a hiring spree. They want our new site to go live ASAP. I won't go into the details but what I need is top reporters who can produce outstanding journalism.'

'Okay,' said Fulton. He felt his phone vibrating in his pocket, again.

'Would you be interested?'

'Well, it's still pretty early in the morning,' said Fulton, distracted. Who was trying to get hold of him? 'I was expecting something but not a job offer. What sort of investigations would you be after?'

'Anything, big meaty exposés like the Crestwell story, or the security breaches at Faslane . . . I also loved the piece you did on corruption at the council. It would be focusing on the stories that matter, all the stuff you do brilliantly – none of the day-to-day news coverage.'

'And who will actually read this stuff? I mean, a website from an organisation that basically no one in Scotland has heard of is hardly a recipe for success.'

'I'm thinking about doing joint ventures with papers – they get the scoop, we get the exposure. We can basically do whatever we want. It really is a blank sheet at the moment.'

Fulton felt his phone vibrating again. He knew he couldn't ignore it for a third time.

'Excuse me,' he said, reaching into his pocket and pulling out the phone. He glanced at the screen. 'I'm sorry, Janet, but I'm really going to have to take this.'

'Something I'd be interested in?' asked Janet, arching her

eyebrows. 'Start the website with a bang.'

'Possibly,' said Fulton, with a sly smile.

'Tell me more.'

'I'm afraid Mum's the word for now. But you can buy the *Siren* and read all about it.'

'Just how I remember you, you're like a dog with a bone. That's why I want you to work for me. But, look, I've ambushed you – why don't you think over my offer and we can speak in the next week or so. We can talk more about terms and conditions.'

'Sounds like a plan.'

'And one more thing,' said Janet, as he stood up. 'In case you're wondering, it will be strictly business. I wouldn't want to abuse my position of authority again.'

'Right you are,' said Fulton, grinning awkwardly. He felt his phone vibrating again. 'Okay, I really need to go.'

He gave Janet a kiss on the cheek and promised to keep in touch. He was intrigued by the offer. It was the first time he'd ever been head-hunted but he would need a lot more info. He also knew that most start-ups normally ended up going bust, although most weren't backed by American billionaires.

Out on the street, Fulton whipped out his phone. He had four missed calls from Elaine, John Millar's sister. Not being able to get through, she'd sent a text: 'I need to give you something. On the train to Glasgow. Will arrive at Queen Street Station at 10:45. Please don't disappoint.'

What could she want? It must be important if she was dragging herself all the way in from Falkirk. He checked his watch. He had fifteen minutes. A black cab was coming over the brow of the hill. He flagged it down.

The taxi dropped off Fulton outside the station. He walked

past the sickly smokers wheezing on their cigarettes, through the double doors, and onto the concourse. The tannoy was announcing the departure of the train to Edinburgh. Fulton scanned the shifting crowd. He saw a pair of university students pawing each other with affection. A couple of businessmen with briefcases were talking loudly about the rugby. But no sign of Elaine. He tried calling but her phone was switched off. Fulton kept looking and eventually spotted her sitting at a table in the Burger King, waving at him. She looked a bit desperate, he thought, like someone drowning at sea.

'Thank you so much for coming,' she said, as Fulton sat down on one of the flimsy metal chairs. 'I know it was all a bit last minute but I just needed to see you.'

'No worries,' replied Fulton. 'I'm glad I could make it. Do you want a coffee or a bite to eat?'

'No, I'm fine, thank you. That's very kind of you.'

Fulton noticed that she was clutching a battered leather handbag on her lap as if she was expecting to be robbed at any moment. Her head was also jerking more than Fulton remembered.

'You okay, Elaine?'

'I'm fine, honestly, I'm fine,' she said. She looked down and fought with her hands to pull open the handbag's zip. She pulled out a small envelope and with it flapping about wildly in her hand, passed it to Fulton.

'What's this?' said Fulton. He could feel there was something inside it.

'It's a flash drive.'

'Do you know what's on it?'

'No, I'm sorry, I don't.'

'Why are you giving it to me, then?'

Elaine sighed deeply. She was no longer clutching her bag.

'Remember how I told you that John visited a month ago and was all out of sorts, that I thought he might do something stupid? Well, he gave me this envelope and he told me that if anything ever happened to him, I was to give it to someone I trust. I thought he was just being silly. But, then, of course . . .'

'It's okay, Elaine.' Fulton reached across the table and held her hand gently. He felt it twitching like a fish out of water. 'I'm so sorry about what happened to your brother.'

Elaine gave him a pinched smile. She pulled away her hand and thrust it into her jacket pocket. 'My brother always said that if you can trust a man with small things, then you can trust them with the big things as well.'

'But you barely know me.'

'I know that you're a man of your word – you didn't run the story. And I just hope, what with you being a reporter, that you might get to the bottom of this and find out who killed my brother. The police don't seem to be getting very far.'

A booming announcement cut through the clamour of the station. Elaine looked up and listened keenly. It was an announcement that the train to Falkirk was leaving in five minutes from platform eight.

'I'm really sorry but I'll need to catch that train,' said Elaine, struggling to zip up her bag. 'Otherwise, I'll need to wait another hour and travelling takes its toll on me.'

'No worries, I understand. It can't be easy with your condition,' said Fulton, slipping the envelope into his pocket. He reached down and picked up Elaine's cane from under the table. She stood up, uneasy on her feet. For a second, Fulton thought she was going to take a tumble but she steadied herself. He took her arm as they moved slowly towards the ticket barrier.

'Are you sure you're going to be okay getting on the train?' asked Fulton, as Elaine struggled to pull her ticket out of her pocket. 'I could come with you.'

'I'll be fine. Don't worry about me. But can you do me one last thing.'

'Sure, anything.'

'I don't mean to be rude, really I don't. You're a good man – a decent man. But please don't contact me again. My nerves can't take it, they just can't – what with everything that has happened. Just do what you think is best for John.'

'Of course,' said Fulton, slightly taken aback by the request.

Elaine swiped her ticket and awkwardly pushed her way through the barrier. Fulton watched her moving up the platform until she was lost in a sea of people. He felt the envelope in his pocket – it triggered a shiver of excitement.

Fulton slipped into the old sandstone library, not far from the station. Carved above the front entrance was the motto: 'Let there be light.' Fulton immediately had a strange feeling of *déjà vu*. He slowly realised it was one of the libraries where his dad had dropped him off on Saturday afternoons when he was a kid. He would devour Enid Blyton and Willard Price novels, reading quietly in the corner so as not to draw attention to himself. Fulton never asked his dad outright where he was going while he was reading, but the proceeds from the shop-lifting excursions would keep them going for another week.

If Fulton was looking for peace and quiet, he had chosen the wrong moment. The library was full of wired primary-school kids on their monthly visit. They looked at him as if he was some kind of animal at the zoo. One little girl, for reasons only known to herself, burst into tears when he walked in her direction. The middle-aged librarian wearing

71

a cartoonish red and white polka-dot ribbon in her mousy brown hair looked like she was on the verge of a breakdown. She was trying to hush a couple of boys who were engaged in a furious tug-of-war over a Harry Potter book. In the corner, Fulton saw a free computer beside a large potted plant. On the wall above it was a poster stating that no external drives should be used. Like any good journalist, he ignored it.

Quickly checking over his shoulder to see if the coast was clear, Fulton slipped the flash drive into the computer's hard drive beneath the desk. It popped up on the screen. He clicked on it. There was a single folder. He dragged it onto the desktop and then ejected the flash drive. He turned round and saw the librarian heading towards him with a face like thunder, her polka-dot ribbon bouncing up and down. But when she was within spitting distance a kid started yelling, 'You're a numpty, you cannae read this book.' She wheeled round and disappeared into the rows of shelves to discipline the children. Fulton quickly slipped the flash drive into his pocket. As he was doing it, the librarian reared, again, into view. But then another kid piped up, sending her scuttling off in a different direction. When the din died down, the librarian returned to her natural position of authority behind the desk.

Fulton clicked open the folder. There was only one video file entitled: 'IN THE EVENT OF MY DEATH.' His heart started racing like he was on speed, which he'd dabbled in as a teenager. He reached into his pocket and pulled out a knotted pair of earphones. When he'd finished untangling them, he checked to see where the librarian was. No sign of her. Result. He slipped the earphone jack into the computer. He took a deep breath and double-clicked.

72

Chapter 9

Davy did not do road traffic accidents; they were way beneath his station. But when he overheard in the canteen that there had been a fatal motorbike crash on a backroad not far from Lenzie and that the driver had no ID on him – it struck him as odd. Who goes out without their wallet?

An hour later, Davy pulled up behind two police vehicles parked tight against the hedgerow, so they wouldn't block the narrow road. He pushed open his car door and was hit by the smell of slurry. God, I hate the countryside, he thought. So much for 'fresh air'.

He walked down to the gate, or at least what was left of it. One of the posts was almost bent back on itself and the rest of the gate was folded over. The motorbike must have been going at a helluva lick, thought Davy. He looked up and spotted a couple of guys from the road traffic division in the middle of the field, which had a slight rise, before sloping away sharply down to a burn.

'O'Neill,' hollered Davy. He waved, still standing on the road. He really didn't want to get his shoes dirty if it wasn't necessary. O'Neill looked up, and when he saw Davy, bounded over. He had barely been a year in the force and his enthusiasm had yet to be bled out of him.

'Good to see you, sir,' said O'Neill, panting.

'Aye, good to see you, son. Now fill me in.'

'On what?'

'On what happened here,' said Davy impatiently. 'I've not got all day and there's no way I'm going any further with these shoes on.'

'Best we can tell, sir, is the motorcyclist hit the gate here,' said O'Neill, pointing at the mangled mess.

'Thanks for that,' said Davy. 'I kinda figured that out for myself. Where did the body end up?'

'See that tree over there, the big chestnut one.' He pointed at a tree, twenty metres away, overhanging the road. 'They found the body in the top branches.'

'Bloody hell!' said Davy. 'Talk about a catapult shot. I don't think I've ever seen one go that far. And who found the body?'

'A local farmer. He said at first he thought it was a plastic bag or something. But then he saw the bike in the field and realised what had happened – says it's not the first time.'

As Davy was listening, he leaned back, nicking his sleeve on the barbed-wire fence. 'Feck's sake, this cost me a hundred quid.'

'Darn it, sir.'

'Do I look like a man who can sew to you, O'Neill?'

Before the young cop could think up a response, they were distracted by a distant medley of moos followed by the sound of hooves. Davy looked up and saw a brown cow appearing over the rise in the field. A few seconds later dozens more were fanned out behind her – and they were heading in Davy's direction.

'What's going on here?' asked Davy.

'It must be milking time,' replied O'Neill.

'How many times they get milked a day?' asked Davy apprehensively, as the animals approached.

'Two or three times a day.'

'So, let me get this straight, we've already had a hundred cows crapping all over the crime scene.'

'Well, they have to use this gate,' said O'Neill defensively. 'It's the only route to the farm. And they need to get milked. I mean it's not as if they can sit and cross their legs.'

One of the cows was now a few metres from Davy. She had big dark eyes and a soaking wet nose from grazing on the damp glass. She looked directly at Davy and gave him a menacing moo. Davy got the message. He took a few steps further up the road so he wouldn't be blocking the cow's path.

'But what do you mean crime scene?' asked O'Neill, moving up the road with Davy. 'We've got it down as an accident. Did I miss something, sir? I've still got a lot to learn.'

'Naw, I'm just toying with you. You're doing a great job.' Davy felt his phone vibrate in his pocket. 'But, look, I've got to get moving.' He pulled out his phone and glanced at the screen. 'Got to take this,' he said to O'Neill. 'But we should go for a pint, sometime.'

Davy turned away from O'Neill and started walking back to the car. When he was out of earshot, he answered the call. It lasted less than a minute. Davy bleeped his vehicle, pulled open the door and got in. He started the ignition. His gut was good. The motorcyclist had been identified. His name was Joey Castle – and he was a known associate of Trilby Tam.

Chapter 10

Fulton was pacing up and down Sauchiehall Street, anxiety rising inside him. He couldn't believe what he'd just seen in the library. The video couldn't be right, could it? Conspiracy on such a scale? He'd watched it five times. Fulton's gut told him the accusations were genuine. If they were, it was the biggest story of his career. But Fulton knew the consequences of exposing it were so grave that he'd need to tread carefully. Standing on the city's busiest shopping street, cold fear was setting in like the blizzard on the mountaintop where Fulton had once been left stranded. He shuddered at the thought. He was distracted by his phone vibrating. Yes, Fulton told Chris, he could meet, and, yes, half an hour in the King's Park Café would be fine.

Fulton sat down in one of the café's small booths with its distinctive yellow plastic leather seats. The only comfort he took from the surroundings was that it was where he'd come with some of the football boys at the end of a big night out. Now Fulton sat with his hand wedged in his pocket, clutching the flash drive as if his life depended on it. He presumed Chris wanted to meet to chew him out about the Elaine interview and his failure to land the scoop. But who the hell was Chris to lecture him about journalism? Fulton could tell Chris about the video but he was the type of editor who would bury the story, saying it was too risky – cowardice masked as caution. Best, thought Fulton, to keep it to himself until he figured out a plan. Back in the library, he'd been careful to delete the video from the computer screen but then a chasm of horror opened up in his mind: he'd forgotten to empty the recycle bin. Oh my God, he thought, what happens if the librarian checks the bin before permanently deleting it? Before his panic could spiral out of control, it was punctured by the sound of a familiar voice.

'Fulton, thanks for seeing me at such short notice – it can be hard to catch you at the office.'

Chris's hair flopped over his brow as he sat down at the quick-wipe Formica table. He used his left hand to sweep it back into place revealing his silver monogrammed cufflinks. There was something about Chris' manner – in fact his entire being – that riled Fulton in a way that he realised wasn't entirely rational.

'You don't get stories sitting in the office,' said Fulton coolly.

'It was a statement of fact, rather than any implied criticism,' replied Chris, with a sigh. Here he was doing Fulton a favour but barely seconds in the door and it was turning hostile. Chris could genuinely never understand the antipathy he stirred in the newsroom. He found the chippiness of Glaswegians flat-out depressing. They loved to profess they were the friendliest people in the world, so long as you weren't English and posh to boot. The I-get-on-with-everyone mob, until they emphatically don't. Chris had lost count of the times he'd opened his mouth only to draw dirty looks and verbal volleys of bugger-off-back-to-where-you-came-from. People barely skipped a beat as they bellowed it out in bars, revelling in the sheer unadulterated joy of letting rip in a public space. Those who really should know better lowered their heads and pretended to have heard nothing or, if caught out, would offer a sheepish smile and excuse it as just banter. Chris could never say any of this, of course; he would simply be dismissed as a patronising English bastard.

'Look, I'm sorry,' said Fulton. 'That was uncalled for. It's just . . . nothing.'

'Okay,' said Chris, wanting to draw a line under the affair. 'Shall we get something to eat? I'm guessing salads aren't on the menu.'

'What are you after? Chips?'

'Yes, fine.'

Fulton waved to Irene, the waitress who had been a familiar face for decades. She lifted up the bar portion of the serving counter, where the battered haddock and haggis were all stacked up in glass cases, and bumbled over to the booth at the pace of someone who would never be rushed. She took down the order on a notepad. As she wrote, a smear of grease on her fingers smudged a shadow over the paper. Once back behind the counter, she dumped four handfuls of freshly cut potatoes into the fryer. The oil roared into life with a hiss. A minute later, Irene gave the basket two good dunts and her thick wrists turned it on its side. The golden chips spilled into the glass display case. With a couple of quick flicks, she sprayed them with salt.

'Enjoy your dinner,' she said, after bringing their order to the booth. Chris took a small bottle of hand sanitiser from his pocket and proceeded to squeeze a dollop onto the palm of his hands. With great precision, he rubbed his fingers taking great care around his wedding ring. He took a paper napkin and laid it across his lap.

'It's been a while since I've had proper chips,' said Chris, after a few bites. 'I won't leave it so long next time.'

'Aye, it's the best chippie in Glasgow. But, look, what do you need to talk to me about?'

Chris looked up and put his fork down. A troubled look swept his face. Even good actors, thought Fulton, can't always disguise their true emotions.

'The accountants have been in . . .'

As soon as Fulton heard the word – *accountants* – it triggered a swell of anger. Here was an editor of a national newspaper, one of the top journalism jobs in the country, and the only thing he could think about was the bottom line rather than the front page.

'I'll get straight to the point, Fulton. Head office has been conducting a review of staffing levels, revenues are sharply down this year and digital advertising has not made up the shortfall.'

'And,' prodded Fulton.

'And I need to make more cuts.'

'And how does this affect me, Chris?'

There was an uneasy silence. Chris picked up his plastic fork, stabbed a pile of chips and popped them into his mouth. His cheeks ballooned. He then screwed off the top of his Orangina bottle and took a swig to cleanse his palate.

'It doesn't necessarily affect you. But I need more out of you. You're one of the highest-paid reporters on the newspaper and when the accountants look at the spreadsheets, your name sticks out.'

Fulton tugged a napkin out of the metal dispenser on the table and wiped the grease off his fingers. He put his hand into his pocket to check the flash drive was still there. Not only would the revelations it contained send shockwaves through the entire British political system, but now it could end up saving his job.

'Just so I'm clear, Chris, you're saying my job is on the line. And just to be doubly clear, you're saying you've got my back? Did I get that part right?'

'Absolutely.'

'Since when, exactly?'

'Do you honestly think I enjoy this?' said Chris, his tone hardening. 'I'm well aware that lies spread faster than the truth, but the reality is journalism costs money: money that we don't have. And at a time when as a society we're more divided than ever, at the very moment when we're crying out for responsible journalism, our industry is being decimated. No one knows that better me, Fulton, no one.'

'But you've never been interested in proper stories.'

'What utter claptrap.'

'What about my story about the Tory leader, him fiddling his expenses? You buried that good and proper, didn't you? Spoke to your pals and the story never saw the light of day. Call yourself an editor? You ended up shitting yourself at the sniff of the first big story on your watch.'

Fulton leaned back in his seat. He realised he'd gone too far – again. Neither man said anything for a while. It was as if they were surveying the smouldering wreckage before them.

'That story was a long time ago, and in the grand scheme of things, small fry. I'm not here to rake over the past. I've always shown you respect and in return I've been the recipient of unremitting hostility. Please don't mistake my kindness for weakness.'

Chris stood up, marched to the till, paid for both of them, and left the café without a backwards glance. Fulton sat at the table, pushing his fingers through his hair.

'What's wrong, son?' asked Irene, clearing away the plates.

'Not much, Irene. I'm fine. It's just there's a lot going on.'

'Who was that fella? Very grand-looking what with his . . . what do you call them?' she asked, pulling on one of her sleeves.

'Cufflinks.'

'Aye, them. That's a first in here. And it's been a while since I've seen anyone use a napkin on their knees – very posh.'

She cackled with laughter. Fulton couldn't help but smile.

'Look, son, sometimes life can get a wee bit overwhelming,' said Irene. 'We've all been there. You feel alone. But do you know what you have to do in these times?'

'What?'

'You reach out to those you love and trust. Do you have anyone, son?'

'Aye, one or two.'

'Well, do yourself a favour and go and speak to them. They might not sort it all out, but they'll definitely help.'

Chapter 11

Fulton was standing on the platform when he heard the soft whooshing sound off in the distance, signalling the imminent arrival of the 07:36 train to Glasgow Central. He watched as the other sleep-deprived commuters glanced up from their phones. They started shuffling forward to form short queues at the spots where they knew the carriage doors would slide open. Fulton hung back. He hated all the passive-aggressive manoeuvring to secure a seat. He'd already resigned himself to the fact that he would be standing for the duration of the journey. He didn't normally head in so early but following yesterday's blow-out with Chris in the café, he thought it best to show his face bright and early in the office. It was his peace offering of sorts.

He was the last to clamber aboard the train and the carriage was stowed out. As they pulled away from the platform, Fulton stared out of the window at the manicured gardens of the elegant sandstone houses he would never be able to afford. The train stopped at Giffnock, Thornliebank, Pollokshaws West, and with each station Fulton was forced further up the carriage. By the time they reached Crossmyloof, he was standing in the centre of the carriage with several folk pressed up against him. It was a mind-numbing experience and Fulton searched for a distraction. He glanced down at a young woman, in her early twenties, who was sitting at a table and scrolling through Twitter on her phone. He felt a brief pang of guilt. He knew he should be doing the same but the torrent of news, information and rumours left him reeling at times. Being offline was considered a revolutionary act these days, but it gave you time to actually think: not that you were ever likely to be inspired amidst the crush of the morning commute.

Fulton was still watching when the young woman with chipped red nail polish stopped scrolling at a post that had already been retweeted 4,000 times – a figure that was spiralling fast. He strained to see the name of the account – @ ThePlotAgainstScotland. He had never heard of it. Perhaps it was a smart advertising campaign for a new streaming series? The woman clicked on the video. It buffered for a second or so and then Fulton saw the face of John Millar staring back at him from the phone screen. He did a double-take. This couldn't be true, could it? It just couldn't be. But with growing horror, he realised it was the video he'd watched over and over again in the library. It was on Twitter and going viral for the whole world to see. He felt as if he was going to explode in the middle of the packed train.

The video showed the gaunt face of a man who looked like he was on the brink of a nervous breakdown. He was standing against a white wall in a room that could have been almost anywhere. The lighting was murky. Fulton grabbed the seat's headrest and leaned over to get a better view. John Millar was talking. Fulton couldn't hear anything as the woman was wearing earphones, but he knew every word, every sentence, every pause.

'My name is John Millar, and if you're watching this video it means I'm dead.'

Millar coughed and cleared his throat.

'I was murdered on the orders of the First Minister, Susan Ward. She repeatedly threatened to have me killed when I worked in her office.

'I knew her well and over the years came to understand what a devious, conniving bitch she was.' His eyes flared with anger. 'She who was prepared to stop at nothing in pursuit of her life's mission: Scottish independence.'

Millar paused. It appeared that he'd momentarily forgotten his lines. 'Why did she want me dead?'

He disappeared for a few seconds, then held up three loose sheets of paper one after the other to the camera but they were too close, the text blurred.

'These three documents are evidence of treason at the heart of the Scottish government. They show transactions from a Russian bank to the Scottish Nationalist party. The party used this illegal funding to pursue its goal.

'And the reason Susan Ward wanted me dead is because I found out about it. I refused to go along with it. She threatened to have me killed to keep me quiet. I admit I was scared, I was a coward and I wasn't brave enough to go public. By keeping quiet, I thought I could save my life but now you know that was not the case.

'Susan Ward is a ruthless killer who will stop at nothing. She is a cold-blooded murderer, but now her secret is out.

'I've left these documents,' he gestured to the papers, 'in the safe-keeping of someone I trust. I've made arrangements for them to be made public in the event of my death. If they never see the light of day, it's part of the cover-up.

'To anyone who may be watching this video, I urge you to seek justice on my behalf – it could be you next. This is not about politics. My only motivation is to protect the great Scottish people. We cannot allow our democratic system to be corrupted by outsiders. The only thing necessary for the triumph of evil is for good men to do nothing.'

Millar stood for a few seconds blinking into the camera. He moved forward, his frame blocking the shot. The screen went black.

Fulton was in a state of shock. How had the video leaked? Who posted it on Twitter? And why? It can't have been the librarian. Could it? He looked up from the screen and realised the news of the video was rippling through the train. He watched as the businessman beside him handed his phone to a colleague. 'You need to watch this,' he said. 'It's bloody unbelievable.'

Further up the carriage, a guy wearing a black cap and oil-smeared overalls shouted, 'That's the bitch done for now.'

'Mind your mouth, there are weans here,' scolded an elderly woman with hawkish eyes, who was holding the hand of a little girl who was oblivious to the bad language. 'And if you believe that woman murdered that man, you're a bigger eejit than you look.'

A man wearing a grey hoodie laughed at her remark, but a young guy standing behind him was growing increasingly agitated. 'It's all a conspiracy,' he cried. 'We're all slaves but we don't even realise it. London will never let us be free.'

A few people in the carriage nodded in agreement while others averted their gaze, not wanting to get caught up in the crossfire of an argument so early in the morning. The train lurched across the River Clyde before pulling into Central Station. Passengers scrambled to grab their bags and tumbled out of their seats. The doors slid open and the commuters piled out. Fulton was the last one off. Standing on the concourse, commuters were surging round him like rapids negotiating a rock. He was at the heart of the biggest story in the world. Cold fear was setting in once more. He felt paralysed; he didn't know where to turn.

Susan Ward, her husband Gordon and their two young daughters were halfway through a breakfast of cereal, toast and scrambled eggs when there was a knock at the door. Before any of them had a chance to react, the door was open.

'Sorry to bother you. I know it's against the rules,' said Brian, giving Gordon a quick glance, 'but, Susan, can I have a moment?'

'Can you give me two minutes?' asked Susan. 'The kids are almost done.'

The girls were dressed in their school uniforms, black-and-yellow ties stuffed inside their shirts to stop them getting covered in jam. They were racing to see who could glug down their orange juice fastest.

'I won!' said the oldest daughter, triumphantly placing her empty yellow plastic cup on the table.

'No, I won!' screamed her younger sister, a second later. 'Mummy, I won.'

'No, I won!'

'Enough, Mhairi . . . Rhona . . .' said Susan firmly. 'It was a draw.'

The girls started giggling, their small hands covering their mouths.

Brian waited for the laughter to die down. 'Susan,' he said, impatiently, 'we really need to talk, like now.'

'Okay,' said Susan, pushing out her chair. As she did so, Gordon stood up from the other side of the table and made a point of slowly refilling his cup of coffee from the stainless-steel pot sitting on the granite countertop. Susan waited until he looked over. 'Sorry,' she said.

'It's okay,' replied Gordon. Susan knew full well he was fuming but he'd just have to lump it: work was work and Gordon knew the score. She kissed both the girls gently on their heads, told them to be good at school, and left the kitchen.

'This had better be bloody serious,' said Susan to Brian.

'Let's go to the drawing room,' he said.

The pair walked through the hallway and Susan could feel her stress ratchet up with every step. She knew something was wrong, deeply wrong. Brian's silence said everything – he normally blurted things without a care in the world. He closed the dark mahogany double doors behind them.

'Have you seen the video?' asked Brian, speaking quietly at first, but his urgency getting the better of him.

'What video? What are you on about?'

'This video,' said Brian, thrusting his phone into her hand. 'It's everywhere. The one where John Millar says you had him killed.'

'What are you on about it? Is this some kind of sick joke?' asked Susan, looking bewildered.

'Just watch it,' barked Brian.

'My name is John Millar . . .' At first Susan was calm, transfixed by the video, but Brian watched as the tough, battle-hardened woman he thought he knew was left reeling. She winced when John said she was 'a devious, conniving bitch'. When he called her a 'cold-blooded murderer' it was as if a slab of concrete had been smashed over her head.

'It's not true, none of this is true,' said Susan, visibly shaking. 'Why has he done this to me? Why?'

'I don't know, Susan, I don't know. I'm sorry, I'm so sorry. I don't know what's going on.'

After a minute or so, Susan wiped away a solitary tear. Brian could see that she was slowly regaining her poise. If being a woman in Scottish politics had taught her anything, it was that you couldn't show any weakness – even when you were shredded inside.

'I'm not going to let that unhinged bastard destroy me and my life's work, Brian. I'm not giving him that power over me.'

'I hear you,' said Brian. 'But you know this changes everything?'

'Really,' replied Susan. 'You really think so?'

A smile crept across Brian's face. Normally, he would have hit back but biting sarcasm under the circumstances was delightful.

'Well, first of all, I think I know you well enough, and I'm going to assume that you didn't order John's hit.'

'Of course not.'

'Good to get that out of the way.'

'Who else has seen the video?'

'Eh, it's more a case of who hasn't seen it. It was posted on Twitter an hour ago and it's gone viral. Everyone wants a comment. The first thing we need to establish is if the video is genuine.'

'What do you mean?'

'If it's a deep fake or not?'

'I know it's genuine, Brian, one hundred per cent.'

'How exactly?'

'His mannerisms,' said Susan. 'The way he pinched his nose and then squeezed his right earlobe – I've only ever seen John do that. He does it when he's under pressure; they can't fake that.'

'Okay, but here's the thing, the public don't know that.'

'What are you suggesting, Brian?'

'We muddy the waters, question the veracity of the video.'

'Are you saying I should lie?'

'Not tell a lie, Susan, pose a question: there's a big difference. You'll simply be planting a seed of doubt in the minds of the public. The internet's awash with deep fakes: why should this one be any different?'

'I'm not pulling a Trump in Edinburgh,' said Susan firmly.

'All right, Little Miss Perfect, what do you suggest then?'

'What if I come clean?'

'Come clean about what?'

'The affair—'

'Christ, are you kidding me? Do you want to be remembered as the woman who delivered independence or as the woman who couldn't keep her knickers on and lost the vote? Because it's your choice.'

'Why do you always need to be so crass?'

'Why do you always need to be so stupid?'

A silence descended. Brian puffed out his cheeks and exhaled deeply. Susan took a couple of steps towards the closed doors.

'Give me a few minutes,' she said. 'I need to speak to Gordon.'

'Okay, but he does know about the affair, doesn't he?'

Susan's face crumpled and she started sobbing.

When Davy woke up his saliva was pooling over the desk. His cheek was wet. After lifting his head, it took him a few seconds to realise where he actually was. He had met an old flame the night before. He had drunk too much, got carried away, and had gone back to her place. She lived beyond the city. When Davy woke up at five in the morning, he had caught a taxi and headed straight into work. But he was so knackered and hungover that he'd promptly fallen asleep at his desk.

He walked over to the sink in the corner of his office. Looking at himself in the mirror, he was shocked, although not entirely surprised, at the state he was in. His eyes were blood-shot from the drinking and all the lovemaking, as he liked to call it. He was wearing the same white shirt and double-breasted suit jacket that he'd had on yesterday. He smelt like a pub at closing time. He turned on the cold tap and cupped his hands to splash water over his face. He grabbed paper towels and dried himself off. He combed his hair. He pulled out a small bottle of cologne that he kept in his top drawer. He sprayed it on his wrist and hand and then smeared it all over his face. It stung his eyes but he felt fresher for it. He checked his phone. There was a message from the boss. 'Have you seen this?' Davy clicked on the link and watched in horror. Why was this video plastered all over the internet? It made no sense. He kept rubbing his eyes. Was this all a bad dream? Was his mind playing tricks on him? Then he heard the click, click, click approaching from along the corridor and a sense of dread settled over him.

'Do you not have a bath at home?' said Larbert, with no discernible sarcasm. He was standing in the doorway. Everything about the chief constable was pristine, thought Davy. His hair was perfectly groomed; his nails were neatly trimmed; there wasn't a speck – not a speck – on his black uniform, and to top it all off his silver buttons were dazzling like jewels.

'Suffering from a touch of the flu.' Davy hesitated. 'Sir.'

'At this time of year, pull the other one, Davy. We'll talk about your carousing and the impact it's having on your work some other time. Come with me, there's someone you need to meet.'

'Yes, sir.'

Davy followed Larbert along the corridor. Both men knew

something immense was underway, that part anyone could grasp. But the police, like politicians and ordinary punters, were waking up to the John Millar video and struggling to make sense of it all. Clearly, it was bad news for Susan Ward and the nationalists. It would surely torpedo their campaign, genuine or not. But were there any other revelations to come? Would the video trigger consequences that few could foresee? The truth was nobody knew, and anyone who pretended otherwise was lying: Scotland was in uncharted territory.

As they stood waiting for the lift, Larbert glanced at Davy and rolled his eyes in disgust. If it had been the army, Davy would have been court-martialled on the spot. The lift bell pinged and the doors opened. Larbert stepped in first with Davy behind. They rode to the eighth floor, home to the top brass. Davy tried to avoid it all costs. He associated this floor of the building with the occasional bollocking and a drinks reception that was once held in his honour after he'd solved a particularly high-profile murder case. He wasn't sure which of the occasions he found more uncomfortable. When the lift doors started opening, Larbert reached forward and hit the door-close button. He turned to Davy.

'A quick word of advice – actually make that an order,' said Larbert, slowly and deliberately. 'You may think you're God's gift to the police but for once in your life, shut your gob and just listen. Have I made myself clear?'

'Aye, sir,' said Davy. He paused while Larbert glared at him. 'You have my word.'

That seemed to satisfy Larbert, who allowed the doors to slide open. The pair walked along the corridor to the conference room. On the walls were black-and-white portraits showing all of Glasgow's chief constables from the past century. Davy glanced at them and felt a surge of contempt. He didn't consider a single one of them a proper polisman. As far as he was concerned, they were all politicians masquerading as polis who had shimmied up the greasy pole out of their own self-interest. Most never knew their arse from their elbow when it came to working the streets and the same went for po-faced Larbert.

Davy walked into the conference room first and instantly recognised the guy sitting at the end of the table.

'Well, well, if it's not the mystery man,' said Davy, who had noticed the guy hanging about HQ for the past few days. The guy lit up, a big grin across his face. He pushed out his chair and walked round the table to greet Davy. He was a powerfully-built man, wearing a Barbour jacket and a pink-and-white checked shirt.

'David Bryant, I've heard a lot about you – all of it good,' he said in a clipped voice that carried across rooms and through walls. 'And from what I've heard, you're the best detective around here.'

'Just so you know, I go by Davy around here.'

'Apologies, Davy, I should introduce myself. I'm Neil Simpson and it's a real pleasure to meet you.'

He shook Davy's hand with a vice-like grip.

'From that English accent of yours, I'm guessing you're not from around here.'

'I see nothing gets by you, Davy.' Another broad grin. 'Born and raised in and around London, for my sins.'

'Don't worry, Neil, we won't hold that against you: welcome to Scotland. What you doing up here? Which department are you with?'

Larbert snorted loudly like a hayfever sufferer who had woken up to find himself lying in a field of cut grass.

'You all right, sir?' asked Davy, glancing over his shoulder.

'Fine.'

'All questions, this one,' said Neil, winking at Larbert.

'Well, that's our Davy and that inquisitive mind of his. But he does solve cases, so we cut him a bit of slack from time to time.'

'I like the sound of that,' replied Neil. 'Chief Constable, shall we get down to business?'

'Yes, let's do that.'

Larbert closed the door and the three men sat down at the conference table.

'Davy, in light of what's happened with the Millar video going viral,' said Larbert, 'we've decided to shake up the investigation. It's absolutely no criticism of you – you're considered the best we've got. But as we're all aware this is no longer just a murder: it's an affair that threatens the political stability of the entire country.

'It's no exaggeration to say that this is the biggest case the Scottish police have ever had to deal with – bigger even than Lockerbie. And with that in mind, we've requested and been granted whatever resources we need to catch those who killed John Millar.

'I'll be liaising closely with Neil. For the purposes of transparency, Davy, Neil is an MI5 intelligence officer. And I should also point out, and again this is only for transparency, that John Millar worked for MI6.'

'Oh, did he now?'

'Yes, while he was stationed in Moscow. But he left the service several years ago under somewhat of a cloud. But, Davy, I don't want any of this discussed outside these four walls. It's on a strictly need-to-know basis and the last thing I want to do is stir up more hysteria. Are we clear on that, Detective Sergeant?'

'Absolutely, sir.'

'Neil here can smooth over any issues when they arise – just let me know. It goes without saying that on a case of this magnitude we can't afford to screw it up. But, Davy, I will stress this again, within the confines of the law we need to secure a suspect and we need to charge them as quickly as possible. The public want answers and it's our job to provide them. Time is truly of the essence. Neil, do you have anything to add or have I covered everything?'

'I'd just like to reiterate, Davy, I'm here to help – my door is always open, my phone is always on. Don't think twice about running anything by me. As the chief constable said, catching the killer or killers is the absolute priority. I'm heading through to John Millar's flat in Edinburgh later this morning, so perhaps you could join me?'

'Aye, that sounds like a plan.'

'Davy,' asked Larbert, 'do you have any questions relating to the case? Or is everything clear?'

Davy rubbed his eyes. 'There is one thing, sir, that I don't quite understand,' he said, leaning back in his chair. 'But maybe it's because I'm a wee bit slow.' Davy wasn't sure whether to follow through but why duck it? 'If we were the only ones with the John Millar video, how exactly did it leak and go public?'

The two men opposite looked at each other uncomfortably, with Neil signalling that he would respond.

'Davy, I understand your concerns and I know you're leading the investigation. But, and please don't take this the wrong way, that doesn't mean you need to know everything. Sometimes secrets are safer in other people's hands.'

Susan was standing in the hallway behind Bute House's main entrance. Once the front door swung open and she walked out, she knew there would be no going back. She would long for the days when she was criticised for being a cold and calculating politician, who put politics before her family, rather than a murdering whore who cuckolded her husband while in high office.

'How big is the crowd?' she asked.

'Big,' said Brian, scrolling through social media on his phone.

'Are the girls back from school yet?'

'Yes, I just checked. They got back a couple of minutes ago.'

'Are they okay?'

'Aye, they're fine. A bit confused about why they got pulled out of school but Gordon's with them. Look, are you really sure you want to go through with this?'

'Yes, Brian. Just give me a minute.'

She gazed again at the photo she was holding. It was a framed school picture of Mhairi and Rhona. She placed it on the side table. Outside, dozens of journalists watched as the black door beneath the fan-shaped transom window slowly opened. There was a swarm of clicks from the photographers' cameras as the First Minister appeared and then carefully negotiated the steps in her high heels.

Susan smoothed out two pieces of paper on the lectern positioned on the pavement. Brian fleetingly placed his hand on her shoulder and whispered in her ear, 'Give 'em hell,' before moving out of shot. Susan looked down at the papers, cleared her throat, and looked straight ahead into the battery of cameras.

'Good morning,' she said. 'Like all of you, I'm shocked by the allegations made against me. In the interests of our country at this critical moment, it is only right that I'm frank with the Scottish people.'

Her voice was strong and steady; she appeared to be in command.

'To be absolutely clear, neither my government nor I had anything to do with John Millar's murder. The allegation that I ordered his murder, or was in anyway involved in his death, is preposterous. It is a lie and it is a lie designed to destroy my life's work.'

She coughed. 'Excuse me . . . So too are the allegations that my party received money from the Russian government. Again, that is a lie designed to destroy the cause of independence. We can account for every penny of the party's spending and will be doing so in the coming hours.

'What happened to John is a tragedy. He was a good man who was clearly disturbed in the last few months of his life. I knew John well – better than most. We worked closely together on a number of issues. We became very close. And that relationship . . .'

Susan faltered. She stared down at her speech for a few seconds while she composed herself.

'And that relationship became something else. John and . . .'

She stopped again. She looked skyward in the hope it would somehow summon help. But on this stage, there was no hiding.

'John and I had an affair.'

A pulse of energy surged through the crowd.

'I make no excuses, it was wrong, and it has caused terrible pain to my family. I have apologised to them and will do all I can to make amends. I take full responsibility for my actions.

'This is the background to the video. John did not want to end the affair and he threatened to hurt me in any way possible. And by accusing me of his murder he is trying to destroy me from beyond the grave.

'We do not know why John was killed. We do not yet know who murdered him. But Police Scotland have reassured me that they are doing all they can to catch his killers. We must ensure there is justice for John.

'But we cannot ignore the fact that these are extraordinary times. Our democracy is being tested as never before. We must remain calm during this difficult period. My personal failings should not detract from the historic choice we have to make in the next few days. I want to reassure you that the independence referendum will go ahead, as planned, next Thursday. The people cannot, and must not, be denied their voice. I thank you for your time this—'

Before Susan could finish, a horde of journalists pushed forward, surrounding her in seconds. It was so quick that the couple of cops standing close by had no chance to react. 'Are you going to resign?' shouted a woman, thrusting her microphone into Susan's face. 'First Minister, do you have blood on your hands?' shouted another. 'Should the vote be cancelled?' 'Is there a conspiracy, First Minister?'

Panic was sweeping across Susan's face. She felt she was being set upon by this mob. Through the sea of faces she saw Brian fighting his way towards her. He elbowed a cameraman in the ribs. The camera on his shoulder toppled into the back of another journalist's head. Brian reached her. Susan felt him pushing her towards the steps. A journalist planted his hand on Susan's shoulder and tried to pull her round. Brian ripped the fingers off her shoulder in a fury. Susan then stumbled on the stairs but Brian caught her, stuck his arm around her waist and, positioning her like a battering ram, pushed her into the house. The policeman at the entrance shoved a couple of journalists out of the way and slammed the door shut.

'People are going to think we're lovers, if we keep meeting like this,' said Tam.

Davy chuckled but then realised the old man wasn't joking. Tam picked up his hat from the weathered park bench and wiped the rim a couple of times before placing it on his silver hair.

'Take a seat, Davy,' he said, with the stern tone of a judge speaking to the accused. Kelvingrove Park was largely deserted, apart from a couple of dog walkers and a young lad who had taken a fancy to Tam in order to pay for a fix.

'Did you see that bum boy over there?' asked Tam, pointing towards the footpath running alongside the river. 'The ginger one? He kept winking at me, thinking I wanted to go into the bushes with him. If he pulls that stunt again, I'll get one of the boys to come down here and slit his throat.

'You know, I used to bring my Maureen down here when we were courting. First time I came here must have been around 1964. There was a jazz band playing on the bandstand. I can't remember the name but, by God, they were fantastic. We had our first kiss that day. She was a good woman, my Maureen, a loving mother, and now we've got bum boys jumping out of the bushes. There's no fucking decency any more.'

'I'm sorry for your loss, Tam, I really am. It can't be easy.'

'Aye, what can you do?'

Tam struggled to pull out a crumpled packet of Benson & Hedges from his pocket. He offered one to Davy before lighting up. The smoke caught on the brim of his trilby before billowing upwards. After a couple of draws, Tam wheezed violently, and for a few seconds he couldn't catch his breath.

The purple veins on his face erupted like raspberries. But then he gulped down a couple of breaths of air and tossed the cigarette onto the grass. He placed his hands on his knees and coughed violently, spitting out a dollop of yellow mucus onto the ground.

'So, what gives me the pleasure of a visit from Strathclyde's finest twice in two days?' asked Tam, as if nothing had happened. 'What you after?'

'I was just wondering if you'd had a chance to think over my wee proposition from the other day? As I'm sure you're aware from the news today things are getting a bit more urgent.'

'I don't watch the news, Davy, I find it too depressing. They've never got anything good to say. Remind me again, whit were you after?'

There was a smile on Tam's lips. Davy felt like grabbing the man's head and smashing it on the arm of the bench. He took a deep breath. 'Tam, I really don't have time for these mind games. I guess you heard what happened to your boy, Joey?'

Tam's smile dissolved. 'Aye, Joey was a young, daft boy who enjoyed his drink a wee bit too much. He was a good lad, high on life – but accidents happen.'

'Are you sure it was an accident?' asked Davy. 'Or perhaps them who paid for the hit wanted to tie up a few loose ends – and, as we both know, Joey was the driver.'

Tam pursed his lips. He leaned forward and pretended to pick a speck of dirt off his trouser leg. He sat back up again. 'What do you want to talk about, Davy?'

'I was wondering if you'd managed to speak to Charlie.'

'Aye, I spoke to the boy.'

'And what did he say? Is he prepared to come down the station?'

'Charlie realises he made a mistake on the job by wearing a shirt that was covered in bunnies. And he also knows that because of it he's now a person of interest. And what with this whole political carry-on, he's prepared, I believe, to go down to the station and make a statement.'

'You believe?'

'I cannae force him, Davy. It's the boy's decision if he wants to talk.'

'Okay. So, when do you think Charlie may be prepared to talk, then?'

'He mentioned something about tomorrow morning.'

'I can't wait that long.'

'Well, Charlie may change his mind. I can't speak for the boy but I could ask him for you ... to see whether he'll go down to the station a bit sooner than he wanted.'

'I'd appreciate that.'

'But, Davy, favours don't come for free,' said Tam, sensing he'd regained the upper hand. He smiled, revealing his chipped, stained teeth. 'I'm a businessman after all. I don't do something for nothing, especially not for the polis. You understand me?'

Davy let out a deep sigh. He rubbed his chin. He needed results. 'No promises, Tam. We'll have to see what Charlie has to say for himself and then we can talk.'

'Fair enough,' said Tam. 'But I've waited a long time for this moment.'

'What moment?'

'When we go into business together.'

The atmosphere at the *Siren's* office was normally that of a poorly attended church coffee morning on a dreary winter's day. But today the place was thrumming with the excitement and anticipation that only such a story can generate. Everyone was in, everyone was engaged, and everyone's adrenaline was pumping. Fulton's colleagues were smiling. Helen, a features writer, even gave him a thumbs-up. Previously, they had barely exchanged more than a dozen words in as many years. But this was a history-making moment and any hack worth their salt wanted a shot at posterity.

The news editor, Max Miller, was like a small-time conductor who suddenly found himself thrust in front of a full orchestra – and he wasn't going to let the opportunity go to waste. He was working up a frothy sweat, hurling orders with flailing arms to the news desk, the political desk and even the arts desk, urging them, begging them, to find out whatever they could about what was going on. When the First Minister appeared for her speech, he scrabbled through all the papers on his desk, sending them flying as he searched for the TV remote.

Dozens of staff gathered round the TV perched above Max's desk to watch the historic speech. Even Chris came out of his office to be part of one of the rare moments when the newsroom felt truly united, rather than tearing itself apart. When Susan Ward finished her speech, Max exclaimed, 'First a sensational video, then an affair, and now a fight – I've never seen anything like it. The First Minister is a dead woman walking and independence has gone doon the swanny with her!'

He rounded it off with a joyous clap of his hands above his head – not because he was necessarily against independence but because it was such a stunning change of fortune. Just a day before, several polls had all shown the Leave vote edging it.

Max's jubilation about the story was in stark contrast to

Fulton's growing fury about how the video had leaked. He'd handed it over to Davy the night before on strict instructions that it was purely for safekeeping only for it to appear on Twitter hours later. Fulton had spent most of the morning trying to get through to his friend, his efforts increasingly taking on the desperation of a parent trying to find their missing child. He called every ten minutes, but Davy's phone was switched off. He sent him more than a dozen text messages – 'Call me' 'Where are you?' 'What's going on?' 'DID YOU LEAK THE VIDEO?' – but they all disappeared into a chasm of electronic silence. In the absence of any response, Fulton was thrown deeper into a gulley of despair, where every possible explanation for the leak grew darker the more he thought about it. He could feel a surge of rage inside him. Had Davy hung him out to dry? Had a man he trusted all his life shafted him in the most spectacular way possible? If so, for what?

A couple of minutes after the First Minister's speech, a message pinged through. 'Sorry. Mad busy. See you at the usual place. 7.' Davy. At last. Fulton felt relieved. Finally, he would get some answers. But his stress spiked again when he saw Chris approaching his desk.

'Fulton, a quick word in my office.'

'Eh, sure.'

The pair of them threaded their way through the desks to Chris's corner office. The editor shut the door behind himself: never a good sign. Fulton slunk down into a seat and tugged on his ID badge. Despite both the men having been in the office since the morning, this was the first time they'd spoken since the argument at the café.

'I'm going to be blunt, Fulton. What did you know about the John Millar video?'

'What do you mean?'

'When did you first see it?'

'I saw it like everyone else on Twitter this morning.'

'Are you sure about that? Or did you know about it before today?'

'No, I did not,' replied Fulton emphatically. 'I don't know where you are going with this.'

'Okay,' said Chris, leaning back in his chair with his hands behind his head. 'Have you heard anything from John Millar's sister yet?'

'No, still trying to get through.'

'Fine, but we're running that piece today – her memories of her brother.'

'I just need to run it by her first, make sure she's okay with it. She's so fragile, Chris, I don't want the piece coming as a surprise to her.'

'Let's be clear, Fulton, we're running the piece. It's a world exclusive and it's ours. We're journalists, not boy scouts. Your word means nothing after the video – everything has changed.'

'But—'

'But nothing, Fulton. You've got an hour. I need it for online and first editions.'

'Okay,' said Fulton quietly. He was a cornered man with no choice. He got up to leave.

'One more thing,' said Chris.

'Yes,' replied Fulton, glancing over his shoulder.

'Don't take me for a fool. Now get that piece done.'

Chapter 12

Davy was looking out over the Meadows from the window of the top-floor flat when he heard the living-room door open.

'Sorry, I was feeling a bit peckish and popped out for a bite to eat,' said Neil. 'I got you a sandwich. I'm guessing you're not veggie.'

Davy screwed up his face in disgust.

'Coronation chicken, it was all I could find – they'll be worried about me going native.'

'Fat chance of that,' said Davy with a grin. 'I'm guessing you're more of a Prêt man. Very kind of you, sir, I've already had my lunch but this will fill a hole later.'

Davy took the sandwich and laid it beside a stack of *Economist* magazines piled up on a low coffee table. He rested both his hands on his hips. 'To be honest with you, I was expecting something a bit grander. This place is more like student digs.'

'We did find enough meals-for-one in the freezer to feed an army. But his drinks cabinet,' said Neil, pointing at a vintage globe beside the window, 'is a thing of great beauty: take a look.'

Davy delicately cracked open the globe, revealing several bottles of whisky.

'All single malts,' said Neil. 'John Millar had taste, I'll give him that.'

'And, apart from the drink, have you found anything else of interest?' asked Davy as he gingerly closed the globe, trying not to trap his fingers along the equator.

'Nothing particularly pertinent but we did find this in a shoebox under the bed.'

Neil picked up a photo from the dining table and handed it to Davy. It was a picture of a group of students, wearing black gowns. Some sported big eighties hair and the kind of smiles that were common before orthodontics came into fashion.

'What's this?'

'That's John in the middle,' said Neil. 'It was when he was elected president of the Oxford Union.'

Davy recognised the face instantly. While the other students were either laughing or looking away, John was looking directly at the camera – his stare so intense that Davy almost felt it burrowing into the back of his head. 'Sounds like a big deal.'

'It means your odds of becoming prime minister have significantly shortened.'

'Impressive,' said Davy, turning over the photograph to see whether anything was scrawled on the back.

'I never actually knew John personally – we're about ten years apart – but we studied at the same college and as it turns out were both recruited by the same history professor. Small world, eh?'

'Closed shop, more like,' said Davy, with an eye roll. 'But apart from the trip down memory lane, what's the significance?'

'Well, Professor Rutherford said something rather odd to me about John. He said that John understood that power lay in controlling the perception of an event rather than the reality.'

'And that's Oxford for what exactly?'

'That John was adept at the dark arts.'

'How so?'

'Well, apparently, John ran a disinformation campaign when he was elected Union president. He doctored a picture of his main rival snorting coke and then fly-posted it all around town in the middle of night. It caused a bit of a stink at the time.'

'Seems like our Johnnie boy was quite the saboteur,' said Davy, chuckling.

'Absolutely. His rival dropped out and John was elected with a huge majority. But Professor Rutherford said that John didn't actually enjoy being president. He said John loved the power but hated the limelight.'

'Riveting stuff, but, bringing it back to my reality,' said Davy, 'have the neighbours here said anything of interest?'

'Nothing of note. Here, I need to show you something else.'

Neil walked out of the living room into the hallway. Davy followed. His shoes squeaked on the laminate floor. He noticed a cat-litter tray tucked below a radiator. 'Recognise anything?' asked Neil as he pushed open a bedroom door. Davy looked around the room: white wall; a mirror in a wooden frame; a single bed with no sheets; and an IKEA table with a metal lamp.

'Nope, if I'm honest.'

'It's where he recorded his video. Here, against the wall?'

'And how do you know it was this precise wall?'

'Our analysts took a look at it and spotted this hairline crack,' said Neil pointing up at a section of plaster just below the cornicing.

'What else did the techies say? There are a lot of folk banging on about how the video is a fake.'

'He was blinking, wasn't he?'

'Aye, but so what?'

'Well, that's always a good indication that a video's not a fake. It's very hard to fake blinks. There are no shadows on the wall apart from John's and the audio analysis indicates that he was the only one in the room – meaning we're sure as we can be that he shot the video himself.'

'Okay,' said Davy. 'And any word on those documents, then? The ones he held up in the video saying the Nats were on the take from the Russians?'

'Not yet. But we're searching his sister's place. I'm heading there now: do you want to come?'

Chapter 13

The spot where John Millar was murdered was a grimy back street, best avoided in the early hours of the morning. It was a place where homeless men with scouring-pad beards and heroin-haunted eyes would fish through large green bins for a half-eaten kebab or bag of chips. They would rub up against the skinny teenage sex workers turning tricks. But in the hours since John Millar's video went viral, this forgotten corner of the city had been transformed into a makeshift shrine.

A few metres from where three bullets were pumped into John Millar's head, a large blown-up portrait of him was now propped up against the blackened brick wall. In the picture, Millar was wearing a suit and tie and staring impassively into the camera. He looked like the grey civil servant many assumed him to be: not exactly the stirring stuff of martyrdom. A piece of cardboard was propped up in front of the cheap lacquered brown frame and written on it were the words: *John Millar – Unionist Martyr – May He Rest in Peace.*

Standing in the shelter of a fire escape, Fulton watched as a couple of young guys, clearly the worse for wear from drink, both took off their blue-and-white Rangers scarves and laid them on the floral carpet rapidly spilling out from the shrine.

'That's fir you, big man,' said one of them.

'Fuck the IRA!' said his pal. 'God save the Queen. They'll never break the Union.'

Fulton shook his head in despair as they staggered away, hanging off each other. The inanity of the city's sectarianism never ceased to amaze him. He had only come to take a look at the shrine because he had time to kill before his meeting with Davy. He checked his watch. He needed to get going – he was running late. He looked up and saw a hunched elderly woman, wearing a headscarf, edging her way up the lane. A young lad supported her with an arm under her elbow as she inched towards the portrait. The woman slowly bent down and placed a bunch of cheap yellow carnations on top of a dozen other bouquets. She stood for a moment, head bowed, the guy gently rubbing her back in affection. They turned and slowly walked back towards Bath Street. As she passed, Fulton noticed her eyes were glistening. She tugged on a handkerchief tucked under her watchstrap and wiped away the tears. It was a private moment and all the more powerful for it. At times it was easy to forget the personal tragedy at the heart of this political crisis. Fulton thought of Elaine and her loss. And he felt even guiltier about the story he'd turned in barely half an hour ago based on her memories of her brother. He hadn't got her approval. He couldn't reach her on the phone. He knew it was a betrayal but what else could he do?

'Where the hell have you been?' grumbled Davy, standing at the end of the bar, a thin creamy moustache on his top lip.

'Where the hell have *I* been?' replied Fulton angrily. 'Where the hell have *you* been more like? I've been trying to get hold of you all day.'

'Just calm it.'

'Calm it? Who the hell do you thinking you're talking to?'

'Give me your phone,' barked Davy.

'What for?'

'Just do as you're told.'

It took Fulton all his self-restraint to stop him putting on his hands on Davy. A few of the regulars sensed as much, raising their heads from the other end of the bar in anticipation of it all kicking off.

'This ain't footie training,' said Fulton, glaring at Davy.

'Look, if you want to talk, you need to give me your phone: it's as simple as that.'

Davy held out his hand. Fulton was seething, but after holding out for a few seconds, handed his phone over. He stared daggers at Davy who picked up his pint of Guinness and downed the remaining half in two quick gulps. He then licked his lips.

'Denise?' he said. She was kneeling on the floor behind the bar, refilling one of the fridges.

'Aye, Davy?' she said, standing up.

'Could you do us a favour and look after these for me.' Davy gave her the phones. 'We need to pop outside for a wee chat.'

'No bother.' She wedged the phones between the cash register and the mirror behind the bar. 'They'll be safe here.'

'Cheers, darling,' said Davy, with a wink. He turned to Fulton. 'Let's get going.'

Outside the Empire, they crossed a busy road and headed up the street, passing a garage where a couple of motorists were getting their tyres topped up. The blast from the air compressor was so noisy that neither of them said a word until they were a decent distance from the garage.

'Where the hell are we going, Davy?' yelled Fulton. 'What's going on?'

'Just keep walking,' said Davy, who was outstripping his normal pace, and with every step was becoming redder in the face. The only reason Fulton was going along with it was out of residual loyalty, otherwise he'd have told Davy to go screw himself. When they reached a multi-storey car park, Davy ducked inside a fire exit. The two men climbed up a back stairwell. Davy was gasping by the time they reached the top floor. He leaned over the wall and stared down at the street – it was quite a drop. He was trying to catch his breath but the view made him feel dizzy. He pulled back and with two of his sausage-like fingers undid the top button of his shirt and loosened his striped polyester tie. For a moment, Fulton thought his friend might be having a heart attack and a part of him didn't give a toss if he was. He waited until Davy steadied himself before launching his attack.

'Why the hell did you leak the video? Why did you do it, eh?'

'I didn't,' said Davy defensively.

'What do you mean you didn't? It's all over Twitter.'

'Calm down, will you.'

'I'll calm down when you tell me what happened. And what's the crap with all the phones?'

'Look, there's some serious stuff going down at the moment, and we need to be careful. You do know those things are listening devices?'

'Aye, I've heard that, but you weren't very careful with the John Millar video, were you? "No worries, Fulton, safe as houses with me," that's what you said. And then I wake up this morning and it's plastered all over the internet.'

'Look, Fulton, you've got to trust me,' said Davy, raising his hands in a plea. 'As soon I watched that video, I knew I couldn't sit on it. I just couldn't, I'm sorry.'

Fulton shot him a filthy look.

'I'm sorry, mate, I really am. But if the boss found out I

had it and never told him, it would have been like a bomb going off under my desk. I'd be finished in the force. I was in an impossible position.'

'What the hell happened, then?'

'I gave it to one of the bosses and then, like you, I woke up to find it all over the place. The bastards leaked it. I don't know who did it but I don't think it was the top brass. They leak, of course, but they don't leak this kind of stuff. Even they're not that stupid.'

'What, and I'm supposed to just believe you?' said Fulton angrily. 'That you're somehow innocent in this whole affair?'

Davy's face instantly flushed. 'Are you accusing me of lying?'

He took a step forward. The men were less than a foot apart, eyeballing each other.

'Who told you about the story in the first place? Me – that's right, me. Do you know your problem?' said Davy, pressing his finger hard into Fulton's chest. 'You can be a prize prick at times – an absolute bell-end.'

'If it wasn't for us, you boys would be running riot,' said Fulton. 'The polis need a good kick in the balls once in a while to keep you in line.'

'There you go again, always got an answer. Give me a break. Am I hearing right? A journalist giving out about ethics? Christ, I've never heard such crap in all my life.' He looked away before glancing back at Fulton. 'And from you of all people. Spare me the lecture.'

Rage flashed through Fulton. He clenched his fist, but was distracted by the sound of a shopping trolley echoing through the multi-storey. A slender woman, wearing a white trouser suit, rounded a corner. She pulled up at a red Mercedes sports car and they watched her unload the shopping bags into the boot. It was only when she was getting into her car that she noticed them. She immediately went for the locks before pulling out of the parking space with a screech, her car flying past Fulton and Davy, its red tail lights disappearing down the ramp.

'I'm right to be pissed off,' said Fulton quietly, not looking Davy in the eye. 'But I should have given you the opportunity to explain yourself.'

'All right,' said Davy, taking a step back. 'But don't ever question my motives again. We've got to trust each other in this situation. Understood?'

Fulton eventually gave him a sullen nod. 'Aye. So who leaked the video, then?' he asked. 'If it wasn't you or the top brass.'

'I don't know for sure but I think it was probably MI5. One of their guys is floating about at HQ and my guess is the boss gave it to him. It's the kind of stunt they would pull.'

'The spooks are involved? Jesus.'

'Tell me about it. But, seriously, Fulton, none of this stuff is making sense. Remember those documents that Millar held up in the video? That he said were proof of Russian payments?'

'Aye, what about them?'

'Well, we can't find them. We went through his flat in Edinburgh and found nothing. And we also searched his sister's place today.'

'You saw Elaine?'

'Aye.'

'How is she?'

'You know, still upset about John – to be expected really. And she wasn't happy that we had to turn her place upside down. But I've seen people in a worse state. To be honest, I'm beginning to wonder if those documents even exist. Maybe it was some kind of a ruse to throw us off the scent.'

'What? John Millar just made it up?'

'Well, it's only when you actually find them that you can say they exist. Until then it's like chasing fairies. Elaine never gave them to you, did she?'

'What sort of question is that?'

'Just that: a question.'

'No, she didn't.'

'All right,' said Davy. He was deflated. 'The whole world is going mad – right is left, north is south, nothing makes sense any more.'

'You're telling me.'

'How's my goddaughter?' asked Davy.

'She's fine,' replied Fulton haltingly.

'What's happened?'

'Nothing.'

'C'mon.'

Fulton puffed out his cheeks. 'She's gone off again, staying at her aunt's place.'

'Ach, chin up, pal, it'll be fine. She's that age. Teenage girls are a nightmare, but it'll pass, it always does. Just try not to be so hard on her.'

'What do you mean by that?' asked Fulton, squaring his shoulders.

'Nothing – just go easy on her. She's been though a lot and, fundamentally, she's a good kid – remember that. Look, pal, I need to get going,' said Davy, reaching out to tap Fulton on the shoulder. 'We're expecting trouble tonight. I suspect a few neds are going to use this crisis to do a spot of shopping.'

Chapter 14

The plan was executed when most of the city was asleep. Edinburgh's cobbled streets were largely empty at four in the morning apart from a few late-night stragglers, tottering home from the pubs and clubs. Two cameramen on the grave-yard shift were staking out Bute House in the unlikely event that the First Minister made a move. But when Brian peeked out from an upstairs window, he saw one of them shuffling down the street – presumably to find a coffee, or use the toilet in a nearby hotel. His colleague was sitting on a folding chair with a tattered black cap pulled down over his face. One pro-tective hand was resting on his camera. He was fast asleep. Brian knew it was now or never.

Five minutes later, a battered red Vauxhall Corsa pulled up the ramp from an underground car park. If the media had been watching at that moment, they would have captured the extraordinary sight of Brian at the wheel and a passenger, covered by a tartan blanket, lying in the back of the car. At the top of the ramp, Brian grimaced as he crunched through the gears and stalled the vehicle. He turned the key in the ignition and the engine emitted a horrible grating sound. He tried again – no luck. He started panicking when he realised how close he was to the sleeping cameraman. Please God, let me get away with this, he said to himself, please Lord don't let him wake up. He turned the key again. He was in luck.

The car bucked into life so quickly that Brian almost ended up stalling it again but instead he managed to fly past the man at such a speed that the screeching acceleration jolted him out of his sleep. But the man was so disorientated at finding himself waking up on a dark street in Edinburgh's New Town that he didn't have a clue what he'd missed. Brian breathed a sigh of relief. They were on their way. He carefully followed the signs out of the city, desperate not to make a wrong turn. When he stopped at a traffic light close to the zoo he gave the all-clear.

'You absolutely sure?' came the muffled reply.

'A hundred per cent.'

Susan pulled off the blanket and dumped it on the seat beside her. She was hot and flustered and had found it difficult to breathe under the rug, which was covered in dog hairs. She knew the whole situation was ridiculous. It was a bit like being a hostage except she'd staged her own kidnap. She ran her fingers through her hair as she watched the traffic light turn green. Brian hit the accelerator. But from the shadows a young woman, tottering on her high heels on the pavement, suddenly tumbled out into the road.

'Watch out!' screamed Susan.

Brian swerved the car, slamming Susan hard up against the window. She howled as she sunk her teeth into her lip. For a terrifying second, Brian feared the car was going to flip. He felt it riding up on two wheels. It was out of his control. But then the vehicle righted itself. He glanced in his rear-view window. The shape of the young woman was rapidly receding in the distance. He knew he hadn't hit her. Even if he had, he wasn't sure whether he would have stopped or kept on driving. It was only when they got on the motorway to Glasgow that he began to relax.

'That's all we need at the moment,' he said. '"Fleeing First Minister Kills Young Woman". Just imagine that headline!'

Brian realised that he'd overstepped the mark when there was no reaction whatsoever.

'I'm sorry, Susan,' he said, trying to make eye contact in the mirror. 'It was meant to be a joke.'

Three hours later, the car edged up the ramp to board the first ferry of the day. A bleary-eyed attendant in a high-vis vest directed them to park in the first lane, marked by the white lanes on the deck. As the car came to a halt, Susan pulled up the fur-lined hood of her coat and put on huge designer sunglasses. Her disguise was the sort that draws attention to the person who's trying to go incognito. Susan knew it was ridiculous but she had no experience of playing this game. She opened the car door and was careful not to trip over a coiled fire hose. She squeezed herself out of the vehicle and pulled herself up the steep stairs onto the upper decks.

She was standing alone below the bridge of the CalMac ferry as it pulled out of Ardrossan harbour, producing a thick, creamy wake. The blue-and-white saltire, flying from the prow of the ship, was pulsing in the wind. The ever-changing sea comforted her. She watched as the darkening squalls danced across the Clyde and the gannets hung in the air before slicing into the sea.

The idea for the getaway had been hers. She could, of course, have closed the curtains in Bute House and refused to have shown her face in public. But that would have meant contending with her husband, Gordon, who was simmering with rage. He had only just found out about the affair, and that was awful enough. But now it was playing out in public, adding to his pain and humiliation. He had always supported her career in politics from the very start. They had fallen in love during her first failed campaign, a year out of university. He took time off work, diligently knocking on doors for twelve hours a day, for a seat they both knew she would never win.

And Gordon had been thrilled for her when she became First Minister. It was her life's ambition – the girl from Fife who, against all the odds, was now leading her country. She was going to make life better for folk with working-class backgrounds like herself. Now she had repaid Gordon by being unfaithful and her two young daughters would face taunts at school. At that thought, Susan took off her sunglasses and turned into the wind. She leaned over the rail and looked at the murky churning water below. She knew she was never going to jump. But this might be the closest she would ever come to considering it.

She still didn't know why she had the affair with John Millar. She loved Gordon: he was kind, he was attentive, and he made her laugh. And she still found him attractive. Even in his mid-forties, he drew admiring looks from women. He was generally clueless about these overtures, but Susan always noticed and it stung. It was when the girls came along that they'd grown more distant. They had an unwritten deal: Susan focused on work, speeches, meetings and conferences, while he stayed at home changing nappies, cooking dinner, and keeping their domestic life on track. Perhaps that was why she had the affair, she thought. Maybe she wanted to punish him for doing so well what she should be doing herself. Or perhaps it was because she was lonely. Or perhaps she wanted something different. Or perhaps there was no one answer.

The affair had lasted only three months. It had sneaked up on her. John was smart, good-looking and flattering. They first slept together in her hotel room during an annual party conference in Perth. She knew it was wrong. The unfamiliar, despite what all the trashy romance novels say, was definitely not fulfilling. She felt guilty and cheap. But affairs often take on a momentum of their own: they are easier to get into than out of. She repeatedly told John it was over but then he threatened to go public. He begged her to leave Gordon. It was never going to happen. She told him it was finished and refused to see him or pick up any of his calls. It was three weeks after they last spoke that she had learned she was pregnant.

Chapter 15

It proved to be a very long night. Despite Glasgow's reputation for violence, riots were rare in the city. But unfortunately for Davy, his instincts were right and as dusk fell, the rioters began their rampage. It quickly gained ground, erupting across the city. Anyone with a grievance was taking a pot shot. The first police report came into HQ at 8:43 p.m. marked 'URGENT Looters breach House of Fraser. Location: Buchanan Street'. A short distance away, rioters were having a tougher time with the Apple Store's reinforced glass windows. But by the time three vanloads of cops showed up they were left chasing youngsters in black balaclavas whose pockets were bulging with iPhones and the latest accessories. One looter had laptops stacked up like pizza boxes. Most of them got away. Out-of-shape cops were taunted, and from that moment on, it got worse. It was a free-for-all. The police were a ghost-like presence. John Millar's assassination had ignited a powder keg of discontent, pent-up fury and frustration. A cascade of reports flooded into HQ from Balornock, Cambuslang, Easterhouse, East Kilbride, Maryhill, Possilpark, Parkhead, Shawlands, Stepps. All calls for backup went unanswered.

Davy was at his desk in HQ all night. The scale of violence left him dejected. This was not the city he grew up in; it was not the city he knew. No doubt it would be said the riots were triggered by Susan Ward's speech. That may well have been the case but it wasn't the cause of the violence: at its heart were people saying to the establishment you've screwed us around for too long. It was about poverty; it was about communities hollowed out by unemployment and ravaged by drugs; it was about people who felt they had nothing to lose by grabbing whatever they could lay their hands on. It was, in essence, a cry for help. Not that you would ever hear any of the worthies describing it as such. The politicians would pile in with platitudes that violence gets you nowhere. But that is – and always has been – the establishment's big fat lie. They always say that, because they're terrified that violence will snowball and suddenly the entire system they've benefited from will be destroyed.

Davy watched as dozens of rioters were rammed into the holding cells. One of them, a boy of fifteen or so, lamely kicked out at one of the officers. The comeback was swift and brutal. The sergeant head-butted the teenager, his forehead connecting perfectly with the bridge of the lad's nose. It instantly blossomed like a red rose, spraying a crimson mist across the cell. Some of it caught Davy in the eye. He delicately wiped it away and left. When asked about the incident weeks later, he denied seeing anything. It was not the time for legal niceties. Now was the time to bring the city back under control. By five in the morning, the charge sheet was sobering: 370 arrests; 90 shops looted, more than a dozen set on fire; 15 people stabbed – three of them fatally. Davy was done at this point. He swept the papers off his desk, laid his head down, and fell fast asleep.

He was jolted awake three hours later by his mobile phone alarm, which was live-streaming the radio breakfast show, *Good Morning Scotland*. A former Scottish First Minister was on the radio calling for calm. 'I appeal to our better angels, our sense of reason; only the ballot box can determine the fate of our nation. We cannot, we must not, allow violence to triumph over reason. We reject this violence. It was not done in our name. Yes, we believe in the Union, yes, we believe in unity rather than division, because the Union gives us clout in the world . . .' Davy turned it off. As far as he was concerned it was the politicians who had got them into this mess in the first place, and, now, because they were such egotistical pricks they naturally thought they were the only ones that could resolve it.

There was a knock on his door.

'C'mon in.'

It was Constable Price. With his pudgy baby face, he had all the authority of a Teletubby.

'Morning, Davy.'

'What?'

'There's some guy called Charlie who wants to see you.'

'Charlie who?'

'Eh, sorry, I forgot to ask him for a surname. He said a guy called Tam had sent him. He said you'd know what it was all about.'

'Where is he?'

'He's sitting in reception.'

Davy sprang from his desk, shoved Constable Price out of the way, and hurled himself down the corridor. He banged the lift button furiously, but realised it wasn't coming anytime soon. He careered down the stairs taking three or four at a time – grabbing the banister at each turn to wheel himself round. Panting into the reception, he saw Charlie sitting like an abandoned orphan on one of the plastic seats. He was wearing a suit that looked like an Oxfam job. He was clutching a Starbucks cup.

'This is fir you,' he said. 'Courtesy of the big man. A couple of sugars if you need them.'

Nice touch, thought Davy. Tam might be a killer but he could also be a gent. 'C'mon with me.'

They wandered through the corridor to a chorus of moans from the holding area. The door of a meeting room was ajar and Charlie spotted a young guy with a bruised face. 'What's goin' on in there?'

'I'll ask the questions, Charlie. You've seen nowt. Is that clear, pal?'

'If you say so.'

'Good to see you've finally found your tongue. Now you can put it to some use and tell the truth for the first time in your life.'

Charlie cringed.

In his office, Davy told him to take a seat. Charlie swung on the swivel chair like a child in a playground. I'm dealing with a simpleton here, thought Davy. He almost felt sorry for the bloke. Out of blind loyalty or stupidity or a combination of both he was here to take the fall for everyone else – although he had pulled the trigger.

'So, Charlie, what's the deal?'

'I'm here to confess.'

'To what?'

'The murder of John Millar.'

'You did it?'

'Aye. It was me.'

'Why did you do it?'

''Cause I was told to.'

'Why?'

'I don't know. I was just told to.'

'By who? Who told you to do it?'

Charlie said nothing.

'You lost your tongue again?' asked Davy. 'Who was riding the bike then? Was it Joey Castle?'

Charlie remained silent.

'Do you want to smash into a tree as well?' said Davy. 'It would be a real shame to ruin that pretty face of yours. Here's the thing, Charlie – I can't protect unless you're honest with me. You hear me?'

Charlie was so glaikit that you could almost hear the gears crunching in his brain. 'Tam told me to say nothing but confess. So, I ain't saying nothing about Joey . . . eh, the other guy.'

Jesus wept, thought Davy. 'But how do I know it was you? Other than you just saying it was you?'

'Tam told me to say I can get you the gun.'

'All right. Where is it?'

'It's in the canal.'

'Do you know where in the canal?'

'Aye.'

'How do you know where it is?'

'Because I threw it there.'

'So where is it?'

'I can't remember exactly. It was dark. But it's in the canal.'

'Okay,' said Davy in exasperation. 'But you can show me roughly where?'

'Aye. I think I can dae that.'

Davy let out a long sigh. With the gun and confession, he knew he'd have a cast-iron conviction. 'Do you want a lawyer?'

'Tam told me he would send one round after we finished talking. He said you'd let me make a call.'

'Okay, you can use that phone there.'

Charlie pulled a piece of paper with a number on it from his jacket pocket.

'He says he'll be here in half an hour,' said Charlie, putting the phone down after a brief conversation.

'Okay. Stay here. And don't bloody touch anything. You hear me? I'll be back in a minute.'

Davy lumbered out of the room and along the corridor. He was heading to the top floor to break the news to Larbert. He had his man, of that he was sure. But these were strange days and Davy knew he had a major problem: there was still no motive.

Chapter 16

The sun blinded Fulton as he emerged from the dark under-belly of the Caledonian Railway Bridge onto the corner of Renfield Street. It was around ten in the morning. The pubs were yet to open but there was a mood of mindless violence in the air. It felt as if people were walking quicker than normal, heads down, anxious to avoid giving a look that could pro-voke a nasty reaction. Eye contact is everything in Glasgow. If you see a guy walking down the street at midday in slippers and his dressing gown, look at him, by all means, but for God's sake don't make eye contact. It is on such encounters that Glasgow's reputation is made.

Strolling along Argyle Street, Fulton lost count of all the beefy cops in stab vests, fingering their truncheons with a little too much affection. Their itchy fingers knew that heads were going to get smashed, bones were going to get broken, and blood was about to flow. The youngest among the ranks were secretly looking forward to the rammy. All police leave had been cancelled, reinforcements were being sent up from the north of England, and rumours abounded that the army would be deployed. Publicly, London had ruled out such a move, knowing it would be accused of imposing martial law. The official line from Downing Street remained that the ref-erendum would go ahead as scheduled.

The police were guarding all the shops whose windows

had been smashed the previous night. Sales staff were sweeping up tiny shards of glass, which blanketed the pavement like ice. Fulton saw dozens of shoeboxes scattered across the street. Quite a few kids would be trying on new trainers that morning. Meanwhile, joiners were hurriedly hammering plywood over shop fronts.

Fulton was still stewing over Davy Bryant's role in the Millar video being leaked. But he had to give it to his pal, he could read a situation better than most. He was bang on about the eruption of violence. As Fulton turned left onto Queen Street, he started to hear the gathering storm. There were thousands of protesters in George Square. The call to save the Union had attracted the city's staunchest elements. Chief among them were hundreds of members of the Orange Order wearing black suits, orange sashes and white gloves. Fulton spotted a few of them tussling with the police who were confiscating their ceremonial swords. In a corner of the square, a marching band was playing 'The Sash' and a band of lager louts were belting out its lyrics. Nearby a man was holding up an effigy of Susan Ward with a noose around her neck. The placard read: 'Russian Whore'. That was one of the politer offerings on display but it was a sentiment shared by most of the crowd. Amid the din of the flutes and drums and chants of 'God Save the Queen', a rent-a-gob politician on the back of a flatbed truck stacked with speakers was exhorting the crowd to attack the perfidy of nationalists who wanted to smash the most successful Union the world had ever seen – a line that drew cheers and applause.

Fulton pushed into the crowd, absorbing the atmosphere. Into the mêlée appeared a young guy wearing a black hoodie, wheeling his granny's tartan shopping bag. Nobody batted an eyelid. Fulton saw him pull out a homemade Molotov cocktail and before anyone else could clock what he was up to, he had lit the fuse and chucked it. Fulton watched as the flaming milk bottle arced over the heads of protesters and then exploded a few metres from a mounted policeman. Instantly, there was a carpet of red flickering flames. The horse reared away from the burning petrol and the police officer lost control. She fell off and landed with a smack on the pavement. The beast wheeled around and charged into the crowd, bucking in pain. A couple of protesters were felled by the panic-stricken horse's kicks as it cut a path through the square and, then, sensing space, bolted through Mandela Place and raced up West George Street, forcing astonished motorists off the road.

Fulton had never experienced anything like it before. He felt as if he was a war reporter except that this story was happening at home rather than in some dusty, faraway country. He found the violence oddly exhilarating. It made him feel alive. It was the first time in his life that everything from parliament to other institutions, all the old certainties, seemed fragile and might be smashed to pieces. Fulton reached down to pull his phone from his pocket. He would record a video of the day's events and send it over to the social media desk. It would keep the editor happy. He liked to call it living the story. But as Fulton raised the phone above the crowd to get a top shot, a flying bottle of Buckfast knocked him out cold.

Chapter 17

'Christ, you heard the latest?' said Neil, bursting into Davy's office. He closed the door behind him.

'What? The ruckus at George Square?'

'No, the border.'

'What's going on there?' asked Davy. 'I've been tied up with other stuff.'

'Some bloody Nats are trying to close it. They've hired tractors and trailers and already blocked off the A1 and A74. They've got banners saying they're stopping imperialist infiltration from England.'

Davy chuckled.

'Why are you laughing?' asked Neil. 'It's not funny.'

'Because laughing is the only thing keeping me sane at the moment. And this is clearly a lunatic fringe who will probably disappear as soon they cobble enough money together to buy a bag of crisps.'

'You don't get it, do you?'

'Get what?'

'It always starts like this before it falls apart,' said Neil. 'First the queues, then the shortages, and before long people start bringing out the guns.'

'All right, all right, Scotland's not Northern Ireland. You need to calm down.'

'Have you ever seen a colleague die?'

'What? Are we going to swap war stories now?' asked Davy in astonishment.

'Seriously, have you seen a man die?'

'Eh, I've turned up places where people are either dead or about to join the other side.'

'But someone bleed out in front of you?'

'No, Neil, I haven't seen that.'

'It happened to me in Belfast, at the start of my career. I was holding a friend as he died in my arms. It was weeks before I could bring myself to wash his blood out of my jeans.'

'Sorry, Neil, that's awful,' said Davy. 'It really is. But what's that got to do with today?'

'It's bigger than us, Davy, always remember that: it's always bigger than us.'

'Okey dokey,' said Davy. He watched as Neil opened his Barbour jacket and pulled out an envelope from an inside pocket. He dropped it on Davy's desk.

'We found the John Millar documents.'

'The ones he held up in the video?'

'Yes.'

'Where'd you find them?'

'I can't say.'

'All right. So what can you tell me then?'

'The documents here show a list of transactions made over the past two years. The payments were funnelled to the nationalists from an offshore account in Jersey.'

'Jersey?' said Davy, with surprise. 'And how did the nationalists get their hands on the cash?'

'We believe it was directed to a PR firm in Scotland, which then used the cash to fund a social media campaign on Facebook.'

'We believe?'

'It will all stack up; it's only a matter of days.'

'I'm kinda busy, Neil, and I really don't have the time or expertise to look into this. Can you not—'

'I'm not asking you to investigate. I just thought your journalist friend might be interested in seeing the documents – would make for a pretty sensational scoop.'

'What friend?'

'Fulton.'

'Oh, aye, Fulton. That's purely social,' said Davy. 'Family friend. I'm not in the business of leaking – never have, never will be.'

'Davy,' said Neil firmly. 'That's about as ridiculous as me denying I'm English.'

Chapter 18

Susan and Brian bumped down the ferry ramp onto Brodick pier, then drove through the town, passing the crazy golf centre with its miniature pyramids, mazes and windmills. Attached to the lampposts were weathered signs for the Highland Games with pictures of muscle-bound strongmen grimacing as they tossed enormous cabers. And then one of Arran's handful of golf courses came into view. But everything was deserted. It was still early for most people and, anyway, it was the quiet end of the summer season.

A couple of minutes later, Susan saw Brodick Castle peeking out through the woods on the left-hand side of the road. She remembered how as a child she'd run through the castle's dining room, with its chandeliers and candelabras, squealing with delight, much to the horror of her parents who were chasing after her. And then how she'd planted her hands on the cold sandstone walls as she climbed to the top of the castle's tower – a twisting, dizzying climb that she wished would never end.

Those memories briefly cheered her, as did the weather. It was the beginning of a wild and beautiful day. The clouds were racing across the Clyde estuary like battleships heading for a showdown. The wind was whipping up the waves, which slammed up against the stone wall and sent spray high into the air. As they approached Corrie, with its assortment of properties set back from the road overlooking a pebble beach, Brian swung a sharp left onto a gravel track and started climbing up the steep hill. He revved the accelerator and the car shuddered violently and stalled. He tried again and seemed to get the knack of it. A short way up the track he got out of the car and untied the frayed rope that kept the gate shut and the sheep from wandering down into the village.

Further up the hill they reached High Corrie. It was a jumble of whitewashed cottages with stunning views to the mainland. Goat Fell's barren, boulder-strewn slopes loomed large over the cottages. High Corrie had once been a colony for artists and poets who drew inspiration from the wild setting. Now, it had been tamed and bent to the will of families from Glasgow who spent small fortunes on turning the rustic cottages into weekend getaways – apart from one building.

'I probably should have told you this sooner, but I have no idea what state the house is in,' said Brian as he pulled up to a cottage, the door to which was blocked by a patch of waist-high nettles. Several of the building's black roof tiles were missing and a small windowpane was smashed and covered by spider webs. 'Auntie Irene died a couple of years ago, and I'm not sure anyone has been here since.'

'I guess we'll find out,' said Susan.

After getting out of the car, Brian dug out a large rusty key from his rucksack. He pulled his jacket sleeve down over his knuckles and scythed at the nettles. He then flattened them with his feet to beat a path to the cottage. The red paint on the door was flaking like it had been badly sunburnt. Brian put the key in the lock and tried to turn it. It wouldn't budge. He struggled with both hands to apply pressure, fearing it would snap. Much to his relief, it turned. Brian gave the door a good shunt with his shoulder, and they were in.

It was pitch-black inside, the only light coming through the thin slit of a wooden shutter on the other side of the living room. He could make out a wood-burning fireplace but not much else. Running his hand along the rough, white-washed wall he found a light switch. Despite repeatedly flicking the switch, no bulb lit up. In despair, he looked down at his feet and realised that he was standing on brown pellets – sheep droppings. What the hell? he thought. How did they get in here?

'Eh, Susan, you're going to have to give me half an hour to see if I can make this place presentable. There are a few teething issues.'

'Teething issues?' she said.

Brian was relieved to see she was grinning. 'Aye, just a few. Why don't you go for a walk and I'll see what I can do.'

'Fine. I could do with stretching my legs.'

Susan began climbing the hill that rose beyond the cluster of cottages. After a few minutes her calves were burning and she was wheezing for breath. She passed a rope swing with a tyre hanging from the bough of a crooked tree. It made her think of the girls and how much they would love it here. Trying to shake the thought, she pushed on. After twenty minutes or so, she reached the top of a ridge and turned back to look at the view. She hadn't realised quite how high she had climbed. She felt almost giddy. The cottages down below looked like tiny salt-and-pepper shakers on a table.

Far off, she could just make out the towns of Troon, Irvine and Ayr on the mainland. She had grown up in a town similar to them; it was where her socialist grandfather's teachings had shaped her entire political life. He'd spent thirty years down the pit in Longannet and the twenty years after that coughing up coal dust. 'The salt of the earth are those who work the earth,' he used to tell her. 'They need their champion; the rest can take care of themselves.'

Closer to shore, she spotted what at first she thought was a pod of orcas. They'd been visiting the Clyde in recent years, although they remained a rare sight. But Susan's elation soured when she realised what she was looking at was the menacing black hulk of a nuclear submarine powering through the waves. Barely visible were two small dirigibles carrying men from the special boat service. They were escorting the submarine out of the estuary and would then watch the beast sink beneath the surface of the Atlantic Ocean – the start of a three-month mission. Despite Britain's main submarine base being in Scotland, Susan wasn't privy to the details of where the submarines went on patrol. Foreign policy and national security were not within her remit, much to her frustration. But she'd always known that London was never going to be forthcoming with a First Minister from a party that was committed to scrapping nuclear weapons. In the event of a successful independence vote, the Faslane submarine base would be closed down. Susan was steadfast on that point: anything else would amount to a betrayal of her supporters. The billions used to buy weapons would instead be spent in classrooms and hospitals. She knew the London establishment loathed her all the more for it. She was viewed as that 'nippy sweetie': a Scottish woman who was too big for her boots, and who needed to be put back in her place. Who was she to reverse three hundred years of history?

If anyone had murdered John Millar, she thought, it was those patronising public-school bastards who thought they knew what was best for her country. They'd stop at nothing to destroy her and the dream of independence. They'd got away with it the first time and they were intent on making damn well sure that Scotland wasn't going to slip through their grasp at the second attempt. But what tore Susan apart was that she knew she'd helped them achieve their goal. One moment of weakness and her credibility was shattered – the cause fatally wounded. Nothing she'd done before or since would ever change the fact that she'd forever be associated with the murder of John Millar, killing off any hope of Scottish independence under her leadership.

How can you fight an allegation that is almost impossible to disprove? She had asked herself this over and over again. You can't argue with a voice from beyond the grave. The claims are immutable. Sure, a full investigation might prove otherwise but it would take months, if not years, and never wipe the slate truly clean. Susan knew she was living in an age of unreason, one where facts were treated as fiction, where logic was treated as lousy. It was a period where honesty and decency didn't stand a chance. She only had one answer for it. Susan stretched out her arms and let out a guttural cry that left her throat burning. It was swallowed up by the howling wind; the seagulls continued circling overhead, undisturbed.

She sank to the ground and pulled her knees close to her chest. The wind battered her face. Susan didn't know for how long she sat on the ridge lost in her thoughts, but when she felt spots of rain on her face, she knew it was time to leave. She moved quickly down the mountain, but as she passed the crooked tree close to the cottages, she spotted that her shoe-lace was coming undone. As she was kneeling down to retie it, she noticed a robin yanking a worm out of the ground. It was struggling a bit but was almost there. But then Susan saw a sleek magpie swoop into view and land. The magpie barrelled down on the little bird, squawking loudly, his claws ruffling the robin's feathers. The robin stood its ground. The magpie couldn't believe the insolence. Susan watched in astonishment as the robin suddenly launched itself at the magpie. The bigger bird jumped backwards and cocked his head left and right. Should I give it another go? But there was something about that wee bird that was not to be messed with, and the magpie thought better of it and took off.

Susan couldn't believe what she had just witnessed. She wanted to get close to that brave, little robin. She took a step forward but her movement startled the bird. It flew off.

She walked over to the cottage, careful not to brush up against the remaining nettles as she pushed open the front door. Brian was sitting on the edge of a mangy old couch in front of the fireplace.

'I got it going,' he said, using an iron poker to shift a log. It began to burn with a satisfying crackle. 'Just one problem.'

'What's that?'

'I forgot to bring tea or coffee, so I can't make us a brew.'

'It doesn't matter. We need to catch the last ferry. We're going back to Edinburgh.'

Chapter 19

Davy was leaning back against the canal lock, becoming increasingly pissed off with each passing minute. The rain was already coming down hard when the waters of the canal started jumping to the tune of hailstones. Davy adjusted the hood of his Gore-Tex jacket and rubbed his forehead, which was numb from the cold. His fingers had turned as white as the roots of vegetables freshly pulled from the soil. He didn't have any gloves on him, thinking he wouldn't need them in early September. How wrong could a man be? For the past three hours, he had watched as a team of police divers took turns to search the canal. They looked like giant otters with their slick black wetsuits covering their heads and giant hooded diving masks obscuring their eyes. Every so often there was a flurry of excitement; one of the otters would bob to the surface with his hand held high, holding what may or may not be a gun. The first time, Davy rushed up to the side of the canal. 'What you got?' he shouted at the police diver who was swimming over to him. 'You got the gun?'

The driver then lifted out what Davy realised was the rusty end of a garden hoe. He slunk back to the canal lock utterly deflated. Ten minutes later, his hopes were raised again but this time they crashed to the ground quicker than a punctured hot-air balloon.

'What the hell,' he muttered under his breath as he watched

a diver pull a submerged shopping trolley through the water towards the towpath. 'Come on! Give me a break!' he yelled at the diver. 'Do you know what we're up against here?'

The diver struggled to remove the regulator from his mouth. 'Those are the regulations,' he shouted. 'A greener Glasgow and all that. We need to pull anything we find out of the canal.'

'A greener Glasgow, my arse,' said Davy, turning away in disgust. 'I need that gun.'

It was only a few hours earlier that Davy had informed his bosses that they had found their man. He expected whoops and hollers and backslaps. Instead all Davy got was the top brass stroking their chins. The charitable view was that they were knackered from dealing with last night's riots. But Davy knew they were only concerned with covering their own arses.

'We can't make this look like a stitch-up,' Larbert told him. 'At the moment, it's too neat and tidy. The public are going to think we beat it out of him. We need something that definitively ties Charlie to the murder . . . Get the gun.'

Get the gun. The phrase had been rattling around his head like a bad rap song ever since. It was driving him nuts. Davy was staying away from the sergeant in charge of the diving team. He was a big lad with a puffy face and ginger stubble, and as far as Davy was concerned a jobsworth of the highest order. He knew that harassing him would probably slow the job down. But when Davy saw him sitting on a bench with his wetsuit pulled down to his knees he thought he might offer a gentle word of encouragement. That was the plan, anyway.

'Why the hell is it taking so long?' barked Davy.

The sergeant took a drag from his cigarette and was briefly enveloped in a cloud of smoke. He wasn't a man you could hurry along. 'You ever lost a bar of soap in the bath?'

'Aye, but what's your point?

'It can take a while to find the bar of soap especially if it's stuck up yer arse. Well, this is bigger than a bath and so it's going to take a bit longer.'

'All right, pal,' said Davy. 'Just find the gun.'

'No need to get lippy, son. You sure your man has the right spot? Those junkies are not always the most reliable.'

Davy wanted to smack him one, because he knew he was right. The lack of sleep, the stress of the investigation was all setting him on edge. He had brought Charlie up to the canal earlier in the morning to identify where he might have thrown the gun.

'I can't be sure, boss,' Charlie kept saying. 'It was dark.'

Davy urged him to think carefully, but even he realised it was a big ask for a man so stupid that not only would he confess to murder but he would help the cops gather the evidence to put him away for much of the rest of his life. They walked along the worn towpath strewn with discarded beer cans and cider bottles in the long grass and stopped at several of the locks. Davy gently tried to coax Charlie into revealing what he remembered from the night John Millar was shot dead. The road or the path he had taken to the canal . . . was it an exposed area or were there bushes . . . was it close to streetlights or not? Davy knew there was no point pressuring Charlie as he would agree to almost anything. It was an approach that required the patience of a saint and Davy was at breaking point. But close to one lock with a row of tenements backing onto it, Charlie stopped. Initially, Davy didn't notice and kept on walking ahead. But when he looked back, he saw Charlie talking to himself.

'Aye, I think this might be it here,' declared Charlie. 'Just let me think.'

Davy bit his lip hard. He wanted to interrupt but had learned long ago that when somebody wants to talk it's best to let them find their own words.

'Aye, I remember that,' said Charlie, pointing to a rock scrawled with graffiti, including the surprisingly exotic VERSACE LOVES QUENTIN in a heart shape pierced by an arrow.

'How?'

''Cause I sat down here and had a wee spliff. You know – to celebrate a job well done.'

It wasn't the concrete certainty that you would build a case on. But in terms of Charlie, Davy knew it was the best they were going to get. Davy asked him whether he was absolutely sure. Charlie assented with an 'Aye, boss, never been surer'. Davy patted him on the back, gave him a tenner, and told him to go and get some lunch. Davy would give him a call when he needed him. With Trilby Tam on board, he knew Charlie wasn't going to do a runner, and if the gun turned up it would be his last few hours of freedom.

A tiny part of Davy felt sorry for Charlie. But as the day wore on, his contempt for the man only grew stronger. The cold was settling into his bones. By now the divers had not only pulled out the garden hoe and the shopping trolley, but a kid's bike, a lawn mower and a toaster. You could kit out a house with all this stuff, thought Davy.

The divers were only allowed to work an eight-hour shift. The jobsworth sergeant had reminded Davy several times that they wouldn't be doing a minute longer. By the eighth hour, Davy had stopped pacing along the towpath. The adrenaline and anger that had fuelled him throughout the day were spent. He slumped on a bench and struggled to keep his eyes open. He kept nodding off and then waking up with a jolt when his chin struck his chest. A couple of kids walked passed calling him a jakey. He didn't have the energy to tell them to piss off. He nodded off again and was awoken by a heavy hand on his shoulder.

'I hope you're not sleeping on the job, officer. That's a disciplinary offence.'

It was the ginger sergeant and he had a grin on his face. 'You owe the boys a pint,' he said.

'And why's that?'

'Because we got the gun.'

Chapter 20

Fulton cracked open one eye and then the other, slowly focusing on his surroundings. There was a pounding pain in his head. He realised he was in a hospital ward but it looked more like a field hospital after a major battle. The five guys filling the beds around him were all in various states of disrepair. One young man was lying on his side, his right buttock bandaged up; the blood was seeping through as if someone had thrown a tomato at his arse. Another patient was sitting bolt upright up in bed with a head bandage that made him look like some kind of down-and-out Easter bunny.

'How are you getting on, Mr McKenzie?'

Fulton gingerly turned and saw a young nurse standing beside his bed. She had soft brown eyes and freckles on her nose.

'I need to check your responses, see if you need a CT scan,' she said.

'Sure.'

She leaned over and shone a pen torch in his eyes.

'It's okay,' said the nurse soothingly. 'Just a nasty cut. A couple of inches and you could have lost an eye. And there's no sign of concussion now. You're a very lucky man.'

She patted him on the shoulder, smiled, and moved to check the patient in the next bed. Fulton looked over at the window and saw the golden light of dusk. He calculated that it was roughly ten hours since he'd been at the protest in George Square. He didn't know exactly what had happened but it was clear from what the nurse had said that a bottle or something similar had knocked him out. Not wishing to move, he slid his hand down the side of the bed and patted the sheet to see whether his phone was there. Nothing.

'Sorry, nurse, but do you know where my phone is?'

'Give me a minute,' she said. She was adjusting the adjacent patient's intravenous drip.

Fulton lay his head back down on the pillow. He closed his eyes but his head was spinning so fast that he opened them again.

'Here it is,' said the nurse, taking the phone out of the drawer in the cupboard beside the bed and handing it to Fulton. 'Your wallet and ID are all there as well.'

'Cheers.'

The nurse smiled back at him, a well-worn expression she'd probably delivered to thousands of patients – even so, Fulton felt a lot better for it. As she walked out of the ward to continue her rounds, he tried to turn on his phone. The battery was flat. He wondered whether anyone knew he was in hospital. Chris would probably assume he'd gone AWOL after their bust-up. He hadn't told the news desk that he was off to cover the protest. And, Jesus, what about Alana? Surely she'd be worried sick, but then she was probably still at her aunt's.

Fulton tentatively touched his scalp. He could feel the ridge of seven or eight stiches through the dressing – serious but nothing life-threatening. He wondered how long he would need to stay in for. Surely they'd want to turf him out to free up a bed. He glanced up at the TV, which was on mute. It was showing one of those banal evening shows where some nonentity was promoting their self-help or cooking book and the presenters were being wildly enthusiastic. He gently rolled over onto his side. His head felt better in that position. He heard someone entering the ward.

'Nurse, sorry to bother you again, but I was just wondering if you had a phone charger I could borrow.'

'Well, we'll see what we can do for you,' said a man with an English accent.

Fulton tried to squint over his shoulder but he was too stiff. He pulled himself up and positioned a pillow behind his back to make himself more comfortable, then looked at the man standing at the end of his bed.

The guy held up a plastic bag full of bananas and grapes and said, 'These are for the wounded soldier. How are you doing? It looks like you got a nasty injury this morning.'

'Had better days but I'm on the mend. Look, do I know you? I think you might have the wrong person.'

'No, we've never met before but we do have a mutual friend.'

The man pulled the curtain round the bed and dragged one of the chairs closer to Fulton. 'May I?' he asked.

'Aye, sure. What's your name?'

'Neil.'

'And who's this mutual friend of ours?'

'Davy Bryant.'

Fulton relaxed a bit, figuring he was on neutral territory. 'Oh, right, and how do you know Davy?'

'We work together.'

'You a copper as well?'

'Not exactly,' said Neil, with a tight smile.

'So what do you do, then?'

Neil weighed up his words before dropping his voice. 'Let's just say security matters.'

'Okay,' said Fulton, pulling himself up a bit more on the pillow. 'Have they pulled you up here for the crisis?'

'Yes, I think that would be a safe assumption to make.'

'And that's how you knew I was here?'

'Ah,' said Neil, equivocating for a second. 'Yes, we have our ways.' He reached over, pulled a banana from the plastic bag and offered it to Fulton. 'You hungry?'

'No, I'm fine, thanks. A bit queasy.'

Fulton watched as Neil turned the banana upside down, so that its stem was pointing at the floor. Neil used his thumb and a finger to squeeze the nubby tip of the fruit, splitting the peel without creating any mess.

'Do you know this is how monkeys eat a banana?' said Neil, delicately pulling back the skin. 'From the bottom up, it's a lot more efficient that way.'

'I didn't.'

'It's amazing how many of us are fooled by the purpose of the stem.'

Neil took three quick bites before tossing the skin into the bin.

'So, I'm guessing this isn't a social visit?'

'Ah, yes, very sorry to intrude like this but I'm afraid I've got some bad news.'

'It's not Alana, is it?' asked Fulton, fear sweeping through him.

'No, no, your daughter's absolutely fine.'

Fulton's heart rate began to ease. But how did Neil know he had a daughter? And how did he know her name?

'So what is it, then?' asked Fulton.

'It's Elaine.'

'Elaine?'

'John Millar's sister.'

'What about her? Is she okay?'

'She was found dead in her house this afternoon.'

Dead. Fulton was confused. He had seen her a few days ago. Sure, she was sick, but she was hardly at death's door. 'What happened?'

'She took an overdose.'

An overdose? None of this was making any sense. She didn't seem the type to kill herself, thought Fulton; she hadn't given him the impression she was a quitter.

'Did she leave a note or anything?'

Neil briefly looked at the floor before casting his eyes back to Fulton. 'No, she didn't leave a note. Look, I came down here because I didn't want you hearing about it from anybody else. I just wanted to check up on you and make sure you're doing okay. We're still investigating the death but there's no suggestion of any foul play.'

'Why would there be?' asked Fulton.

'Well, given her brother's murder, and it's just . . . We're living in strange times, that's all, and there's a lot at stake.'

'Eh, okay.'

'You might not see it this way, but we're actually on the same team.'

'Same team?' said Fulton slowly. 'Sorry, am I missing something here? I'm just a journalist trying to figure out the truth.'

'Of course you are. It's just that the public doesn't need to know how the video leaked. It will only confuse things, and in the current climate wouldn't be helpful to the cause.'

'The cause? I thought the referendum was for the people to decide.'

'Well, people don't always know what's best for them – sometimes they need a nudge in the right direction.'

'Oh aye, and that's your job? By leaking the video, you were nudging people in the right direction?'

'Think of it as a paternalistic gesture, nothing more. Now I better let you rest up – we wouldn't want anything to happen to you.'

'Are you threatening me?'

'Come on, Fulton, that's not how we operate,' said Neil, with a pained expression. 'We're not living in a police state. I guess with all the drugs in your system, you're not thinking straight. But when you're better, think over what we've just talked about it. It would be best for us all.'

Neil stood up from his chair. He opened his brown leather satchel and pulled out a phone charger.

'Keep it,' he said, throwing it onto the corner of Fulton's bed. 'You can return the favour sometime.'

Chapter 21

By the time they got back to Edinburgh it was nighttime. The same camera crews were still stationed outside Bute House; they just looked a little more dog-eared than before. And, again, they missed her. Susan was in the passenger seat – she wasn't even bothering to hide this time around. The extraordinary fact of the matter was that the media hadn't found out about her escapade to Arran. They knew nothing about Brian's cottage or Susan's climb up Goat Fell. The official records would forever be silent on an excursion, which, had it been discovered, might have been hailed as a dramatic turning point in the nation's history: a journey from which the First Minister returned to fight for independence. As far as the media was concerned, Susan Ward had been holed up in her official residence refusing to face the public and, depending on the political bent of the newspaper, that made her either a coward or a victim.

Brian pulled the car into a tight parking spot in the gloomy underground garage – without having to reverse. He looked rather pleased with himself.

'You're finally getting the hang of this,' said Susan. 'I should hire you as a driver.'

'Thank you, First Minister, for what I may say is a rare compliment.'

They both looked at each other and burst out laughing

before climbing out of the car.

'Susan, if you don't mind, I'm going to head home and see the man. Tom will be wondering what's happened to me. I'll be back here early doors, but any problems, just give me a buzz. And, whatever you do, don't speak to anyone from the media – let me handle it.'

'Yes, boss,' said Susan, with a flash of irritation.

Brian patted the roof of the car and chose not to return fire. 'Okay. See you tomorrow.'

As Brian's footsteps echoed through the garage, Susan pushed against the fire escape door that led to a flight of stairs. It took her up into an office block located behind the official residence. She darted across the lane separating the buildings and banged on the back door of Bute House. She glanced left and right, worried that a member of the paparazzi may have been lurking behind a bin and snapping away. She wouldn't put anything past the tabloids. FIRST MINISTER LOCKED OUT OF OFFICIAL RESIDENCE! She watched as one of the security cameras whirred and turned in her direction. It reminded her of the prison visits she'd made as a junior government minister – the nausea that formed in her stomach as the fear grew about what waited for her beyond the door. She gave the camera the evil eye. The door sprang open. A young lantern-jawed police officer greeted her.

'Afternoon, ma'am, I'm James Robert, part of the new security detail,' he said.

'Good to meet you – sorry about my absence.'

'Yes, we were wondering where you'd gone but good to see you're back in one piece. First Minister, in the future—'

'I know, I know. It won't happen again, trust me. Now, you'll have to excuse me.'

She climbed up the back stairs, which creaked with each

step, into the main hallway with its polished wooden floor that shone like a pool of honey. It was offset by a huge Persian rug, which Susan had chosen when she moved in. On the wall were the portraits of her predecessors – all white middle-aged men, with the predictable comb-overs and teeth that resembled tombstones in a neglected cemetery. Susan stared at one of them who had beady eyes. She remembered how even when she was a government minister, he'd insist on referring to her as 'the girl'. He had been mansplaining decades before it even became a term. Most of them had had affairs but being a woman made it different. It somehow made you loose and lacking in judgement and therefore unfit for politics. If she could have had her way, she'd have torn down every last portrait but you can't play with the past.

From deep within the residence, Susan heard her daughters shrieking with laughter. She was briefly cheered by the noise but then a wave of despondency swept over her. Perhaps they would be better off without me, she thought, before the moment passed. Susan walked towards the kitchen, the girls' laughter growing ever louder. She paused at the door. She knew she had caused so much pain and anger and was now about to shatter another happy time. The laughter faded. She turned the door handle. The look on the girls' faces was one of surprise followed by delight.

'Mummy, Mummy,' they cried as they slid off the breakfast stools and raced towards her. They both wrapped their arms around her waist and squeezed her tight. Susan closed her eyes and savoured the moment. She could feel the stress draining out of her as soon as she felt the warmth and weight of her daughters pressing into her flesh.

'Mummy, can we play games on the iPad tonight?' asked Rhona.

'Please, Mummy,' chimed in Mhairi.

'It's an ambush!' said Susan. 'You'll have to run it by your dad. He's the boss.'

'Daddy, please, please,' the girls pleaded in unison.

Gordon was looking out of the kitchen window at the narrow garden that ran down to the lane. He turned round and quickly averted his gaze from Susan to the girls.

'Okay, but only for half an hour and then bed. My iPad is in the living room. Play in there. Me and your mum need to talk.'

The girls were mollified. They chased each other screaming out of the kitchen. Susan and Gordon were left alone in the room. The silence that followed was fathoms deep. Neither of them knew what to say or do. Eventually, Susan felt compelled to make the first move. It was her deceit that had created this gulf. Even though she had known and loved Gordon for years, she had no idea how he would react.

'How are you?'

'I'm okay,' he said, looking up. 'How are you?'

'Fine. Sorry about leaving.'

'It's okay.'

'I just needed to get away.'

'I understand.'

Silence once again filled the room. It was as if everything that had gone before was no more permanent than footprints left in the sand.

'I'm sorry, Gordon. I'm so sorry. I can't say that enough. But if we're to get through this we've got to be honest about where we went wrong.'

Gordon clenched his jaw. He looked down at his feet. 'I wasn't the one who was out shagging someone else,' he said, looking up at her. 'I wasn't the one out pursuing their career.

I was at home, taking care of the girls. Our girls. Tell me, Susan, where did *I* go wrong? I've done nothing but support you. I loved you, I wanted the best for you, I wanted the best for us, for our family, and this is how you repay me. Was it because I wasn't man enough for you?'

'No, please, Gordon, it was my fault not yours. I'm so sorry. I wish I could take it all back. I never stopped loving you. I don't know why I did it. I felt lonely, somehow, I guess.'

'*You* felt lonely? What about me? Was he the only one?'

'Yes.'

'Tell me the truth.'

'Yes. But—'

'But what?'

'I'm just so sorry, Gordon. So sorry.'

'What, Susan? I need to know.'

Susan watched as he crossed the kitchen. At first, she thought he was going to leave the room. But he walked straight up to her and grabbed her shoulders. He shook her once, hard and sharp, before pulling away. Susan was scared momentarily, but then she saw that he was crying. She had never seen him cry before. She doubted that his father or even his grandfather had ever cried. With those tears he crossed a threshold. There are no words that can soften that kind of pain.

'I'm sorry,' said Gordon, wiping his face with his hand. 'I shouldn't have done that but you need to tell me everything. I need to know every last detail.'

'Okay. But can we please sit down.'

They sat on the stools. Susan passed Gordon a box of tissues. He tore out three and wiped his red, raw eyes. Susan stared at his chest to avoid looking him in the eyes. She loved and respected him and because of that she was now going to cause more pain than he would ever deserve.

'I don't know how to say this.'

'Just say it. No more lies.'

'You remember when I was in Canada for an official visit?'

'Yes.'

'And they took me to the hospital for severe food poisoning?'

'Yes.'

'It wasn't food poisoning.'

'What was it?'

'I miscarried.'

'Whose baby was it?'

'John's.'

Susan tensed for an explosion that never came. Gordon remained calm. It was almost as if he'd half-expected the revelation.

'Did he know?'

'Yes, but when I told him I'd miscarried he didn't believe me.'

'Why not?'

'He thought I had an abortion to make the problem go away.'

'And then what happened?'

'The last time I saw him—'

'What happened, Susan?' demanded Gordon. 'Tell me what happened. I need to know.'

'He grabbed my throat and said he was going to destroy me.'

Chapter 22

Fulton wasn't the paranoid sort, but the more he thought about Elaine's death the less it made sense. He just could not believe that she'd commit suicide. He usually rubbished conspiracy theories but, maybe, just maybe, the security services had killed her. Neil said it himself: the public were never to find out how the video leaked. It was all about nudging them in the right direction; it was about saving the Union. And then there was the veiled threat: 'We wouldn't want anything to happen to you.' Those weren't words of compassion – they were the words of a man who made terrible things happen to other people. First John Millar and then Elaine – who next? The thought of returning to an empty home in Clarkston filled Fulton with a fear he had never felt before. Would they jump him as soon as he opened the door? Or would they do it when he was asleep in his bed? They could easily string him up and pass it off as another self-inflicted tragedy. The police report would almost write itself: middle-aged man who lost wife and son in car crash decides to top himself. Case closed: no point wasting resources on that one. Even Davy would have a hard job prising open the case file in light of those cold hard facts. Sweat formed on Fulton's hairline. He knew for his own sanity that he needed to get out of the hospital and as far away from Neil's presence as possible.

The nurses were predictably dead set against the idea. Just stay one more night, they pleaded. They even got a doctor to lecture him about how irresponsible he was being after a head injury. Fulton's mind was clear, though, and it was screaming get the hell out of here. He grabbed his things and discharged himself.

It was a chilly night, the cold cutting to the bone. Fulton walked briskly to the Merchant City, a product of Glasgow's past that had been yuppified long ago, with its boutique hotels, fancy restaurants and a smattering of luxury cars on its quiet streets. He walked into one trendy bar with dim lighting, a ridiculous chandelier and purple leather barstools. He ordered a Diet Coke. It was mid-week, and the place was deserted, apart from a brunette woman wearing a black sequined top, who was sitting at the other end of the bar. She looked up and smiled demurely at Fulton. He smiled back and went back to staring at the streams of bubbles in his drink. He tapped his wedding ring on the glass. He glanced over again.

'No need to be shy,' she said.

She picked up her glass and knocked back the last of her white wine. 'Oh, look, it's empty now,' she said, with a cheeky grin. 'And I'm really thirsty.'

Fulton pushed his fingers through his hair. The truth was there had never been anyone after the accident. He'd shut down that part of his life to focus on Alana. As for during the marriage, well . . .

'You from around here?' the woman asked. 'You look a bit Italian or something?'

'Glaswegian born and bred,' said Fulton quietly. He stood up from his stool. The woman smiled, expecting him to join her.

'Sorry,' said Fulton. 'I really don't mean to be rude but maybe some other time. Have a lovely night.'

As he headed to the exit, the woman rolled her eyes. She wasn't used to knockbacks. Outside, Fulton realised he had left without any thought to where he was going. He wandered aimlessly for a few minutes before sitting down at an empty bus stop, in front of a church. He saw a guy stumbling up the street. His head was steady while the rest of his body was wildly gyrating. Fulton called an Uber.

He thanked the driver as he got out the car. The unruly hedge brushed up against him as he opened the gate. He stood for a moment in the darkness and looked up at his house. The curtains were all open. It gave his home the appearance of a wide-eyed orphan hiding in the shadows. He placed his bag on the doorstep and rummaged through it for his keys. He pushed open the front door. It was quiet in the hallway. Then he heard something. Was his mind playing tricks on him? He remembered that the house sometimes creaked as if it was stirring from its sleep. But then he heard it again. Footsteps. His breathing quickened. They were coming from upstairs.

'Dad?'

Fulton instantly relaxed. He looked up and saw two frightened eyes gleaming in the dark at the top of the stairs.

'Dad, is that you?'

'Yeah, it's me.'

He flicked on the lights and saw Alana standing there in a tank top and shorts. Her messy blonde hair obscured her sleepy face. She ran down the stairs and hugged him with such force that she almost knocked him off his feet.

'Dad, you scared me. Where have you been? I was worried about you.'

'Working.'

'This late?' asked Alana, pulling out of the embrace. She spotted the dressing on the side of his head. 'What happened? Were you fighting?'

'Fighting? Me?' said Fulton. 'When have you ever known me to fight on the street?'

'What happened then?'

'I got bottled while covering the protest in George Square. It's nothing,' he said, gently touching the side of his head. 'The doctors say it will be fine.'

'Okay,' said Alana softly. 'But you've got to take care of yourself. Do you need anything? There's some paracetamol in the cabinet.'

'Honestly, I'm good.'

She let out a loud yawn and stretched her arms above her head. 'Dad, I've got a test tomorrow. I really need to get some sleep.'

'Go, then . . . Love you so much. See you in the morning.'

'Love you too,' said Alana, giving him a quick hug and a peck on the cheek. 'Shout if you need anything.'

Fulton watched as she climbed the stairs. When she was almost at the top, he heard himself saying: 'And tomorrow we'll have to talk about what happened earlier this week.'

Alana's body immediately tensed. She rounded on the stairs as if about to swipe some prey.

'We weren't having sex, okay?' she yelled at her father. She glared at him. 'And even if we were, it's none of your business.'

She stomped to her bedroom and slammed the door.

Chapter 23

Ian Larbert wandered through the ranks of grey gravestones. Some were towering, ornate affairs with winged angels resting on their tops, but most were modest, barely waist-high, whose plaques were weathered, making the engravings difficult to read. Beneath a willow tree, Larbert knelt down and placed a bunch of white roses on a grave. He stood up and read the inscription: LANCE CORPORAL STEPHEN LARBERT – KILLED IN ACTION – 21 MAY 2007. His nephew had been killed on a foot patrol in the Iraqi city of Basra – a bullet straight through the head. Today would have been in his birthday.

Larbert never spoke to his colleagues about the tragedy, he only ever talked shop. He knew he wasn't the best street cop and that self-awareness was part of the reason he'd climbed so high in the force. If Larbert had any talent, it was for knowing which way the wind was blowing. But the John Millar investigation was a whole different league. It was scrambling his senses. Normally, he called the shots; now he was being forced to collaborate with MI5 and it wasn't always clear what they wanted from him. But late last night, Larbert had been given a pretty good idea.

'Can you spare a minute?' asked Neil, sticking his head round the door.

'Sure, come in – take a seat,' said Larbert, who was going through the last of the day's paperwork. As Neil pulled out a chair, Larbert scrawled his signature on a form before laying down his pen. 'How can I help you?'

'I just wanted to say that you and Davy have done absolutely superb work in hunting down Millar's killer. We can't thank you enough.'

'That's very kind of you,' said Larbert evenly. He was always wary of flattery but this praise struck him as honestly earned. 'As you know, Davy can be hard to handle. But if you point him in the right direction, he normally comes up with the goods.'

'I can see that and I'm sure your efforts will be appreciated. I think I'm right in assuming that you'll announce the arrest of the killer at a press conference tomorrow?'

'That's the plan.'

'Great. It's going to be a huge moment – one for the history books, that's for sure.'

'Yes, there will be a lot of interest.'

'But, look,' said Neil, concern creeping across his face, 'we've got the hitman but no idea who paid him to actually do it: the real culprit, as it were.'

'Agreed. But Davy and I are busting a gut to get to the bottom of this. We're following all the leads and I'm confident we'll turn up something fairly soon.'

'Ian, please don't think I'm questioning your professionalism, because I'm certainly not, but what with the riots and the referendum in a few days, what we don't have at the moment is the luxury of time – an assessment I'm sure you'd agree with.'

'What are you suggesting?'

'We're increasingly confident there is a link between the

Russians and this murder. Clearly, Moscow thought Millar had gone off the rails and we believe they took him out because he discovered their secret slush fund to help the nationalist cause.'

'Okay,' said Larbert, with a degree of surprise.

'We need to amplify that fact to the press. We need people to understand that this murder didn't come out of the blue. We need to create a narrative that the public understands. Because if we don't, we'll end up only sowing more confusion and that's the last thing either of us wants.'

What is it with these guys? thought Larbert. Do they ever question their own judgement? Do they even know that self-doubt even exists? 'I hear you, Neil, but what's this assessment actually based on? Neither Davy nor I have seen any evidence that would remotely suggest Russian involvement in this case.'

'Intelligence we have.'

'And this intelligence *you* have, could you share it with me? As the lead on this investigation, I'm sure it would come in useful.'

'Ian, I respect you, and if it were up to me, absolutely.'

'But?'

'But the Director-General specifically told me not to share. It's highly sensitive. My hands are tied, they really are.'

Larbert sat perfectly still. He said nothing. He didn't even blink.

'I understand your dilemma,' said Neil. 'I'm not asking you to do anything I wouldn't do myself. As you know, such intelligence is not always conclusive, but, Ian, this is as good as we're going to get. We have it from multiple sources. It's credible and needs to be acted upon.'

Larbert continued staring at Neil, saying nothing.

'We need to give the public a motive for this killing. Our

161

intelligence strongly suggests it was Moscow. It's as simple as that. Do you want to see more violence on the streets?'

'Of course not,' said Larbert impatiently. He undid his top button and pulled off his black tie. He rolled it up and dropped it in his top drawer. 'But that's not the issue here, is it?'

'I shouldn't need to remind you that the top job in Scotland is coming up,' said Neil, the faintest quiver in his voice. 'If you play your cards right then you'll be a shoo-in for that promotion. Just think it through. It really wouldn't be fair if someone else sneaked in ahead of you. Isn't this what you've worked for all your life?'

'I think we'd better call it a night,' replied Larbert.

Glancing back at the gravestone, Larbert thought about his nephew. He'd died before he'd barely got going. So much of life, he thought, comes down to luck. How many times are we an inch from death and yet never realised it? Larbert felt close to tears. Stephen's friends and fellow marines may have taken comfort that he died doing what he loved, doing his duty, but Larbert was never swayed by that – he felt burned by the emptiness, the waste of it all. He checked his watch. Larbert knew his reputation would be on the line at the press conference. Play it how Neil wanted and the top job would be within his grasp – unthinkable just a week ago. Crises throw up once-in-a-lifetime opportunities. But if Neil was playing him along, if the intelligence was dodgy, Larbert would be made the scapegoat when this crisis blew over. Most of his colleagues would cheer on his fall. As he turned away from his nephew's grave and trudged back to his car, Larbert still didn't know what he was going to say in two hours' time.

Chapter 24

Davy stared out of the double-glazing van at the housing scheme. The second support vehicle had failed to turn up, hence the hold-up. It was now 6:45 a.m. and Davy knew that in fifteen minutes he would have to call the whole thing off. You need to get the suspect sleeping. If he's up and about and making himself a coffee it can all get a bit messy. He may have the chance to flush the drugs down the toilet. And Davy tried his best to avoid busting into homes when he knew the kids might be up. He didn't like children seeing their parents being held down over a table while being handcuffed by the police – although many of his colleagues didn't share his reservations.

As the minutes ticked by, Davy grew more agitated. 'I'll kill that stupid bastard,' Davy said to nobody in particular. '"My car won't start," my arse.' His colleagues sitting in the back of the van cradling upturned black helmets with protective goggles inside said nothing. They knew better than try to placate the gaffer when he was in a foul mood. Davy wound down the window and started tapping his fingers on the door in a rhythmical fashion. He hoped it would calm him down. Instead, the tapping got angrier and more discordant. He glanced at the clock on the car's dashboard. 'Bloody hell.' 6:59 a.m. Davy knew he would need to call it off. Then, in the wing mirror, he saw the second van approaching along the street. It flashed its lights. Davy picked up his radio when the vehicle stopped behind his van.

'You enjoy your fry-up?'

'Sorry, gaffer.'

'Good to go?'

'Aye.'

'Right, show-time. Go, go, go.'

In seconds, the team had pulled on their helmets and tumbled out of the two vans with Davy sprinting into the lead. It was only a few metres to number 46 but he was feeling it in his chest and knees. Outside the front door he silently counted his men. There were six in total: four from his van, two from the support vehicle. He gave a nod. All the guys pulled down their goggles. Davy tugged at the hidden panel on his blue jacket and pulled it down. It read: 'Police.' The two policemen carrying the battering ram positioned themselves just beside Davy – one on either side of the door.

'This is the police!' shouted Davy. 'Open up!'

Before he'd even finished the sentence, the battering ram took the door clean off its hinges. It was left marooned in the middle of the hallway as the team barrelled into the house. Most of them moved upstairs, taking two or three stairs at time. Chris McLaughlin was the target: one of Glasgow's biggest cocaine and heroin dealers. Surveillance had seen him dropped off by a taxi at this address, late last night. He normally lived in Bearsden, ensconced in a mansion of middle-class respectability with his wife and their two twenty-something daughters. But Chris had a weak spot for the ladies and, on the pretence of doing business, would spend a night with his latest fling as often as he could. Also, McLaughlin happened to be Trilby Tam's top rival in the city – hence the raid this morning.

When Davy burst into the bedroom the first thing he saw

was the man's hairy arse waving in the air. Chris was scrabbling around on the bed sheets trying to find his underwear. Knowing that the game was up he turned to face Davy, cupping his balls. He wore a thick gold chain and his gut was like a mossy boulder rolling down a hill.

'How we doin', Chris?' asked Davy from across the room. 'You after these?' Davy held up a pair of boxer shorts with his index finger. He swung them over to Chris. 'Put them on. And if you behave yourself, I'll let you put on the rest of your clothes before I take you out of here.'

'I want a lawyer,' said Chris, pulling on his pants. 'You've got nowt on me.'

'I'll be the judge of that,' replied Davy. He then heard screaming from the bathroom across the hallway. The shrieking woman, he thought, prepare yourself.

'Chris, what the fuck is going on? Is that the polis?' The door cracked open and Davy saw a woman with wet brown hair staring directly at him with undiluted hatred.

'Just put a towel around yourself. One of the boys will be in to see you in a second,' Davy told her.

'Who the fuck do you think you are?'

'The polis. Now, shut it. I'm trying to be nice. Be good and we won't mess up your house too much.'

She slammed the door in his face.

From down the corridor, two of the team were tearing through the chest of drawers and wardrobe in a kid's bedroom. There was a *Paw Patrol* poster on the wall. Thankfully, the kid wasn't there.

'Gaffer, we've got something here,' said one of the policemen. He handed Davy a package wrapped in plastic containing a white substance. They had found it stuffed at the back of a sock drawer.

Davy flicked open the Swiss army knife he kept in his trouser pocket and sliced open the top of the package. He gently squeezed it and some of the powder spilled out. He dabbed it with one his fingers and took a quick taste. It was the real deal – cocaine. By Davy's reckoning, it was a kilo of the stuff. That was ten years' jail time there and then.

'I thought you'd be smarter than stashing your gear at your girlfriend's house,' said Davy, glancing at Chris who was still in nothing but his boxer shorts.

'It's hers, not mine. Nowt to do with me,' protested Chris.

He was allowed to put on his clothes and was taken out of the house peacefully enough. But his girlfriend hollered and screamed as the police tried to drag her down stairs, and kicked one of the officers in the groin.

At the door, Davy realised that some of the neighbours were already out on the street to enjoy the spectacle of an early morning arrest.

'Just get her in the van, will you,' he told his two officers who were still struggling with the woman. She was refusing to walk. So they carried her out of the house like a rag doll, feet dragging on the path, and hauled her into the back of the van and slammed the doors.

One of Davy's team came up to him and patted him on the back. 'Good job, gaffer. He's going down for a long time.'

'Aye, that he is.'

But Davy didn't share the boys' jubilation at a successful bust. Instead, he felt sick to his stomach. He knew the John Millar case was the biggest of his career. It ranked right up there with terrorism. The bosses didn't want to hear what he was up to: they just wanted it done. It was a charter to break as many rules as he wanted. But when the dust settled on this case as inevitably it would, the lawyers and journalists would start asking questions. And Davy knew that if anyone found out about his association with Trilby Tam, he'd be hung out to dry.

Chapter 25

The briefing room at Police Scotland HQ was stowed out with more than a hundred journalists and photographers in a space designed for barely half that number. Those present were sweating profusely and growing increasingly short-tempered. A pair of cameramen almost came to blows over where to set up their tripods and were only separated after an officer reminded them that they were inside a police station.

Away from the mêlée, Larbert was poring over his final statement in a small, windowless room down the corridor. He was trying to make it as succinct as possible and iron out any contradictions. While Larbert had no trouble projecting an air of authority, what really concerned him were the questions that might be asked after he made his statement. He had war-planned in advance, writing down possible talking points. But his greatest fear was that a single, carelessly tossed-out word might trigger a free-for-all.

One of Larbert's assistants was sitting beside him, twiddling away on her phone. She knew better than to interrupt the boss when he was deep in thought. He was the master of the disapproving stare. She was startled by a knock at the door. She jumped to her feet, seeking to head off the danger. She opened the door a crack and explained that the chief could not be disturbed. Larbert spoke as soon as heard Neil's voice.

'Let him in,' he said with a sigh, looking up from his statement.

'I hope I'm not interrupting you,' said Neil, flashing a smile.

'Absolutely not,' replied Larbert. 'Gayle, if you wouldn't mind giving us a moment, and tell the guys I'll be good to go in a couple of minutes.'

'Will do, sir.'

The assistant grabbed her bag and left, closing the door behind her.

'What can I do for you, Neil?'

'I just wanted to offer you some moral support in front of the big crowd.'

'Thank you.'

'And just to reiterate what we spoke about last night – it's absolutely vital that you give the Russian angle a push. I know you have your doubts, but there's a lot riding on it. I just got off the phone with the Director General and she wanted me to pass on her personal appreciation for your sterling efforts on this case. As I'm sure you're aware, she's from this part of the world.'

'That's very kind, and, yes, I know better than to disappoint a woman like her.'

'Thank you, Ian. I'm sure you'll be rewarded for your remarkable service. Now I'll leave you be,' said Neil, raising an eyebrow with a theatrical flourish, 'I believe you have a press conference. *Bonne chance, mon ami.*'

The door closed and Larbert was left alone. He knew the time for worrying was over. He picked up his peaked cap and slapped it twice on his trouser leg to remove any dust. Then positioning the rim on the back of his head he carefully brought it down over his hair. He tweaked the cap, so it was tilting upwards ever so slightly. It improved his profile on camera. His fingers moved on to his black tie. The knot was firm: the tie was straight. On to the pewter buttons, his fingers working fast – one, two, three, four buttons done. Then for the final check. He ran his fingers down his black jacket. Smooth as a bowling green, he thought. Time to go.

'Good morning, ladies and gentlemen. My name is Ian Larbert and I'm Acting Chief Constable. We here at Police Scotland welcome you today. I'll start by making a short statement and then take a couple of questions: one from the local media, the other from the international press. I apologise in advance but that is all we will have time for today.'

Larbert detected an air of discontent in the room as restless journalists manoeuvred to catch his eye. He took a sip of water and placed the glass back on the lectern.

'At approximately eight thirty this morning, a twenty-five-year-old male was arrested and charged with the murder of John Millar.'

There was a whoosh of clicks as a bank of cameras sought to capture the dramatic moment.

'The suspect, Charles Easter, is from the Pollok area of the city. He confessed to the killing of John Millar. Mr Easter provided us with valuable information that allowed us to retrieve what we believe to be the murder weapon. A team of police divers located a gun in a canal close to Firhill football stadium in the Partick area of the city. Our forensic unit is currently examining the weapon. I should state for the record that our inquiries are ongoing in what remains a complex and sensitive case. I repeat my calls and ask you all to report this case in a responsible fashion. But make no mistake, we here at Police Scotland are determined to deliver justice for John Millar and his family. I'll now take the questions.'

A forest of hands shot up followed by a harsh chorus of shouts from the journalists. But Larbert simply ignored them and scanned the crowd for a familiar face. He pointed at Fulton who stood up from his seat.

'Is the First Minister still being investigated in regard to this case? And is the death of John Millar's sister, Elaine, connected in any way? Thank you.'

'I said one question, Fulton, but I'll let you away with it this time. To answer your first question, the First Minister, Susan Ward, has been interviewed in relation to the murder of John Millar and remains a person of interest in our inquiry. I should stress for the record that it does not make her a suspect. But I can't say any more on this matter.

'On the second point, the procurator fiscal released a report this morning on the death of Elaine Millar. The conclusion was that Miss Millar's death was the result of an accidental overdose. We here at Police Scotland have no reason not to accept those findings. Our condolences go out to Miss Millar's family and friends.'

The shouting broke out once more much to Larbert's frustration. 'Ladies and gentlemen, this isn't a circus. I'll take one question from the woman at the front.'

'Thank you,' said the journalist, in an American accent, as she rose from her seat. Everyone in the room strained to catch a glimpse of the exotic creature wearing a red suit and sporting big blonde hair.

'I'm Lara Banks, CNN,' she declared, with a star reporter's confidence. 'The Russian Foreign Ministry has put out a statement denying it ever gave money to the Scottish Nationalist Party in response to the claims in John Millar's video. Is it your opinion that no Russian money has been used in this campaign?'

Larbert took a sip of water. Neil, who was leaning up against the wall at the back of the room, gave Larbert a nod. Larbert looked down at the lectern again. He gently kicked it with his feet.

'We take these accusations very seriously, Lara. Any illegal funding of parties during the referendum is not only an attack on democracy, but on our country and our way of life. If there is a British way, if there is a Scottish way, it is to play by the rules. Our nation was founded on law and order and our institutions are admired the world over for their independence and fairness. We will do our utmost to prevent hostile nations from subverting the democratic will of the people in order to sow chaos.'

He paused. He thought of his career. He took the plunge.

'At this time, Police Scotland cannot rule out the possibility that Russia was trying to interfere in the referendum. It is our position that it is more likely than not that Moscow sought to affect the outcome of the vote. We cannot rule out the possibility of Russian involvement in the killing of John Millar in order to conceal its alleged financing of the Scottish Nationalist Party. Our investigations into this matter remain ongoing. Thank you for your time.'

Pandemonium broke out in the briefing room. Larbert moved swiftly away from the lectern to avoid being taken hostage by journalists. They were shouting out questions: 'Do you have proof the Nationalists took money from the Russians? Are you saying Moscow murdered John Millar?' A couple of them tried to block Larbert as he exited the briefing room. He firmly brushed them aside. Two policemen stationed at the door prevented them from going any further.

As Larbert marched down the corridor, he sensed someone coming up behind him.

'Great performance,' said Neil, slapping him on the back. 'The Russians are now centre stage.'

Chapter 26

'How's your head?' asked Chris, leaning back in his office chair, his tan leather brogues casually propped up on the desk.

'Could be better, if I'm honest,' said Fulton, standing at the door. 'But it'll heal quick enough.'

Fulton had just returned from the police conference and decided it would be best to run his piece by the *Siren*'s editor before committing words to the page.

'I've been thinking,' said Chris, 'and please don't take this the wrong way, but I think the thrust of your question was wrong.'

'How exactly?' replied Fulton. 'Asking whether the First Minister was still being investigated in regard to the murder? Sorry, but that's the story, unless I'm missing something.'

'Close the door,' said Chris firmly. He pulled his feet off the desk and motioned for Fulton to take a seat. 'It's not a criticism of you but I think our coverage has been too emotional.'

'Emotional?'

'I think we've been blinded by the human drama.'

'A man's dead, Chris, and the First Minister's accused of killing him – if that's not drama then what the hell is?'

Chris clasped his hands tightly. 'Yes, point taken, but let's look at this another way, do you honestly believe that Susan Ward had John Millar killed?'

'No,' said Fulton. 'She doesn't strike me as a heartless killer and, anyway, she was ahead in the polls, so why should she?'

'Exactly.'

'So, what am I missing then?'

'I think CNN got it right: it's the Russian angle – that's the story we haven't looked into.' Chris bounced his clasped hands on the desk. 'Do you think the Nats could have been taking money from Moscow?'

Fulton exhaled deeply. 'It's possible, I suppose. Anything's possible. But other than Larbert saying they're still looking into it, where's the evidence? It appears to be a classic case of whataboutism. Someone's pointed the finger and said what about this?'

'Thank you for the definition, Fulton, I wasn't aware of the term,' replied Chris, sarcasm discernible in his voice. 'A bit like nationalism, it's fast becoming the last refuge of the scoundrel. But in this case, it's not just Larbert saying it – we have the dead man pointing the finger as well.'

'Yes, you're right but, again, where's the evidence? I know there are a few freelancers banging on about the nationalists being on the take but they're on the lunatic fringe. On the flip side, there's one guy pumping out reports that John Millar was killed by MI5 to frame the nationalists.'

'And who's to say that guy's not right?'

'Sorry?' said Fulton.

'And who's to say that's not true?' repeated Chris, this time a bit louder as if he was speaking to someone who was hard of hearing.

Fulton was flabbergasted by the remark. Chris was making even less sense than normal. 'Sorry, but are you really suggesting that MI5 was behind the hit?'

Chris stared through him. He then held up his hand,

angling his signet ring so it glinted as it caught the light. 'This ring means a lot to me,' he said finally. 'It belonged to my great-uncle Harold.'

'The foreign secretary?'

'No, that was Charles,' replied Chris, with a grimace. 'A truly ghastly man, but Harold was delightful. His great love was Persia; he was stationed there during the Second World War. He spoke fluent Farsi and used to regale me about his trips to Persepolis and Isfahan. God, he loved it there, but in the end the country broke him.'

'How exactly?'

'He was an intelligence officer and he was involved in the 1953 coup – when the Americans and Brits overthrew the prime minister, Mossadegh. It was all part of the Cold War calculations and Mossadegh was seen as a dangerous social-ist. But Uncle Harold used to describe it as the most shameful chapter in British history and there's a fair few candidates for that prize to pick from.'

Chris gently tapped his ring on the desk. 'All I'm saying is we can't afford to be naïve; let us not forget that some conspiracies are, in fact, true.'

'Well, when you put it like that . . .'

'And let's not allow prejudices to cloud our judgement, Fulton. This story is far too important for that.'

Fulton dearly wanted to show a flash of defiance but reluc-tantly conceded that his editor was right on this occasion. 'What do you suggest, then?' he asked.

'I think you should put aside John Millar for now and focus on the Russian angle. See what Russian money was coming into the country and whether any of it was being funnelled to the nationalists – that needs to be our priority.'

Fulton couldn't help but look irritated this time. Now Chris was suggesting he go on some wild Russian goose chase. 'And apart from googling it, how do you suppose I do that? I've never done a financial story in my life, never mind one with an international espionage angle. We'd need a specialist – a forensic auditor.'

'Just do what you always do, Fulton: get out there and speak to people.'

'Well, I know plenty of guys down the pub who're never short of an opinion or two.'

'I'll help you out,' said Chris impatiently. 'Take down this number.'

He slowly read out the digits as Fulton keyed them into his phone.

'Start with Bill,' said Chris. 'He was a friend of my dad's. He knows everything there is to know about Russia. You'll find him helpful and you'll like him as well.'

'Why's that?'

'Because he's Scottish and he isn't posh.'

Chapter 27

Davy Bryant resembled an overweight flamenco dancer as he approached the turnstile. He was holding two pies aloft like castanets and he used his hips to barge his way through.

'Wouldn't want to get peckish during the game,' he said with a grin before taking a greedy bite of pie. The hot, juicy grease trickled down his chin. Davy unashamedly wiped off the offending stain with his sleeve.

'C'mon, I've got us good seats right behind the dugout, so we'll get two shows for the price of one.'

'What are you on about?' asked Fulton, who'd passed on Davy's offer of a pie.

'Oh, the new manager always puts on a good show especially when we're losing. He's pure class, a real firecracker. It's often the only entertainment I get watching the Jags.'

The two men were carried along the pitch-side by the flow of fans pushing in behind them as kick-off neared. They climbed the concrete stairs and reached their seats about ten rows back from the pitch. Fulton was a bit squished as Davy wriggled to make himself comfortable in his seat.

'God, I missed this, sitting in a stadium. Magnificent, isn't it? But how you doing anyway, pal?' asked Davy. 'Been avoiding those flying bottles?'

'Aye, you could say that,' replied Fulton. 'Look, I need to speak to you about something.'

'Fire away.'

But Davy was immediately distracted as the two teams ran onto the pitch, raising a roar from the crowd. The home team were wearing their distinctive red and yellow striped tops and were taking on Caledonian Thistle in one of the first cup-ties of the season. Davy was soon on his feet, bawling at the top of his lungs, 'C'mon, the Jags, give 'em hell, boys!' He only stopped screaming himself hoarse when the referee blew the whistle to start the game.

For a few minutes, Fulton resigned himself to the fact that he was being spurned for the football. Davy was like a dog chasing a slip of silver paper blowing in the wind. 'Away ye go, ref,' he cried, jumping from his seat in pure rage. A nasty-looking tackle on a home player was provoking similar howls of protest around the stadium. But there wasn't anyone who was giving out quite as much as Davy. His face was puce.

But the man in black simply waved play on and was barracked by abuse every time he approached the touchline. 'We're going to lose ... Decisions already going against us ... I can feel it in my bones,' Davy moaned.

'Why do you support Thistle?'

Davy looked at Fulton as if it was the daftest question he'd ever been asked. 'Because I'm not some kind of glory hunter. And, anyway, when we do win it's that wee bit more special.'

As the minutes ticked by the tempo of the game dropped, with both teams heaving long kicks back and forth to each other from their own halves.

'It's supposed to be a game of football not a tennis match,' said Davy, with barely disguised disgust. 'Anyway, what is it you need to talk about?'

Fulton looked around him. He was in a stand with hundreds of other fans – not exactly the place to have a private

179

chat. But then most fans don't go to a football match to eavesdrop.

'Do I need to worry about my safety?'

'It's a family club; there are no hooligans here.'

'Is anyone going to try and kill me?'

'What, at Firhill? What the hell are you on about?' asked Davy, arching an eyebrow in astonishment.

'Neil . . .'

'What? The MI5 guy?'

Fulton nodded.

'A real smarty pants but not a total bell-end. What's he's been up to?'

'He came to see me at the hospital.'

'He did?' said Davy, with a degree of surprise in his voice, before his gaze drifted back to the pitch.

'Aye.'

'And what was he after?'

'He told me about Elaine Millar's death.'

'And?'

'And he said he wouldn't want anything to happen to me.'

Davy turned awkwardly in his red plastic seat and his knees were now digging into Fulton's legs. 'What happened to that woman was a sin,' he said. 'I felt for her, but Neil is just messing with you – it's what those guys do, they play mind games.'

'So, you don't think they killed her?'

'Nah, I don't think so.'

'How come you're so sure?'

'Because I spoke to a couple of boys I trust. They were the first at the scene and said it wasn't a fit-up. But it's messy, Fulton, I'll give you that.'

'But if they wanted to, could they have pulled it off – MI5?'

'Maybe. Anything's possible. But we've got to keep our heads; it's the only thing keeping us out of the loony bin at the moment.' Seeing that he'd fail to convince Fulton, Davy continued: 'Look, I remember when I first started out in the police and there was a young woman who'd hanged herself. The gaffer immediately wrote it up as suicide. I wasn't so sure. I thought she'd been strung up but none of the boys would listen to me. I kept banging on about it. Do you know what happened?'

'What?

'Two days later they found a suicide note that had fallen down the back of the headboard. It said she'd been raped as a kid and it first happened on her eleventh birthday. And do you know what, Fulton? She had hanged herself on her birthday – two decades on and she had never got over it. The reality is that Elaine was a sick woman; she had just lost her brother, and she probably overdosed because she didn't have anything to live for. That's the brutal truth of it.'

Just then a surge of energy pulsed through the crowd and Davy's attention was away again. A neat ball slipped through the opposition's defence and Partick Thistle's star striker was racing in on goal. He couldn't miss, he just couldn't. And then the ball bobbled in front of him. He still shouldn't miss it. The home crowd were carried off their seats and onto their feet in a wave of expectation. And the striker struck the ball, ballooning it over the bar. He sunk to his knees, holding his head in his hands, probably wishing he was anywhere but a stadium full of his own team's supporters, who made no bones about telling him they thought his effort was beyond pathetic.

'Whit the hell, my granny could have done better than that!' blared Davy, his face flushing a sweaty red again. But then a devilish smile swept his face. He nudged Fulton in the ribs. True to form, the Jags manager shot out of the dugout, his hands held high as if he was begging for some divine intervention all the while letting loose a string of invective that you definitely wouldn't hear in a place of worship.

'That boy's going to have a heart attack if he's not careful,' said Davy, his belly bumping against the seat in front of him. 'At least he'll die doing something he loves. But what were we talking about?'

'Neil.'

'Aye, Neil. I know it's strange times, Fulton. But honestly, they're not going to touch a journalist. If you're really worried, I can get a couple of cars to swing by at night, so you and Alana feel safe.'

'Ach, you're probably right: I'm reading too much into things. But what did you make of what your boss said at the press thing, that they couldn't rule out Russia trying to interfere in the election?'

Davy's facial expression looked like he'd just sucked on a lemon – even ferocious calls for a penalty couldn't distract him now.

'Screw Larbert. He would've sung "The Sash" if he thought it would get him the top job.'

'So, what he said wasn't true?'

'Unless he's seen something I haven't, which I doubt, it's just complete bollocks. He's just saying it so we can claim to be making progress. Remember those documents John Millar claimed tied the Russians to the nationalists?'

'Yeah.'

'Well, yer pal Neil found them and said I was to give them to you.'

'So where are they then?'

182

'The bottom of the Clyde.'

'What?'

'I stood on Jamaica Bridge, tore them into very small pieces and threw them where they belonged.' Davy's gaze drifted back to the pitch. 'Now, less of the work chat, let's watch the game.'

Chapter 28

Susan couldn't sleep. Her mind was like a carousel that never stopped. Gordon, the girls, John . . . Gordon, the girls, John . . . Gordon, the girls, John . . . As dawn broke, she gave up trying and pulled herself out of the bed in the guest room, threw on her dressing gown, and crept downstairs to the kitchen.

She made herself a cup of coffee. She poured in the milk and watched the liquid change colour. Even sleep-deprived, she loved the rhythm of renewal in the mornings – a time to think before the day barged in like an overbearing relative. But the problem with today was that there was no plan, no engagements, only oblivion, as Susan saw it, stretching end-lessly into the distance.

Her thoughts turned to the girls still sleeping in their beds and how much she loved them, how much she had let them down – even if they were too young to know it yet. She fought the urge to sneak into their rooms and kiss them gently on their foreheads. They'd be up and about soon enough. She thought about her conversation with Gordon. Every revela-tion had drawn blood. With time the pain would dull but the scars would always be there.

And, guiltily, because she knew it should be the last thing on her mind, she thought of the political campaign and the vote in three days' time. In her absence, Paul Fielder had taken over the campaign. He was a great number two – loyal and diligent, with no designs on the top job. It was just as well, because before this crisis he would never have had a chance at it. He had the charisma of a goldfish. People remembered his mouth opening but nothing that came out of it. Now, that would be hailed as a virtue. Steady Paul. Susan knew he was never going to win the vote. He would robotically go through his talking points until the referendum was over. And then when the results were announced he would give a dignified speech admitting defeat and call upon the country to come together. Susan couldn't blame him. It was the hand he had been dealt. But it made her feel sick to the stomach that the campaign would end in a whimper and with the establishment crowing.

She went upstairs to get dressed.

Brian spread the latest polls across the mahogany coffee table. 'There's good news and there's bad news,' he said, gesturing to the papers in front of them. He picked one of them up and handed it to Susan.

'This is the bad news. See here,' he said, pointing to the paragraph with a pen he had pilfered from a Hilton hotel. 'It shows we've dropped eight per cent in the polls.'

Susan quickly skimmed the figures and analysis. She didn't share her colleagues' obsession with them. They built whole election campaigns based on the findings and whisperings of the pollsters. But as far as Susan was concerned most polls were fundamentally flawed – there was never any foolproof formula for quantifying people's emotions.

'What's the good news then?'

'The good news,' said Brian, 'is that we're on forty-three per cent and we appear to have hit rock bottom. To be honest, I expected a far bigger fall – something in the region of fifteen per cent. We've seen a collapse but not a complete one.'

Brian fully expected Susan to share in his relief but instead she gave him a cold, hard stare.

'What I'm saying is that we're not going to be embarrassed. That's good, no?'

'If I wanted to avoid being embarrassed, I'd have become an accountant. So, what are we going to do?'

'What do you mean?'

'To close the gap?'

'Sorry, are you taking the piss?'

'No, I'm serious.'

'Are you seriously saying that you think we can still win?

'Yes.'

'For God's sake, Susan,' said Brian, his voice rising in anger. 'You've lost it. It's over. Can't you see that? You need to face facts. Half the population, every Unionist out there, thinks you're a cold-blooded killer. And as for swing voters, can you really blame them for having their doubts?'

'This isn't about me.'

'Isn't about you? It's all about you. It's all about you and John and him getting murdered.'

'I'm not admitting defeat.'

'Woman, you've taken leave of your senses,' said Brian. He reached forward and pushed aside the papers on the table. He toyed with the notion of storming out the room but the moment passed. 'So, what do you propose then?'

'I stop hiding. I give a speech.'

'Where?'

'George Square.'

'Jesus Christ! Saying what exactly?'

'Telling the truth.'

'And that is?'

'That I had nothing to do with John Millar's death.'

186

'You've already bloody said that – out there,' said Brian, gesturing out the window, 'in case you've forgotten. And every time you say it, you remind people of exactly what happened. It damages you, it damages us, it damages the cause – can't you see that?'

'Don't patronise me, Brian. Remember, I hired you.'

'All right, First Minister,' he said sarcastically. 'But what on God's green earth are you going to say that will make any difference?'

'I'm going to tell people this is about them – and not me. It's about their children, their grandchildren, who will look back at all of this and wonder why so many people were fooled by what is so clearly a travesty of justice.'

'It won't make a blind bit of difference. We're still going to lose.'

There was a knock at the door. They both looked up.

'Come in,' said Susan.

The door opened. It was Gordon. His face was raw and creased, like a muddy walking boot left to dry in the sun. He'd clearly had a rough night too, she thought.

'Can I come in?'

'Of course,' said Susan, surprised that he wanted to be anywhere near her.

Brian got up to leave. But Susan's expression told him that he was going nowhere. His anger turned to unease. Political rows were his forte. He felt alive when it all kicked off – he loved the thrust and parry of battle. But domestics were civil wars – messy, protracted affairs, driven by emotions rather than pragmatic interests, you had no idea where the battle-lines were drawn. When it came to domestics his instincts always screamed scarper.

Gordon pulled up a chair between them. This wasn't going

to be a casual drive-by.

'Sorry, I couldn't help but hear your conversation.'

'Sorry for the shouting,' said Susan.

'It's fine. But I've got something to say to both of you and please hear me out. Brian, let's just be honest for a moment: do you think Susan had anything to do with John's murder?'

'Of course, not. It's just—'

'Okay, Susan is right then. This isn't the time to lie low: love her or hate her, she's a fighter. The John Millar video is a tissue of lies and it's being used by the establishment to destroy the case for independence. We can't let that happen. If we're going to go down, we need to go down fighting. Susan should make that speech, she should tell them it's about them and not her. It's what her whole life has been about.'

Brian leaned back in his chair. There was no way to fight himself out of this ambush. 'I guess I've been outvoted,' he said, glancing at both of them. 'But we're still going to lose and lose badly – mark my words.'

Chapter 29

Davy pulled into the country club's car park and found a spot beside the sleek blue Bentley convertible he instantly recognised as Tam's motor. One of the crime boss's boys was behind the steering wheel listening to the radio and brazenly smoking out the window. At the club entrance, Davy was greeted by a receptionist whose fake tan was darker than the stain on a wooden fence. He asked for the restaurant and she pointed through the double doors. Davy saw a couple of old dears picking at their fish and chips and one guy, still in his gym gear, eating a salad. But no sign of Tam. Inside, Davy stopped a waiter and was shown through another set of double doors to an area with a small fake waterfall, used for exclusive evening dining.

It was empty apart from Tam who was sitting alone at a window table. His napkin was stuffed down the front of his shirt and he was staring vacantly into the distance. As Davy approached, Tam tried to stand up but his legs got tangled under the lavish tablecloth. He looked embarrassed and offered his hand instead.

'I thought a wee celebration was in order,' said Tam, reaching for a bottle of champagne resting in an ice bucket. He filled up two flutes.

'I'm not supposed to drink on shift but I'm always happy to make an exception,' said Davy, sitting down. 'What's the occasion?'

'The arrest of that bastard Chris McLaughlin.'

Tam held up his glass, fully expecting Davy to do the same. But Davy stared at him impassively. The old crime boss slowly put his glass back down on the table. He fiddled for a moment with his chunky Rolex.

'You honestly think you're better than me?' said Tam in a quietly menacing tone. 'You do, don't you? You think the likes of me shouldnae be sitting in a country club in Newton Mearns, don't you, son?'

'It's not that. It's just . . .'

'Lost your tongue, son? Well, you fucking listen to me, Davy. Life chooses you, you don't choose life. Do you think if I'd grown up here, I would have done what I've done? Of course fucking not. I'd probably be a lawyer or a doctor or something else legit. But I did what I had to – *needed* – to do. And do you know what, Davy, I started with nothing and I made something of myself.'

'Tam, I'm not judging you.'

'Aye, you are – that's exactly what you're doing. But since we're from the same place, I'm willing to let it pass as an unfortunate misunderstanding. I wouldn't want to create a scene in a nice place like this. That's manners for you. Now, let's try that toast again. Pick up your fucking glass.'

Davy reached for his glass. The two men toasted and took a sip.

'Sorry about that, Tam.'

'Okay, but Davy . . .'

'Yes, Tam.'

'Never fucking disrespect me again.'

Tam's fist bounced off the table, jolting his knife and fork. Davy was silently cursing himself for the enormity of his mistake. Why the hell hadn't he raised his glass? Given all the compromises that he was being forced to make on this case, a private toast paled into insignificance.

'Do you know why I wanted that bastard arrested, Davy?'

'No.'

'You probably think it was business, that I wanted his turf.'

'Aye, if I'm honest.'

'You'd be wrong, very wrong. I'll tell you why I wanted that bastard taken down. He was rude to my Maureen in this very restaurant. If you cannae hold yer tongue you shouldnae fucking drink in the first place. Do you know what he said to my Maureen?'

'No.'

'That bastard said she had a neck like a turkey. A neck like a turkey, can you fucking imagine it? My Maureen has a beautiful neck. If I'd had my way, that stupid bastard would have been deid the next day. But the other bosses wouldnae let me do it. I'm a reasonable man, Davy. I forgive but I don't forget. Now shall we order?'

'Yes.'

Tam hollered for a waiter, who came running from the kitchen in a panic. They both ordered the soup of the day. When it arrived, Davy watched Tam's spoon shoogling as he fed himself. He was getting more on the napkin than in his actual mouth. By the end of lunch it would look like he'd been garrotted.

'How's your case doing?'

Davy was briefly taken aback by the change in tone. It was like they were now a father and son catching up on the week. 'Slowly, way too slowly. You know, Tam, I was hoping you could do me a favour.'

'I told you if you brought in that bastard Chris I would return the favour, didn't I?'

'Aye, you did.'

'So, what do you want then?'

Davy quickly checked the restaurant to see that a waiter wasn't loitering. He dropped his voice. 'I need to know who paid for the Millar hit.'

'Is Charlie not enough?' Tam didn't bother lowering his voice.

'To be honest, Tam, not in a case like this one. It's a conspiracy that's turned the country upside down. We can't close the book until we know all the facts.'

'What you mean to say is you can't close the book until you're satisfied with all the facts.'

Tam tugged out his splattered napkin and dabbed his chin. He placed it on his side plate alongside a half-eaten roll. 'It's not that simple.'

'With all due respect, Tam, why is that? Charlie did carry out the hit?'

'Aye, it was Charlie. Don't worry, you got the right guy. I would never suggest one of my boys go down for something they didn't do. I don't believe in that kind of behaviour. I find it dishonourable.'

'Absolutely.'

'The thing is, and this may come as a surprise to you, I don't actually know who paid for the hit.'

'What? You don't know who wanted John Millar dead?'

'That's what I said, son. No need to repeat it. I'm not fucking senile.'

'So, if you don't mind me asking, how did it come about, then?'

'Let's put it this way: it didn't come through the normal channels. At first, I thought it was a fit-up by you boys. I know the games you bastards play. But then I checked with a couple of my sources and they gave me the all-clear.'

Tam winked at Davy who refused to take the bait.

'But if you didn't know who you were dealing with, why did you take the job?'

'I'm a businessman, Davy, and when an opportunity presents itself, I would be a fool to pass on it. Let's just say, I had a wee cashflow problem and this job helped fill the hole.'

'How much?'

'I'm not getting into that. But let's say it was a generous amount for a risky job. You know how it is.' He took a sip of water, then gestured to the waiter to bring the bill.

Davy knew he needed to act fast. 'Tam, is there anything you can do to help me solve this?'

'Well, I can't get you a name.'

'I know that.'

'But what about if I get you a phone number and some fingerprints? Would that help?'

'What – of the guy who paid for the hit?'

'Aye. And you boys, I'm sure, can put two and two together. That's not beyond your capabilities.'

They were interrupted by the young waiter arriving with the bill. His eyes widened when he saw the wedge of fifty-pound notes snug in Tam's wallet. Tam pulled out two. He thanked the waiter and told him to keep the change. Seeing Tam struggling to stand up from the table, Davy quickly pushed out his chair and went round to give him a hand.

'Why are you helping me?' asked Davy as he draped Tam's coat over his shoulders.

'Because I'm a man of my word. Unlike the polis, I actually honour my promises.'

'Thanks, Tam.'

'And because John Millar shouldn't have been shot. He was

193

a civvy. He never done nothing to anybody. Nobody is perfect and I want to right a wrong. I made a mistake. You might not believe it, Davy, but even men like me have principles.'

Chapter 30

'Susan, we have a major fucking problem,' said Brian, catching his breath as he ran into the kitchen. He immediately saw the two girls and gasped in horror. Susan glared at him over their shoulders. She was struggling to help them put on their rucksacks.

'Sorry,' said Brian, mortified.

The girls giggled. They probably heard worse on the school bus.

'You need to wash your mouth out with soap, young man,' said Susan sternly. 'Give me a minute.'

Gordon came through to hurry the girls out. Susan kissed them on their cheeks and watched as they raced out the back door. She turned and headed to the living room, where she found Brian. He'd been so flustered about swearing in front of the girls that he had failed to notice Susan's radically transformed appearance. She was wearing a beautifully tailored white dress with black side panels giving the illusion of a trim hourglass figure. The dark shadows under her eyes had magically disappeared. She was radiating feminine glamour and authority.

'I've never seen you look so lovely,' said Brian, mumbling his words. 'Seriously.'

'Thank you,' replied Susan awkwardly. She always found it hard to accept a compliment. 'What's up?'

'They can't guarantee your safety.'

'Who can't guarantee my safety?'

'The police. I just got a call from Larbert and he said you need to call it off.'

'Why? They've known about it since yesterday. It's not exactly a surprise to them.'

'He said they don't have the numbers to ensure it will pass off peacefully. He said it could trigger trouble and they'd be overwhelmed. He was very apologetic.'

'Bullshit. They just don't want me giving a speech and they're using security as an excuse. Who the hell does he think he is, anyway? I never liked him from the first moment I saw him. London must be leaning on him.'

'Look, he's got a point.'

'Why exactly?'

'The riots last week.'

'That wasn't us,' said Susan, growing exasperated. 'That was the Unionists. Can't you see, Brian? They're calling our bluff and expecting us to fall for it. I've never seen such blatant political interference in my life. Larbert thinks I'm down on my knees and he can kick me around. I'd bloody sack him if I could.'

'Susan, I've got a bad feeling—'

'Just stop it, will you.' She put up her hand. 'You've made your feelings clear, but if they think I'm going to back down, they've picked the wrong woman.'

Brian knew trying to reason with her was as much use as throwing water on a flaming frying pan. He thought, again, of just sticking it to her – resigning on the spot and storming out the room. His conscience would be clear. He'd served her loyally for years and they'd simply come to an impasse. Everyone, even Susan with time, would understand why he'd done it. But despite his mounting frustrations, loyalty held him back. Susan was not motivated by ego but a sincere belief that politics should be about improving people's lives. It was a surprisingly rare trait in politicians. And, anyway, Brian knew it would all be over in a few days. The campaign would be lost and they'd both have to step down. He would slip back into the anonymity of private life easily enough. There was no need to jump the gun on a resignation.

'All right,' he said. 'Exactly what should I tell our friend Larbert, then?'

'Tell him the rally is going ahead with or without the police.'

A few hours later, Susan was sitting in the back of her official car, watching her supporters pouring into George Square from every direction. She nodded with satisfaction. She sensed it was going to be far bigger than she could have hoped for. Brian gently squeezed her hand on the armrest. The police, of course, had shown up. They were lining the streets. Susan had sympathy for those on the frontline. They were being asked to referee a game where nobody could agree upon the rules. But that wasn't her main concern. Today was about putting the vote for Scottish independence back on track.

The car was inching forward through the ever-thickening crowd. By now it was obvious that they were going to get no further. The car had hit a wall of human flesh. Faces were pressing up against the tinted windows. One supporter started screaming in delight. With his finger he started prodding the window, leaving greasy fingerprints on the glass. 'It's Susan Ward!' he shouted. 'It's Susan Ward!' As word rippled through the crowd more and more people surrounded the car. The police were helpless. Everyone wanted a piece of Susan.

The mood was anything but hostile, but it was taking on a momentum of its own that could quickly spiral out of control.

James, Ward's young security detail, was sitting in front. He could barely see through the windscreen, which was blocked by a surging number of supporters. One misjudged his footing and was left sprawling on the bonnet. James knew he had to act. He undid his belt and turned to face Susan.

'Listen to me,' he said. 'Forget our previous plans. And whatever happens, Susan, stick with me. Okay?

'Yes.'

James opened his car door, tentatively at first, and then more forcefully as people cleared out of the way. He slid through the gap and pushed his way to Susan's door. As he opened it, a couple of guys tried to jump up on his shoulders to get a better view. Instead, they threw James forward, slamming the door shut. James glared at them. 'Cool it, guys, do you want to hear the First Minister speak or not?' The crowd briefly became more restrained, and James opened the door again. Susan's head popped above the vehicle and James guided her out. But within seconds he lost control. Susan's supporters rushed forward to hug and kiss her, to shake her hand. She was swept away in the tide. James frantically tried to keep up by pushing people away. He grabbed her arm. But they were prised apart again by the sheer weight of supporters. 'Susan, Susan!' he was yelling, but she could barely hear a thing. Suddenly, she was hoisted aloft on a supporter's shoulders. There was nothing James could do – he was too far away. At first, Susan was terrified. She almost toppled over, but a dozen hands appeared to catch her and push her upright on the man's shoulders. A look of sheer joy appeared on her face. As she was carried through the crowd, she slapped people's hands in delight. At one point she was handed a saltire and she whirled it around her head, drawing successive cheers from the crowd. Nearby, the cheeks of a guy wearing a tartan turban puffed out like bellows and the skirl of the bagpipes floated through the air. Susan saw that the square was jam-packed – the image of the hulking, immovable Cenotaph and the palatial City Chambers looked like the backdrop to a revolution.

Susan was moving through the crowd towards a truck in the centre of the square, which was being used as a makeshift stage. When she reached the truck, a couple of local organisers helped her off the supporter's shoulders. She smoothed down her dress and ran her fingers through her hair. She realised she'd left her speech in the car. But it didn't matter. Let it be unscripted. She was going to ride her emotions.

'Ladies and gentlemen,' cried a young party member into the microphone. 'I give you the future Prime Minister of Scotland!'

As Susan took the microphone, the roar from the crowd was electrifying.

'They told me not to come.'

Another roar.

'They told us the cause was dead.'

Another roar.

'Well, I've come here today . . .'

Another roar.

'. . . and by this weekend, our country, our nation, will be free again. We cannot, we must not, let the dream die . . .'

As the roars reached a crescendo, Susan felt a lump in her throat, tears in her eyes and a feeling of euphoria sweep through her body. Deliverance really was at hand. She was the figurehead of a movement far larger than herself. She looked out across George Square and saw a sea of yellow Lion

Rampant flags waving among the statues of the establishment figures who for far too long had kept Scotland down.

Susan knew the pebble had been cast generations before. It had created ripples through society for decades. But today in George Square the ripples were becoming waves, and were finally gathering their full force. The chant began at the back of the crowd. A couple of bare-chested guys with Scottish flags draped over their sunburnt shoulders started shouting it until their voices became hoarse. And then just as they began to wane, their dwindling cries suddenly ignited the crowd. People were pumping their fists in the air. And the noise built and built with such intensity that it became almost impossible to hear. The cries of 'Scotland, Scotland, Scotland' surged around the square. These were people who would not be lied to; these were people who would not be denied; this was their moment, this was their destiny.

'SCOTLAND, SCOTLAND, SCOTLAND.'

Susan closed her eyes to truly savour this moment when the memories of all her struggles were wiped clean. In those few seconds she felt a cold wind sweep through her body. She shivered. As she opened her eyes, she saw the looks of horror on the faces of people around her. In agonising pain, she stumbled headlong onto her knees and collapsed. Susan was struggling to breathe. It was only then that she realised she was coughing up blood.

Chapter 31

Fulton strolled up the ramp of Waverley Station and caught his first glimpse of the craggy outcrop of Edinburgh Castle. It had been a couple of years since he'd last visited the capital but it took just a minute for him to be irritated by the place. A breezy, young Australian tour guide, with mangy dreadlocks and rainbow-coloured bangles bouncing on her wrists, thrust a leaflet into his hand offering a discount for a bus tour. Fulton tossed it into the nearest bin he could find. There was nothing quite like being mistaken for a foreigner by a foreigner. Fulton found the capital suffocating in all its self-preening haughtiness. At best, it was an international tourist attraction, at worst, an English colony increasingly populated by upper-class southerners who had belatedly caught on that it was cheaper than London.

Fulton hurried along Princes Street. He crossed the road when his path was blocked by a group of tourists busily taking selfies in front of the Scott Monument's blackened Gothic spire. None of them had read his books, of that he was sure, but there was a plaque, which made it worthy of a snap. A few minutes later, hot and sticky, he found himself in front of a row of elegant Georgian townhouses. He carefully checked for the address but many of the homes were either too grand to have a number that would spoil their beautiful façades or had been cannibalised into flats. After a bit of toing and froing, he found the right number. He climbed the three steps and rang the brass doorbell.

A bear of a man, well over six feet, with a strangely boyish face opened the door. Whenever Bill Wylie grinned, a dimple appeared on either side of his mouth, creating an effect that made him look like a mischievous street urchin. Fulton was taken aback. He had been expecting something, well, a bit more aristocratic.

'Welcome to my humble abode,' said Bill, ushering Fulton into the hallway. At the top of the mahogany staircase was a huge stained-glass window depicting a sunset on a windswept island, which Fulton pegged for Islay. Bill allowed Fulton to admire it for a few seconds before showing him into a large sitting room with crown mouldings, hardwood floors and floor-to-ceiling windows with views across the street onto the walled private garden shared between the neighbouring properties.

'Can I take your jacket?' asked Bill.

Fulton handed it to him, half surprised that a butler hadn't appeared.

'And can I get you a cup of tea and a biscuit? I fancy a bit of chocolate myself.'

'Aye, why not?'

While Bill was out of the room, Fulton examined the rows and rows of books stuffed onto the shelves that lined the walls. There was a chunky section dedicated to Russian history and the classics, Tolstoy and Dostoyevsky, books that Fulton had always wanted to but never did get around to reading. Beside the marble fireplace was a tasteful black-and-white photograph of the iconic St Basil's Cathedral on Red Square. Fulton also noticed a couple of photographs in the corner of the room. One showed a very young-looking Bill beaming as he stood beside Mikhail Gorbachev. It must have been taken more than thirty years ago, thought Fulton. The other photo was far more recent, and this time there was no smile on his face. He was shaking the hand of a rather puffy, dour-looking Vladimir Putin.

Bill returned carrying a pewter tray with a teapot, cups, a little porcelain jug of milk and a couple of Wagon Wheels. He served the tea.

'My new favourite,' said Bill, sitting down and immediately tearing open the biscuit wrapper with the delight of a child who hasn't had his sugar fix in weeks. 'The doctor says I'm not supposed to eat chocolate because of my diabetes. But what's the point of living if you can't enjoy yourself once in a while? Here, take yours.' He frisbeed it into Fulton's lap. 'Otherwise, I'll be having it.

'So, how's young Chris getting on? I've known him since he was in his nappies – a real bawler, he was. The only thing that would shut him up was a breast.'

'Fine, absolutely fine,' said Fulton hesitantly. 'He's been the editor now for four years and he's doing a decent job. But, as I'm sure you're aware, it's not exactly the easiest time to be in newspapers.'

Bill obviously clocked the fact that they didn't get on. He must have built a career, after all, on trying to decipher what people really meant, and the old pro couldn't help himself from trying to finesse the situation.

'Chris's father, Nicholas, was a very good man – unbelievably posh, though. We used to joke that he'd make the Queen feel like a commoner. But if you could forget that plummy accent of his, you quickly realised that you'd never find a fairer man. We both became ambassadors around the same time and used to catch up when we were back in London. I was very sorry when I heard he'd passed away. I hear Chris is a chip off the same block. I know those fellas can be hard work at times, Fulton – believe me, I know – but you've got to give them a chance.'

Before Fulton realised he'd been gently admonished, Bill had moved the conversation on. They talked about politics, football and rugby, scoping each other out. Fulton noticed that Bill seemed to know more about many of those topics than he did himself. Being away from home often means you're caught between two worlds – not totally comfortable in either and left trying to prove yourself in both. Bill's accent on occasion also betrayed its roots. It had mellowed after years of being overseas, then all of a sudden he would turn a verbal corner and Bill was back down the lanes of his child-hood kicking a ball with his pals.

'Anyway, enough of the small talk,' said Bill. 'I assume you're here to ask about John Millar. Christ, what a tragedy, what a waste. I knew John very well. For a time, we were very close. I guess you could say I was a mentor to him.'

'Chris told me you'd worked together in Moscow when you were the ambassador.'

'That's right. I don't know how much you know but John never actually worked for the Foreign Office – that was his cover. He worked for MI6. As I'm sure you'll understand, I need to be careful what I say.'

Bill took a slurp of his tea and polished off what remained of his Wagon Wheel. He picked up a tissue and wiped the melted chocolate off his fingers.

'You're not going to quote me on any of this.'

'It's up to you but I would like to take some notes.'

'No notes,' said Bill firmly. 'Why don't we chat for now and then discuss what you can use later?'

'Fine.'

'All right, then, against my better judgement, I'll choose to trust a journalist,' said Bill, smiling, his two dimples reappearing. 'Chris vouched for you, so that's good enough for me.'

'What was John doing for MI6?' asked Fulton, diving straight in.

Bill shifted in his chair. He rubbed his eyes. 'I can't talk about all the specifics but let's just say John recruited and ran Russian double agents for us. He was brilliant at it. He probably recruited more high-value agents than anyone else in the history of MI6. I think having always been an outsider gave him an edge and he understood that if you find a grievance then you've found a potential recruit – us Scots are good at grievances. It's gruelling work, emotionally and intellectually, but it was truly extraordinary to witness.'

'So why did he leave Moscow, then? He's not the type of guy you would want to lose.'

It was as if an icy gust from the North Sea had suddenly blasted into the room. For a moment, Fulton thought Bill wasn't going to answer the question.

'He was let go.'

'Sorry, *let go*?'

'He was fired from his job. We all have our weaknesses, Fulton, and John was no different from you or me.'

'Why?'

'God, I really shouldn't be talking about this.'

'Take your time.'

Bill picked up his mug and held it to his lips momentarily. He put the mug back down on the table. 'He got involved with a Russian woman. Now, that's fine if it's part of the job but if it's anything more than that, you need to flag it because you become a security risk. And John went too far and he didn't report it.'

'Too far?'

Bill was quiet for a while. Fulton fought the urge to fill the silence. He knew better than to interfere with the rhythm of revelation otherwise the moment might be lost.

'They had a kid,' said Bill finally.

'A child?'

'Aye, a baby boy.'

'And where's the kid now?'

'The baby died,' said Bill, with a sharp intake of breath. 'He was a couple of months old when he died in his sleep. They never knew what happened; it was just one of those things. And, John, well, understandably he was devastated and he came to me for help.'

'And what happened?' asked Fulton gently.

'I had no choice but to report him,' said Bill, standing up from his chair. 'Sorry, but you're going to have to give me a minute.'

Bill hurried out of the living room without making eye contact. Fulton sat still and listened hard. He heard a stifled sob from the kitchen then Bill loudly blowing his nose. Footsteps sounded in the hallway.

'Sorry about that,' said Bill, settling back into his chair. 'I'm not normally so emotional.'

'I understand.'

'Now, where were we?'

'You had to report John.'

'Ah, yes,' said Bill, fidgeting with his fingers. 'Of course, I wasn't proud about what happened but the brutal reality is that I had no other choice. You can't have spies having children in the country they're supposed to be spying on. We had to let him go and that's how he ended up working for the Scottish government.'

'I can see he meant a lot to you.'

'Yeah, he did, I can't pretend otherwise. I treated him a bit like a son. You know how it is when we're away from home – we Scots look out for each other when there aren't many of us about.'

Bill smiled weakly.

'Did you ever speak to John about his relationship with the First Minister?'

'No, I didn't. Sadly, after Moscow, our relationship was finished. I tried to make amends. I reached out to him through a couple of mutual friends but he never wanted to see me again. He was very bitter, and, to be honest, I don't blame him. He lost his child, his career, maybe the love of his life . . . It would take a remarkable person to recover from those kinds of losses.'

'And what do you make of the accusations that the First Minister may have been involved in his death?'

'It's a fabrication. Just to be clear, I'm not a nationalist, but there isn't a shred of evidence that connects her to the killing. I will say this, though: when he met Susan Ward, I think he truly met his match. Both of them are smart and tenacious and they had similar upbringings. But the one big difference is that Susan was succeeding when John was failing. And I think it would have hurt him deeply that someone from the same background was doing better than him. John couldn't deal with losing; it was pathological with him – in his line of work you simply can't lose.'

'What about the Russians? Could they be behind it?'

'That's a bit trickier: you'd have to ask yourself what they would have gained from killing John. I've heard some people arguing they wanted to silence him because the nationalists were in Moscow's pocket but, again, where's the evidence? And the fact is John's death has made independence less, not more, likely. It's the smart thing to say the Russians are playing by different rules but we all have agency. Moscow understands that you can't create divisions but you can exploit them and obviously they'd be cock-a-hoop if the Scots became independent. Not only would it weaken the UK but, more significantly, it would have implications for NATO – the organisation they see as their biggest threat. But we mustn't fall into their trap; we shouldn't overestimate Moscow's power and influence.'

'How so?'

'Well, here's a question for you: which country has launched seventy-five different military operations to topple legitimate regimes around the world since the end of the Second World War?'

'Not Russia,' said Fulton.

The ambassador appreciatively nodded his head as if coaxing on a reluctant student.

'America.'

'Exactly,' said Bill. 'The Americans have interfered in several elections around the world and yet we're supposed to jump up and down when Moscow interferes in the US vote and perhaps even our own referendum. Now, I'm not defending what Moscow does – it's done plenty of despicable things. But facts are stubborn things, you can't argue with them: so, if they don't fit your narrative, best to ignore them.'

'I know this is going to sound like a naïve question, but if it wasn't Susan or the Russians then who would have wanted John dead?'

'It's not naïve at all and I've given it a lot of thought,' said

Bill. He stood up and went to a bookcase beside the fireplace. He started browsing from the top row and then bent his knees stiffly as he moved down the shelves. He fished out an old leatherbound volume. Sitting back down, Bill carefully flicked through it. The pages were yellow with age, the print slightly smudged but still perfectly legible.

'Here,' he said, handing the book to Fulton. 'Read this quote for me.'

'"No great man lives in vain. The history of the world is but the biography of great men."'

'The words of Thomas Carlyle, one of our greatest thinkers,' said Bill. 'Walter Scott may have created a world but Thomas Carlyle understood the world. He would have made the perfect spy. He understood that global events sometimes pivot with a little push from an individual – that the train of history can suddenly divert along a track that no one was expecting . . .'

They were interrupted by the phone ringing in the hallway.

'You'll have to excuse me for a minute,' said Bill, standing up to get it. A few moments later, Fulton heard him on the phone exclaiming, 'Bloody hell!' before he rushed back into the living room. He was visibly shocked. 'Susan Ward's just been stabbed,' he said. 'She's fighting for her life.'

Chapter 32

The ambulance sped up to the Royal Infirmary entrance, lights flashing, siren blaring. A crowd of doctors, specialists and police were all lined up ready to take the First Minister straight up to the operating theatre. The ambulance's back-doors popped open and two paramedics jumped out. They swivelled round effortlessly, immediately grabbing the stretcher and pulling it from the vehicle. Susan was revealed momentarily, an oxygen mask clamped to her face, torso covered in blood-soaked dressings.

The paramedics swung the stretcher into the corridor and then into the lift. Medics crammed in behind them. All eyes were on the patient. The doors closed.

Larbert was standing nearby watching it all unfold. His head was bowed, his expression sombre. Brian strode up to him. Larbert straightened his uniform and steeled himself for a bruising conversation.

'Can I have a minute?' said Brian. 'In private.' It wasn't a question. Larbert followed him into a nearby disabled toilet. Brian flipped the lock to closed. His eyes were bloodshot, his cheeks stained by tears.

'What the fuck happened?' he screamed in pure rage, getting right up into Larbert's face. Larbert was forced to back up against the mirror behind the sink. He then felt one of Brian's hands on his throat. He was squeezing hard. Larbert's face went purple. He started choking. Spittle blossomed on his lips. Brian released his hand. Larbert slumped onto the sink, the tap jabbing painfully into his back, and sucked in deep gulps of air. Slowly, he pulled himself upright.

Brian backed away.

'Please, please, calm down. Let's talk,' said Larbert.

Brian looked at him with fury in his eyes. 'I'll calm down when you tell me how this happened. If you'd done your job we wouldn't be here in the fucking Royal Infirmary, would we? Susan wouldn't have been stabbed like a dog.'

'I'm sorry, Brian. I really am. This is the last thing I wanted to happen but I told you we were stretched. I warned you about her safety but you wouldn't listen.'

Brian stared him down. 'If you can't protect the First Minister, then who can you protect?'

'I know. It'll never happen again.'

'Happen again!' said Brian. 'There might not be a next time. It's fifty-fifty she'll make it.'

He clenched his fist. He was trying to crush out all the pain he felt in that hard fleshy ball. He then released his grip and took a deep breath.

'Who did this?' he said quietly. 'Who stabbed her?'

'We've arrested a guy. He wasn't known to us. It looks like he was a lone wolf, some nutter with a knife.'

'What's he been saying?'

'It's been barely half an hour, Brian.'

'What the fuck has he been saying?'

Larbert sighed deeply. His eyes narrowed. 'He said he wanted to kill Susan to save the Union.'

'What else?'

'He said she was a murderer and a traitor who deserved to die.'

Brian stood glassy-eyed. He took a step closer to Larbert. Their chins were almost touching. 'Let me be clear about one thing,' he said icily. 'If she dies, I'm holding you personally responsible.'

Chapter 33

Davy had just received a call to meet Tam at the usual place in an hour's time. He looked out of his office window: it was pelting down. The type of rain that no matter how many layers you put on, the water still finds a way to seep in and send a cold shiver down your spine. Why the hell does he want to meet in the park in this weather? thought Davy. Has the old bastard taken leave of his senses? But Davy wasn't going to argue. This was the meeting when Tam was finally going to deliver. Davy pulled on his puffer jacket and made for the door.

At Kelvingrove Park, the river was swollen, thundering under the bridge. Streams were building on the paths, forcing Davy to walk on the grassy verge. At one point, his foot slipped into a murky puddle and kept on going until the water was well above his ankle. When he pulled out of it, his trouser leg and shoe were covered in brown sludge. He cursed at himself. He looked up and saw the park bench where they were to meet. But Tam wasn't sitting there. Maybe he was running late. Instead, there was some guy in a blue anorak with the hood up, hunched over. He was bracing himself against the wind. For a moment, Davy hesitated. But then the guy looked up and waved him over. Perhaps he was a junkie in search of some change. But the fact that they were the only two people in the entire park made it unlikely.

'Do I know you?' he asked. Davy could barely make out his face because his hood was pulled so tight. Only his eyes, nose and mouth were visible.

'Naw, but the boss sent me.'

'Tam?'

'Aye.'

Davy shook his hand and sat down on the bench. 'A fine day for a meeting. Where's Tam at?'

'He said he's sorry. He's a bit under the weather.'

'Aren't we all,' replied Davy.

No response.

'You got a name?'

The question was ignored.

'Here,' said the guy, handing Davy a double-wrapped plastic bag. 'Tam said I was to gie it to you.'

Davy pulled it close to his chest to try and protect it from the rain. He wiped a hand on his sodden trousers in a futile attempt to dry it off. He then opened the bag a crack and slipped his hand in. It reminded him of doing a raffle. He gingerly pulled out a couple of hundred-pound notes.

'What's this?' he asked, with surprise.

'Tam says that's some of the cash that the guy used to pay for the hit. He didnae want to give you all the money.'

'No surprise there, then.'

'He says there's fingerprints on it ye can test fir.'

Davy quickly dropped the notes back into the plastic bag.

'And is there anything else I need to know about?'

'Aye, there's a wee bit of paper.'

Davy rummaged about in the plastic bag and found the paper tucked in one of the creases. He pulled it out, delicately holding a corner so the writing on it wouldn't smudge. There was a string of digits.

'And what's this?'

'It's a mobile number.'

'I could have guessed that. But who's it a number for?'

'For the guy who ordered the hit.'

'Sweet Jesus,' said Davy, with a smile. 'I think we might be in business here. Anything else?'

'Nah, that's it.'

'Did Tam say anything else?'

'Aye, he told me to tell you that you owe him one. He says he'll be in touch.'

Davy's face was at the angle where it was being lashed by the rain. He didn't wipe away the drops running down his cheeks. He felt one trickle down his collar. He shivered.

'Give Tam my best.'

'Aye. All right. See you later.'

The guy stood up to leave.

'And one more thing,' said Davy.

'Whit now?' asked the guy. 'I'll be late for my bus.'

'Tell Tam I'm finished when it comes to business. We're quits.'

'He's no' gonnae like that.'

'I know, but make sure you tell him, every single word of it.'

Chapter 34

The trauma surgeon knew the patient lying in front of him was someone who was about to die. Life was slipping away from her like the water being carried from a cove during spring tide. He had been in this position more times than he cared to count. But this was no normal patient: it was the First Minister of Scotland.

Susan had a single stab wound to her chest. It had punctured her rib cage and there was massive internal bleeding. But before the attacker could plunge the serrated hunting knife into Susan a second time he had been overpowered by the police piling on top of him.

The surgeon pushed Susan's identity out of his mind. He needed to think with absolute clarity – no distractions. *Just do the job you've been trained to do.* The Beatles' 'Something' was being played in the operating theatre. The fantasy that he was somehow the fifth Beatle helped soothe him. He mentally rehearsed the steps he would need to take.

The surgical team were congregated around the operating table, just waiting for the word. 'Scalpel.'

An hour later, the First Minister was stitched up, a livid red scar running under her chest. She was recovering in a private room on the top floor of the hospital with a view over the city's Necropolis. It was, perhaps, some bureaucrat's idea of a joke to build these particular Glasgow landmarks side by side. Two policemen were stationed at the door, a couple more along the corridor and another two at the lift. They were not taking any chances.

When Susan first opened her eyes, she saw Gordon's familiar features: the strong jawline, the brown eyes. He was stroking her hair. He planted a kiss on her brow.

'I love you,' he said. He touched her cheek and she turned so his hand cradled her face. They sat like that for a few minutes while Susan took solace in his presence.

'Where am I?' she asked.

'You're in the Royal.'

Susan registered the beeps of the machines around her and various tubes sticking out of her body.

'What happened? I feel so bleary.'

'You were stabbed at the rally.' Gordon clasped her hand. 'You're going to be fine. I just spoke to the surgeon and he's confident you'll make a full recovery. He says you've just to get plenty of rest.'

'Where are the girls? Are they okay?'

'Don't worry, they're fine. They're at home. My mum's with them.'

'Do they know what happened?'

Gordon grimaced. But he knew the truth with Susan – even in this situation – was always the best option.

'Yes, they know. I couldn't keep it from them. They were at school when the news broke. And I thought it best to tell them rather than leaving them confused. But they're going to be fine. They're tough – they take after their mum.'

Susan smiled weakly.

'I said you'd call them tomorrow, when you're feeling stronger. But don't worry, Sue, they're going to be okay, I promise.'

She started to weep. She tried to raise her hand to wipe away the tears but was too weak. Gordon tugged a tissue from the box on the bedside table, folded it in half, and gently dabbed them away.

'I love you so much,' she said quietly. 'And I'm so sorry for everything. It's all my fault. This is all my fault.'

'It's not your fault. And I love you, too,' said Gordon, bending over to kiss her forehead. He lingered there for a while as he fought back the tears.

'I thought I was going to lose you,' he said. 'But you need to get some rest. Close your eyes and sleep, babe. I'll be here.'

Chapter 35

Davy had given up biting his nails when he was eight years old. His father used to belt him every time he saw a chewed fingernail. It was a useful, if brutal corrective. But his dad was now long gone and Davy was once again biting his nails. Earlier in the morning, he had dusted the fingerprints off the hundred-pound notes Tam's delivery boy had given him. He went downstairs to make a scan and send it off to the national database to be checked.

An hour later, one of the secretaries, Deidre, knocked on his door 'Sorry, Davy, got some bad news for you. There was no match.'

'Any near matches?'

'Nothing. I double-checked because I knew you would ask.'

After Deidre left, Davy slammed his palm on the desk. The only identifiable print was his own fat thumb on the corner of the note he'd pulled out of the plastic bag. Could Tam be giving him the run-around? But Davy's gut told him that probably wasn't the case, especially after Tam had made such a song and dance about being a man of his word at their last meeting. Far more likely was that the suspect who paid for the hit was simply unknown to the authorities and had a clean record. And that suggested this might be the first time this individual had engaged in this sort of activity. Davy felt a wave of stress crashing over him again. It could literally be anyone.

Davy turned his attention to the phone number. He had dialled it earlier and, as he expected, it was switched off. That left the mobile phone companies. Officially, Davy was supposed to fill out a couple of forms for the request. But what was the point of doing all the paperwork for something you didn't know you needed yet? He decided to swerve all the arse-covering procedures and go about things his own sweet way. He knew a guy who could help.

'Stewart, big man, how are you? Family all good?'

'Aye, how are you?'

'Fine. Been flat out at work with this John Millar case.'

'Jeez, must be stressful.'

'You could say that. Look, I was after a wee favour – any chance you can run a check on a number?'

'Nae worries. Just WhatsApp it to me and give me five minutes or so.'

Davy hung up and sent over the number. He leaned forward on his chair and started drumming the rhythm from 'Turn It On Again'. He'd been a Genesis fan since his teenage years. Even after decades in the police the suspense still got to him. The waiting for someone to type some information into a computer that leads to the critical breakthrough. It was the modern way of policing, and Davy didn't like it one bit. He was forced to hand over control to the geeks. Now, it was all about CCTV footage and mobile phone positioning. Davy conceded it worked but the excitement of real police work was now playing second fiddle to the digital realm. His mobile phone started vibrating on his desk.

'What you got for me, Stewart?'

'Unregistered. No contract, so no name.'

Davy had expected as much. It would have been truly a shocker if it had been registered.

'Okay,' he said. 'When was it activated then?'

'A couple of weeks ago. According to the call list, it's only been used twice. Both times to call the same number.'

'Okay, give me that number. We'll need to run a check on it.'

Stewart read out the number and Davy wrote it down.

'Okay,' said Davy, 'the first number: when was it last used?'

'Give me a second . . . Sunday night.'

Bingo, thought Davy, that was the night of John Millar's murder.

'And the exact time?'

'It was 10:27 p.m. The call lasted seventeen seconds.'

'Not a chatterbox, then,' said Davy jubilantly. The timeframe fitted. Tam wasn't giving him the run-around after all.

'And do we know where the SIM card was sold?'

'I should be able to find that out. But, Davy, it may be better if—'

'Don't worry. I hear you, pal.'

'Sorry, it's just the bosses are tightening up on this sort of thing.'

'I know. Why don't you run a check on that second number and I'll get going on the paperwork – should be with you in an hour. Cheers, mate, we'll catch up soon.'

Davy hung up. He leaned back in his chair with hands clasped behind his head. Happy days, he thought, happy days. If he found out where the SIM card had been sold, he would be a massive step closer to identifying John Millar's killer.

Chapter 36

Larbert spent the night holed up in HQ. He felt like a man crawling up a hill with a rock on his back. With every step he was getting weaker, there were spasms in his thighs, and he thought he was going to fall flat on his face. He knew the police were being blamed for the lax security that had led to the First Minister's stabbing. He also knew that his job was on the line.

The suspect was quickly identified as forty-two-year-old Murdo McLennan, unemployed, from the Govan area of the city. His poor mother started sobbing when police officers turned up at her council flat to tell her what her boy had done. 'That's not the way I brought up my son,' she cried, before collapsing in a heap in her living room. It took the officers a good half hour to calm her down and for her to start making any sense. 'He was acting funny in the past few days,' she told them. 'I've been worried that he was going to do something stupid . . . He stopped taking his medication.'

That opened up another line of inquiry. It was soon discovered that McLennan had been released a week before from Leverndale Hospital. He had been sectioned for three years after having been diagnosed with paranoid schizophrenia. Previously, he'd been arrested for wandering the streets wielding a samurai sword. Larbert was relieved to discover that his mental health was the issue. It meant there was no conspiracy. It also meant that neither side of the political divide could use it to stir up trouble. And the press's attention would inevitably be drawn to the fact that a sick man had been allowed to wander the streets. It wasn't just the police who were having to deal with the consequences of the brutal cuts foisted upon them by Susan Ward's government.

When the first light of dawn started creeping across the horizon, Larbert sat down at his desk and began bashing out a press release. It was too important to leave to the press team and he wanted it under everyone's noses when they woke up in the morning. There was no room for complacency. He needed to emphasise the fact that the attack was the work of a lone man who deserved sympathy and treatment – not condemnation. It was done in ten minutes. He read the statement one final time, picked up the phone to the press department and told them to get it circulated as fast as humanly possible. By then it was six o'clock in the morning, the adrenaline that had kept him going had long since run out, and his thoughts turned to where he could get a couple of hours' kip before the day ahead. He heard the rattle of his office doorknob turning.

'Long night?' asked Neil, flashing a look of sympathy.

'Yes, you could say that.'

'Don't worry, it will all be over soon enough.'

'I wouldn't bet against another surprise today.'

'You're exhausted, Ian, but the press release was perfect. It will help calm the waters. You're doing a sterling job.'

'Well, as I'm sure you're aware, we're copping all the blame for the stabbing. It was the First Minister herself who insisted on going ahead. She's a difficult woman.'

'Some might be tempted to use stronger language. But that's the nationalists for you – a hot-headed fanatical bunch who will never listen to reason. They deserve everything that comes their way.'

Larbert thought the comment was a little harsh. But he was so tired he didn't have the energy to object.

'Do you think the vote will still happen? I mean we've just got two days to go. Has there been any discussion about calling it off?'

'There was an emergency meeting yesterday after the incident,' replied Neil. 'Many were in favour of postponing. But then news started filtering though that her operation had been successful and the mood changed. As far as London is concerned, the vote will go ahead. The Prime Minister will be making a statement saying as much this morning.'

'I'm glad to hear that.'

'Yes, I think they just want to put this brutish chapter of British history behind them as quickly as possible. You're not the only one exhausted by all that's been going on. And, anyway, the thinking is: why give up a winning position?'

'London's that confident the nationalists will lose?' said Larbert, with a degree of surprise.

'Put it this way,' said Neil with a grin, 'there's a sweepstake in my office about how big the margin will be. I've plumped for five per cent. In hindsight, I may have been too conservative. But if I'm honest, do you know what makes me really happy about Susan Ward pulling through?'

'What?'

'She'll be alive to witness her own defeat.'

Chapter 37

Davy strolled along Dumbarton Road whistling to himself. He sensed he was on the brink of a breakthrough. He turned onto one of the side streets, searching for the newsagent that had sold the SIM card used before the John Millar killing. He wasn't sure which side of the road it was on, and a line of cars and vans obscured his view. But then he spotted the sign for Mohammed Latif's shop. The window was covered in fluorescent ads for deals on milk, bread and biscuits. When Davy pushed open the shop's door, a bell rang. A young man in his early twenties looked up from behind the counter. His white teeth stuck out a mile in a city of yellow smiles.

'What you after, mate?' he asked Davy.

'Are you the owner?'

'No, that would be my dad.'

'Is he around?'

'Nope. It's his day off. Can I help?'

Davy reached into his jacket pocket and pulled out his police badge. A look of concern swept over the son's face as Davy laid it on the counter.

'Okay, so I'm guessing you're not after a pint of milk.'

'I'm investigating a case. And I believe that one of the suspects may have bought a SIM card here. Nothing for you or your dad to worry about, but I'm going to need to see your footage.'

Davy turned and pointed at the camera attached to the ceiling.

'Fair enough,' said the young man. 'But you're going to have to give me a minute.'

'No worries. What's the name by the way?'

'Bilal.'

'Good to meet you,' said Davy, leaning over the counter and shaking his hand.

Bilal took out his mobile phone and called his dad. From Bilal's animated expressions and eye-rolling, Davy knew this wasn't going to be plain sailing.

'Sorry about that,' said Bilal, slipping the phone back into his pocket. He flashed a smile. 'We have a problem.'

'And that would be . . .'

'The camera isn't working,' said Bilal. 'See the red light on the side of the camera? It's not on.'

Davy felt his chest tighten as if he was being given a bearhug by a friend during a boozy night out. He rubbed his forehead. What should have been routine was fast falling apart.

'When did it stop working?' he asked impatiently. 'I mean who has a camera in a shop that doesn't work.'

'It's a deterrent. If people think they're being watched, they—'

'All right, all right, I get you. But when did it stop working?'

'Dad said a few days before all the looting took place. Thankfully, we didn't get robbed.'

Davy let out a long breath. All was not lost. The timeframe still worked. John Millar's killer had bought and activated the card shortly before the murder.

'And where are the tapes?'

'In the storeroom.'

'Can I take a look?'

'Sure, just give me a minute.'

Bilal lifted up the countertop and put it down behind him. He walked to the door and flipped the sign to 'Closed', then took out a jangling bunch of keys from his trouser pocket and locked up.

'You can never be too careful,' he said to Davy, with a wink. 'Even with the police here. Now come with me.'

He led Davy into the storeroom, which was overflowing with boxes rammed into shelves at almost every angle. Bigger boxes were piled against the wall, well above head height. Davy felt slightly claustrophobic. A space had been cleared on a dusty shelf and on it sat a monitor and video player. Bilal reached over and switched both on.

'And where are the tapes?' asked Davy.

'Give us a minute. I don't normally come in here.'

Bilal stood on his tiptoes and began running his fingers along the tops of the shelves. Whatever he was looking for wasn't on the first shelf, so he shuffled along to the second one. It wasn't there, either. Davy tapped his foot.

'It's definitely here,' said Bilal, trying to reassure himself as much as Davy. 'Just a second.'

On the third shelf, he felt a tattered box. He pushed it out with his fingers, so a corner was hanging over the edge. He then grabbed at it, and managed to flip the box over so all the tapes clattered to the ground.

'Sorry,' said Bilal, dropping to his knees. He turned the box the right side up and started putting the tapes back inside it.

'Don't worry,' said Davy, trying to soothe the situation. But his alarm grew when he realised how many videotapes were in the box – more than two dozen.

'Are those videos all for the security camera?'

'Eh, no, I don't think so.'

Bilal started examining what was written on the tapes and set aside two.

'Here they are,' he said, handing them to Davy.

'What about the other tapes, what's on them?'

'My dad's favourite Clint Eastwood films.'

Sensing that Davy was growing impatient, Bilal showed him how to work the video recorder. He then pulled out a box full of washing powder for Davy to sit on.

'How would I spot when you or your dad were selling a SIM card? I'm going to need to fast-forward through the footage.'

'Dad keeps the SIM cards in a drawer under the counter. You'll see him reach under there to bring them out. The only other thing he keeps there are his reading glasses.'

'Cheers.'

'Okay, I'll leave you to it. Give us a shout if you need anything.'

Bilal closed the door. Davy felt as if he was in a submarine. The room was tiny and the naked bulb was producing a minimal amount of light. It was hot, so Davy took off his jacket and stuffed it on a shelf alongside some boxes of crisps. He pushed a video into the player. It whirred into action. Davy glanced at the monitor. The first image he saw was Bilal's dad looking directly at the camera, checking to see whether it was on. The footage was grainy but of decent quality. On the top right-hand corner there was recording data. It was the date Davy was after. But the timing read 06:08 a.m. Davy sighed. This was going to take a while. He hit the fast-forward button and the video jerked about like a Charlie Chaplin movie. It showed Mohammed opening the shop door, exiting, and then entering, this time carrying bundles of

228

newspapers. He did it again and again. Only the choppy piano music was missing. Later, customers started trickling in. Most were buying the soft morning rolls balanced on a tray on the countertop, which Mohammed tore off in strips. After an hour, Davy was growing exasperated. His back was hurting from squatting on the box. He was interrupted by a knock on the door.

'Can I come in?'

'Of course, it's your shop.'

Bilal entered carrying a mug of coffee and a KitKat. He handed both to Davy, who was touched by the act of kindness and felt a bit guilty about being so impatient earlier.

'So, Bilal, what do you normally do then?'

'I'm studying to be a dentist.'

'Where?'

'At Glasgow Uni.'

'Good for you. Your old man must be proud of you. Explains your teeth. Ever thought about joining the police?'

Bilal laughed nervously. 'Don't think my dad would be too happy.'

'Fair enough,' said Davy, slightly annoyed by the response but deciding to let it drop. 'Anyway, back to the tapes,' he said, tapping one of the boxes. Bilal took his cue.

Left to his own devices again, Davy took a sip from his mug and hit the play button. Watching the video was a truly mind-numbing experience and it was easy to get distracted by people's comings and goings – the old man in the wheel-chair who got stuck in the door; the woman with the kid who was busy pocketing sweets while he thought no one was looking; and the lonely pensioner who must have spoken to Mohammed for a solid ten minutes. But Davy realised all he needed to do was stare at the counter. Nothing else mattered.

Every few minutes he stopped the video to readjust his eyes by blinking furiously. All the intense staring was giving him double vision.

By the third hour, Davy was losing the will to live. He was on autopilot and almost missed the moment when Mohammed reached down to pull open the drawer. When he finally clocked what had happened and scrambled to hit the pause button, the customer had already paid and was out of the shop. Davy pressed the rewind button and backed it up a couple of minutes. He took a deep breath. This was surely it. He hit play.

His heart started racing as he watched the customer entering the shop. A man of average height and build wearing a black baseball cap. Davy couldn't see his face. On the monitor it showed the customer speaking to Bilal's dad. There was no audio. But Davy saw Mohammed becoming animated and from closely watching his lips he thought he recognised the word 'Vodafone'. Mohammed reached down, opened his drawer, and pulled out a shortbread tin with a picture of a shaggy Highland cow on the lid. Even though it was real-time, it felt like it was all happening in slow motion. Mohammed opened the lid, took out a SIM card and handed it to the man. Still Davy could not see his face. The man took out his wallet and paid. Still no clear line of sight on the guy's face. The man placed an old phone on the counter and Mohammed helped him insert the SIM card. *Come on, come on . . .* Davy pumped his fists as if he were at the football. Please, please, surely this isn't going to be a bust.

'Look at the camera, man, give Davy boy a wee smile,' he muttered to himself. 'Just a wee smile for Davy.' But the man wasn't listening. He thanked Mohammed and headed for the door. It's done for, thought Davy, the biggest bloody bust of my career. He leaned back on the soapbox he was sitting on, and let out a moan. But just as Davy lost all hope the man stopped a couple of feet or so from the door and began tilting his head upwards. The movement was barely a centimetre at first but then he kept on going. Slowly the brow of the cap began to peak and Davy saw the man's chin, his lips and nose, and finally his eyes. It was inexplicable. He was staring directly into the camera.

If Davy had framed it himself, he couldn't have asked for a better shot. He hit the pause button with such force he nearly knocked the video recorder off the shelf. Davy stared into the eyes of the hitman who had carried out the most explosive assassination in Scottish history. And the enormity of what Davy was looking at caused his body to start trembling. He braced himself by grabbing the box he was sitting on with both hands. He closed his eyes. Surely they were deceiving him. 'It can't be,' Davy muttered to himself. 'It can't be.' He opened his eyes again. There was no mistake. Davy knew John Millar's killer.

Chapter 38

Brian knew he had to find a way into Susan's hospital room. He had something he urgently needed to tell her. Gordon Ward had explicitly barred him from going anywhere near his wife for the next few days. The two men would never be mistaken for pals but they weren't enemies, either. For that reason, Brian didn't take Gordon's decree personally. It was the act of a protective husband who wanted his wife to recover away from any distractions.

For a few hours at least, Brian fully intended to uphold his side of the bargain. He didn't want to inflame the situation by getting into a rammy with a man who'd almost lost his wife, but Brian's resolve quickly dissolved. He knew he just had to tell her. More than that he saw it as his duty, reasoning to himself that the information he possessed would aid Susan's recovery. He began scheming how to get into the room under Gordon's nose. He was helped by the fact that the security detail were so bored standing around in a hospital that they would take any opportunity to talk to a friendly face. One of them helpfully told Brian that Gordon left every few hours to stretch his legs or grab a sandwich or coffee. He was normally back within half an hour. Brian knew it would be too suspicious to ask the officer to text him when Gordon left the room but the tip was all he really needed.

Brian waited down in the reception area with a view of the

main entrance. He was far enough away from it that he could only be spotted if someone was actively looking for him. But he also brought along a newspaper just in case. He pretended to read it for a minute or so before realising he was acting like some B-movie spy. He folded up the newspaper and dropped it under his seat.

An hour passed with no sign of Gordon. Brian made faces at a young boy with a crayon stuck in his ear. The exasperated mother told Brian that her son had been pretending to be an air-traffic controller. Eventually, the boy was carted off to see a doctor to remove the offending object. By that time, Brian was desperate for a piss but he knew it would be sod's law that he'd go off to the toilet and miss Gordon. He crossed his legs. Another twenty minutes went by. It was becoming painful. Brian was doubtful he could hold on for much longer. Just then he saw the familiar figure of Gordon walking out of the main entrance and Brian made a mad dash for the toilet in the opposite direction.

As he stepped out of the lift on the top floor, Brian was immediately accosted by an officer wanting to see his ID. However, one of his colleagues recognised Brian and waved him through. Brian walked gingerly up the corridor not knowing what to expect. He poked his head inside the room. When Susan saw Brian, her face lit up. She was sitting up in bed, eating what looked like lasagne from a food tray.

'That looks worse than the slop we dole out at the party conference,' said Brian. 'But how the hell are you? I've missed you – you're looking like you're on the mend.'

She stretched out a hand and he leaned forward and kissed her on the cheek.

'So, when do you get out?' asked Brian.

'I should be out in a few days.'

'Really, that quick?'

'Yes, that's what the consultant says. I'll need to take it easy for a couple more months but he says I'll make a full recovery.'

'Great stuff.'

'So, what's been happening?'

'All fine my end. The hubbie is well—'

'No, with the campaign!'

'Aren't you a bit fragile for all that,' asked Brian, a hint of mischief in his voice.

'Save me the nonsense, with two days to go to the vote. Where do we stand?'

Brian picked up his briefcase from the floor and pulled out a sheet of paper. 'Well, First Minister,' he said with a flourish, 'while I would never suggest it as a campaign tactic, this whole pallaver turned out to be a great move.'

Susan gave him a mock disapproving stare.

'I present you, madam, with this morning's polling data and respectfully suggest that getting stabbed is worth a five per cent swing.'

He handed the paper to Susan who studied it carefully.

'We're back in the game,' she said finally. 'We're only three points behind the Unionists: the question now is how do we close the gap?'

'If I'm honest,' said Brian, 'I don't think we can win—'

'But you said it,' interrupted Susan. 'Almost dying was a game changer. So could we generate a bit more sympathy?'

'I'm not following.'

'Why don't you phone up one of your tabloid mates and tell them I've relapsed and I'm fighting for my life. Make sure it's one of the more disreputable rags, so we can deny it if it becomes an issue.'

'Well, well, my own Lady Macbeth, and here was me thinking I was the devious one,' said Brian. 'Are you absolutely sure?'

'Of course I am,' replied Susan. 'I've not come this far not to win.'

Chapter 39

Fulton felt his body stiffening as the Golf GTI climbed the steep hill running through the conservation village of Eaglesham and up onto the edges of the moor. He knew Davy couldn't have been thinking straight, otherwise he would never have suggested this location. He'd been so curt on the phone that Fulton had realised there was no point in protesting. The urgent message had read: *Meet on the moors @ 7.*

Just beyond the last houses in the village, Fulton drove past the sign for Bonnyton golf course and then the white-washed water treatment plant beside the small reservoir where a breeze was rippling the surface. His mood grew darker as the bleak, unforgiving moors opened up before him like a map. This was the scene of his nightmares. It was the first time he'd been up here since the crash and the memories were flooding back.

As he climbed another hill, he saw the moors being thrashed by what looked like some kind of monstrous farm machine. It was only when he crested the hill that he saw the dozens of wind turbines stretching for as far as the eye could see. Fulton kept on the winding, single-track road until he swung a left into the Whitelee Windfarm visitor centre. He pulled into the car park beside the low-slung building, which had large picture windows so that visitors could enjoy the view from the café. There was one other car in the parking lot, a red Skoda, which Fulton immediately recognised as

Davy's. His friend was leaning against a wooden fence. He looked lost in thought.

'You all right, Davy?' asked Fulton, as he walked up to him.

'You left your phone in the office?'

'How many times did you have to tell me? Of course I did.'

'It's just I cannae take any chances on this one. C'mon, we're going for a walk.'

Davy started along a muddy track leading away from the visitor centre. Fulton followed in silence. The path ended at the base of a wind turbine sixty metres high. Three giant blades sliced through the air. Fulton looked up and felt giddy. It was like an optical illusion: they swung so hard and fast it was as if they were going to slice you between the eyes only to then swing up and over your head.

'Do you think here will work?' asked Davy.

'Work for what?'

'Nobody will see us up here?'

'Davy, we're in the middle of a moor,' said Fulton incredulously. 'Can you see anyone?'

'Aye, all right,' he said, dipping his head sheepishly. 'I'm just being careful.' He rubbed his hands hard. 'Feck, it's cold up here.'

'Well, we're about a thousand feet up. But, come on, what are we doing here?'

Davy stared at the ground for a moment. He looked up, fastening his eyes on Fulton. 'I know who did it.'

'Did what?'

'Killed John Millar.'

'What the hell,' said Fulton. 'Are you serious? Who?'

'The video accusing Susan Ward and all that Russian stuff, it was just designed to bamboozle us.'

'All right, so who killed John Millar, then?'

'John Millar.'

'What do you mean John Millar killed John Millar?'

'He ordered the hit on himself,' said Davy. He rubbed the back of his neck. 'Honestly, you couldn't make it up.'

'Seriously, Davy, are you sure? You're sounding crazy.'

'It's true, and I can prove it.'

'How?'

'We know Charlie did the dirty deed.'

'Tam's boy?'

'Aye. He was the one who pulled the trigger. But we never knew who paid for it.'

'Go on.'

'Well, Millar was the one who paid for it.'

'And how do you know that?'

'Tam gave me some of the cash that Millar used to pay for the job, and his fingerprints were all over the notes. The careless prick probably thought we'd never get this far so he never put on any gloves to handle the cash. Everyone makes mistakes – even the smartest ones.'

'But how did he pay for the hit? I mean did Tam not know who ordered the job?'

'This is where it gets even stranger, if you can believe that. Tam told me he never knew who wanted the job done other than it paid well. He was just being a greedy bastard. And according to Charlie, who picked up the cash, the guy never showed his face.'

'What do you mean?'

'They met at a bus stop across from the Citizens' Theatre. It was late at night. Charlie says the guy was wearing a scarf round his face, glasses. He says the guy didn't say much apart from handing him the cash and a piece of paper with instructions written on it.'

'And what did it say?'

'It was instructions for the hit. That it was to happen that Sunday night at eleven on Bath Lane, the entrance just down from the Film Theatre. Clearly, Millar knew it would be quiet then.'

'What, and Charlie just showed up and shot a guy standing there?'

'Hold your horses, will you, I'm not finished yet,' said Davy, raising his hands. 'It was agreed the hit would be confirmed half an hour before it took place. And the caller would use a code word to confirm it.'

'But even so, how would they know they'd got the right guy?' asked Fulton.

'It was agreed that the guy would be wearing a sprig of something on his lapel – like you do at weddings.'

'And was he?'

'Aye, but it was a sprig of juniper.'

'Juniper? Who wears juniper to a wedding?'

'No one, that's the point. Apparently in Russian folk tradition, they'd use juniper to chase away evil spirits at funerals. That sick bastard knew he was going to die.'

'And what was the second thing then,' asked Fulton.

'A Curly Wurly.'

'A what?'

'A Curly Wurly, you know, the chocolate bar. Millar gave Charlie a Curly Wurly in a plastic bag.'

'Christ, so you're telling me the fate of the country hung on a Curly Wurly?'

'I am. It's beyond surreal.'

Davy cupped his hands and blew a couple of short, hard breaths on them. He rubbed them together vigorously, trying to generate some warmth. The cold, clear sky was beginning to darken as the sun started slipping beyond the horizon, silhouetting the two men. Davy would normally have been bursting with bravado at a moment like this but instead he was staring off across the moors.

'Chin up, big man, you've done a great job. What's the matter?' asked Fulton.

'Ah, nothing.' Davy unzipped his puffer jacket and pulled out a manila envelope.

'This is for you,' he said, handing it to Fulton.

'What is it?'

'It's the police report.'

'What does it say?' asked Fulton, peeking into the envelope.

'Everything I just said. I wrote it up.'

'When are you guys going to make it public?'

Davy looked away again. He sighed. 'After the referendum.'

'What,' said Fulton. 'What are you on about?'

'After the referendum. You heard me right the first time. Larbert wants to sit on it, says it could spark trouble before the vote.'

'But he can't do that. People won't know the truth before the referendum.'

'And since when has that ever been an issue? The public safety argument is just complete and utter bullshit. They just don't want to give the nationalists a bump a day before the vote.'

'But that's outrageous.'

'Aye, but that's not going to happen, is it, because you're going to get it published. Your editor will jump at it, no?'

Fulton didn't respond. He kicked a clump of heather.

'What?' said Davy, growing irritated. 'What's the problem?'

'I just don't know if he'll publish it.'

'What do you mean? He's a journalist, isn't he?'

'Sort of. But he's super cautious.'

'And . . .'

'And what?'

'He's English.'

'What's that got to do with anything?' said Davy, looking aghast. His cheeks were growing redder, and it wasn't because of the cold.

'Nothing, I suppose,' said Fulton, feeling embarrassed.

'Look, sometimes those guys surprise you, even the posh ones. This needs to be published.'

'I know, I know,' said Fulton, exhaling deeply. 'Let me handle it. I'll fix it. It's just . . .'

Davy placed both his hands on Fulton's shoulders. 'Listen, mate,' he said, giving him a good shake. 'You need to get it together. What's happening is wrong. I've got no love for that Susan Ward. But whatever she's done, she isn't a murderer. She has nothing to do with any of this. Nobody deserves that hanging over their head – the people need to know the truth.'

'Davy, I said it's a problem. I didn't say I couldn't fix it. When have I ever let you down?'

'Okay,' said Davy. 'I hear you. Now let's get it done.' He began walking along the track back towards the visitor centre. When he was a short distance away, he turned and hollered, 'You coming?'

'Give me a minute,' replied Fulton.

Davy threw up his hands in the air in protest, shook his head, and continued walking.

Fulton knew he needed to get the story published but how exactly? Bellington was a coward, not the best quality in a newspaper editor. He stared out at the heather and listened to the gentle but firm whoosh from the blades as they harnessed the winds blowing in from the North Atlantic. He thought about how life comes down to these moments, how we're pulled along by currents we cannot resist. He lifted his head and looked across the bleak landscape. He was only a couple of miles from where Clare and Daniel had died, where his life as he'd known it came to an end. He closed his eyes for a few seconds and saw their faces. He felt something inside him collapse. The wind picked up. He started to hear soft whispers from the past. Slowly, they started to make sense and, finally, Fulton remembered what he and Clare had argued about that night in the car.

Chapter 40

Chris Bellington stared hard at Fulton. He twirled a Mont Blanc pen in his fingers. Fulton wasn't sure whether Chris was being defensive or struggling to find the words – probably both.

'What?' asked Fulton, unable to hide the annoyance in his voice. He'd had enough of all the pussyfooting around.

'We're going to need a second source on this,' said Chris impassively. 'I can't go out to bat on a story of this magnitude without a second source.'

Fulton's shoulders sank as if the scaffolding holding up a building had suddenly collapsed. He rubbed his eyes, which were red with tiredness.

'If we don't run this story, you might as well sack everyone and shut up shop here and now, because otherwise this whole set-up is a lie. We're pretending to be journalists. If journalists won't tell the truth, then who will? If we don't stand up to the establishment, then we *are* the establishment. And I'll tell you something, that's not me, that's not what I signed up to.'

'Is your diatribe finished?' asked Chris, with more pushback than Fulton expected. 'I need ten minutes.'

'Ten minutes so you can bury it good and proper like you did last time?'

Chris glared at him. He didn't want to get drawn into another one of their dogfights.

'Fulton, not now, not tonight. You're not the only one who's under the cosh. Remember who's in charge here. I'm going to have to make a few phone calls. We can run this; I just need to be sure.'

It was a politician's plea, thought Fulton, on the surface very measured and rational but designed to fob you off. He stood up. Chris looked at him expectantly but he turned away in disgust. Leaving the office, he whispered a single word under his breath.

'What did you say?'

'Nothing,' replied Fulton, closing the door of the glass-walled cubicle. As he turned to walk away both men eyed each other warily, not wanting to make a move until the other was out of sight.

The office was empty apart from a couple of guys from the social media team. Fulton didn't know their names. They were so young he referred to them as the acne crew. Fulton slouched over to his desk and pulled open his top drawer. Under a mound of brochures, briefings and business cards he found his stash. He took out the packet of Marlboro Lights and opened it. There were seven cigarettes and a cheap purple lighter. Fulton pulled out a cigarette and stuck it between his lips. He lit the cigarette, taking a deep draw. He turned so he was facing in the direction of Chris's office, shaped his mouth as if was making an 'O' and blew three perfect smoke rings. Fulton watched as they floated across the office, the smoke rings expanding and then quivering, before breaking apart. He walked to the fire escape, pushed it open and sat down on the cold stairs. He pushed out another couple of smoke rings and watched them collapse against the wall. Fulton wasn't surprised by what Chris had said but on these stories there is never a second source. It's all or nothing, and Fulton knew Chris was a nothing man. Then it hit him.

'Janet,' Fulton said slowly to himself. 'Rottweiler Rae will run the story.'

How could he have forgotten? She wanted to start her new website with a bang – and you didn't get much more explosive than this.

Fulton took a quick final draw of the cigarette before stubbing it out on the stairs. He'd left his mobile on his desk. He pulled himself up on the banister only to see the fire exit opening.

It was Chris. 'I've been looking all over for you,' he said. 'Come on, we've got a story to write.'

'Sorry?'

'We're going to publish the police report, so let's get moving before I change my mind.'

Fulton was in a daze as he followed Chris back to his office. He couldn't believe what he was hearing.

'Let's bash it out together,' said Chris, swivelling in his chair. 'You dictate. Let's get a few paras out first and then we can build up the story later.'

Fulton stood behind Chris, the words falling effortlessly out of him. He'd crafted thousands of stories over the years but he knew his entire career would come down to a handful of sentences. Chris read aloud the four short paragraphs. He suggested one change, which Fulton agreed improved the copy.

'Happy?' asked Chris, glancing up from his chair.

'Aye.'

'We're good to go then,' said Chris, dragging the arrow over to the website's publishing software icon with his mouse. He double-clicked on it and copied and pasted the text into a box. He did one final silent read through for any typos. His cursor hovered over the publish button. He clicked it.

'This changes everything,' he said, with no emotion. He brought up the *Siren*'s homepage. 'The story's gone live.'

Fulton stared at the story on the screen – EXCLUSIVE: JOHN MILLAR ORDERED HIT ON HIMSELF – before collapsing onto the brown leather couch. He was exhausted. He glanced up at Chris. Now that the story had been published, neither man quite knew what to say.

'I got you wrong,' said Fulton, finally, his voice cracking ever so slightly. 'I got you very wrong and I'm sorry for that.'

'It's okay,' said Chris. 'Having a chip on your shoulder is part of what makes you a great reporter, but sometimes you've got to put it in your pocket.'

Chapter 41

Larbert was leaning back in his chair, feet up on the desk. He had briefly closed his eyes. The door burst open. For a few seconds, the police chief was disorientated by the commotion in his office. But slowly he realised the strange figure standing on the other side of his desk was the MI5 man, his right eye twitching like an old-fashioned cinema projector.

'Have you seen this?' asked Neil, so quietly it was almost as if the words were burning his throat. He kept jabbing at his phone. 'Have you seen it?'

'Seen what?' asked Larbert. 'I've no idea what you're on about.'

Simpson held up his phone. 'The story that's just gone live on the *Siren*'s website.' He began reading aloud in staccato fashion. 'Breaking news . . . a bombshell police report . . . reveals that murdered civil servant had in fact ordered his own assassination.' With each sentence he was thrown deeper into despair. 'The stunning revelation was disclosed in a Police Scotland report, which has been leaked,' he shifted his gaze from the screen and glared at Larbert, 'I repeat, leaked to this newspaper. The extraordinary development is likely to bolster the chances of the nationalists ahead of tomorrow's historic independence referendum . . .'

Neil lunged forward, slamming his fist down on Larbert's desk so hard that a glass of water tipped over and spilled its contents. Larbert didn't flinch. He rose to his feet, never taking his eyes off Neil. It was how he dealt with a suspect waving a gun about.

'You really need to calm down, Neil. Have a seat and let's talk.'

'Who leaked the report?' demanded Neil with a furious, twisted intensity. 'Who leaked it?'

'Honestly, I don't know.'

'Was it that fat lump Davy Bryant? Where is he? Get him in here.'

'What good would that do?'

'Why are you defending him?'

'I'm not. I'm just saying that you can't accuse someone without evidence.'

'Oh, come on. You and your procedures,' cried Neil. 'Don't you know what's at stake here? The United Kingdom, that's what. And this report' – he started waving his phone again – 'means the nationalists are back in the game. It gives them a chance of winning.'

'Calm down, Neil. It's not over yet – not all is lost. People have yet to vote but at least they know the truth now. And at least the result will not be tarnished by allegations of a police cover-up. Could you imagine how people would have reacted if they thought we'd buried the report?'

Neil was gulping down air as he listened. 'It was you who leaked it, wasn't it?' His body recoiled at the revelation. 'It was you.'

'I swear to God I didn't leak it,' said Larbert, with calm authority.

The certainty Neil felt just a few seconds ago evaporated. He was sure that Larbert wouldn't lie to his face. He saw Larbert as a guy who played by the rules even when everyone around him was cheating. Larbert was a man who confused righteousness with actually being right.

'But . . .'

'But what?' said Neil, struggling to get his words out. '*But what?*'

Larbert wiped his mouth with the back of his hand. 'But I did confirm to the editor that the report was genuine and there was nothing we could do to stop them from publishing it.'

'Why?' asked Neil, in astonishment. He stumbled back a couple of steps. 'Why would you do that?'

'Because we were making a mistake. We were wrong to leak the video in the first place. I was weak and I will forever regret going along with the decision. And I wasn't going to make the same mistake with the police report. You should never have tried to bury it. I was against it from the outset.'

'But the Union, Ian . . . What about the future of the country?' cried Neil.

'You can't build a democracy on lies.'

'What are you on about? The truth is all of us will be far better off in the Union.'

'Maybe if you'd done a better job in Iraq, more people would believe you.'

'What's Iraq got to do with Scotland?' asked Neil, bewildered.

'It's got everything to do with it. You don't get it, do you?'

'Don't get what?'

'Don't get the fact that two decades on most folk don't trust people like you.'

'But it was the assessment of every intelligence agency in the world that Saddam Hussein had weapons of mass destruction. It was—'

'Neil,' said Larbert, interrupting him. 'That may well have been the case but you didn't find any weapons, did you? You were wrong, and young boys died because you were wrong. My nephew died because you were wrong. He was twenty-one. He had his whole life in front of him. A country was destroyed because you were wrong. And not only did you screw it up, what makes it even worse is that not a single person took responsibility for it – no one. You were all too busy covering your own backs. And now you expect it to be all hunky-dory after the fact. You think you're so bloody smart with your fancy degree but I'll tell you something, Neil – and you don't need to be an MI5 officer to figure this out – that's not the way the world works. There are consequences and we're living with those consequences now. You waltz in here and think you can string me along, string the country along – well, you can't.'

Neil slumped down on a seat.

'And just to be clear, I had authority to confirm that report.'

'What are you talking about? Everything was supposed to go through me.'

'Well, it turns out that almost no one in your agency shared your view – including your boss.'

'You spoke to her?'

'An hour ago. She said your behaviour was completely reprehensible and unauthorised. She told me to confirm the leak to the newspaper and she also ordered me to release the full police report immediately. It was signed off by Downing Street.'

Larbert picked up the phone on his desk. 'He's here. Send them up.'

A heavy silence hung between the two men until Neil finally spoke.

'Despite what you may think, this was never about politics for me,' he said quietly. 'It was a question of patriotism, and there's a huge difference. Like your nephew, Millar died because he believed our country was worth defending but I suspect you're too spineless to ever understand that kind of sacrifice.'

Larbert tapped his index finger several times on the desk. He raised his head, gazed at Neil for a while, and slowly said, 'You might be right.'

There was a knock at the door.

'Come in.'

Two suited men walked into the office.

'He's all yours now,' Larbert said, getting to his feet.

Chapter 42

Fulton sauntered through Glasgow's Southside, savouring the warmth of the sun on his face. He was wearing his Ray-Bans and his jacket was slung over one shoulder. Fulton smiled at a kid who was furiously licking a cone, trying and failing to staunch the streams of melted ice cream running down his fingers. He always enjoyed the early calm of a voting day when reason appeared to prevail. It was still hours away from the final results and then, Fulton was sure of it, the rancour that had characterised so much of the campaign would raise its ugly head.

At Shawlands Cross, Fulton slipped into the Granary. The pub had been revamped since his last visit – an aquamarine paint job, a black-and-white tiled floor and seating booths cornered off by oak panels. Davy was sitting on a leather bar-stool with a pint of Tennent's and a cheeky Bacardi and Coke keeping it company. Fulton patted him on the shoulder. 'It's certainly an improvement on the Empire.'

'Aye, they serve food you can actually eat,' said Davy, with a grin. 'What you drinking?'

'Diet Coke.'

'Aw, c'mon.'

'Diet Coke.'

'Barman,' said Davy, to a hungover-looking teenager sitting on a keg, 'a Diet Coke for the lady here.'

The barman nodded and after serving up the drink returned to his perch.

'Thankfully, all's quiet on the Scottish front,' said Fulton.

'Long may it last.'

'Amen to that,' replied Fulton, reaching for his drink. 'Cheers,' he said, holding his glass up to Davy. 'Who would have thought it would be the two of us in the eye of the storm?'

'Do you know what I still don't get, though,' said Davy, 'is what sort of man arranges to get his own brains blown out. I mean that's a whole level of mental—'

'He lost a kid when he was posted in Russia,' Fulton interrupted.

'How do you know that?' asked Davy, the pint glass paused at his lips.

'Someone who was close to him told me.'

'And this source of yours, did he tell you anything else?'

'Aye. He said Millar was never right after that and then he got the boot from MI6.'

'Talk about kicking a man when he's down.'

'But do you know what was really strange?'

'What?'

'The guy took out a book and made me read from it for him.'

'Clearly knew your number,' said Davy, giving him a wink.

'It was a quote from Thomas Carlyle,' said Fulton.

'Tommy who?'

'A famous Scottish philosopher – long dead. Anyway, the quote was: "No great man lives in vain. The history of the world is the biography of great men."'

'And what's your point, caller?' asked Davy, a touch exasperated by this round-the-houses conversation.

'Millar loved everything Thomas Carlyle ever wrote. He

always wanted to be a great man and by getting himself killed he thought he could become a hero by saving the Union.'

'So, an utterly deluded prick,' said Davy, before taking a swig of his lager. 'We bloody nailed him in the end.'

'But he might yet do it and he's still in our heads,' said Fulton.

'Maybe yours, but not mine.'

'What if he meant to get caught?'

'Seriously, Fulton, have you been smoking the wacky baccy? Do you honestly believe that John Millar thought the two of us would work together, discover the truth, and then persuade Lord Snooty to publish the report? That this was somehow his grand plan all along?'

'Might be.'

'Gie us twenty then.'

Fulton held out his hands in front of him and mimicked doing press-ups. They both started laughing when he reached about a dozen. 'Give us a break,' said Davy, taking a large gulp of his drink. He ripped open a packet of peanuts too enthusiastically, sending half of them scattering over the floor. He pushed the ones that had landed on the bar into a little pile and began popping them into his mouth. 'Do you know what, though? John Millar sure put the country through the wringer and it brought out the worst in us. The Nats are blind to reality,' continued Davy. 'Love or hate the English, we've got to trade with them. And I like Scousers and Geordies and Brummies – even the Mancs. They're good honest folk in working-class cities. I know the Prime Minister's a lying buffoon, but if I've got any politics, it's muddle through with as many folk as possible – families need to stick together.'

'Says the man who's been divorced. Twice.'

'Aye, well, nobody's perfect. But it's all swings and

roundabouts – if it ain't your bloody Nigels and Jeffreys, it will be your Anguses and Torquils soon enough. Since when did a fresh start mean a different ending?'

'So, you voted to stay in the Union?'

'How did you guess?' said Davy, chuckling.

The pub's doors were wedged open and the sound of traffic washed over them. They both took a few sips of their drinks.

'You voted yet?' asked Davy.

'No.'

'What do you mean? You've only got a few hours left.'

'I don't vote.'

'What? *Never*?' said Davy, so loudly that he would have drawn stares if there had been anyone else in the pub.

'No.'

'How come?'

'I guess,' said Fulton, swirling the liquid in his glass, 'I've never really felt part of it.'

'Jeez,' said Davy. 'You've always been special, Fulton, I'll give you that. You're the only boy I ever knew that carried a book in their boot bag.'

They both laughed at the memory. Davy gulped down the remainder of his lager. He tapped his empty pint glass. 'Another one?' He saw Fulton hesitate. 'C'mon, another one for the road. Go crazy. Live life on the edge.'

'Honestly, I'd love to,' replied Fulton, sliding off his stool, 'but I really need to get moving. Alana just got home.'

Chapter 43

By the time Fulton got the number 4A bus back to Clarkston, Alana was in the shower belting out songs at the top of her voice. It made him smile – his daughter could hold a tune. She was getting ready for a date. Fulton now knew his name. Darren – the lad who hadn't been able to get out the house fast enough the week before. The teenagers were heading to a late showing at the cinema on the Quay.

In the kitchen, Fulton took a serving plate out of the dishwasher. He opened the cupboard door beside the sink and pushed the heavy cast-iron casserole dish further back to make some space. Its lid slid off. He was surprised to see what looked like a quarter bottle of vodka. He pulled it out. He unscrewed the cap and sniffed. Definitely vodka. I could kill her, he thought. He poured the remains of the bottle down the sink. He grabbed a handful of almonds and settled on the sofa. Should I ground her? Say she can't go to the cinema tonight? Fulton sighed. He really didn't want to have a fight on her first night back.

Fulton heard shouting from upstairs. It was muffled, but Alana must have been on the phone and she wasn't holding back. It went quiet. Fulton wondered whether he should check on her. But after a minute, he heard footsteps marching down the stairs.

'I'm not going out,' declared Alana, sweeping into the living room in her black dressing gown.

'Why not?'

'He says he's busy, says he needs to go out with his pals.'

'You all right?'

Alana's bottom lip started to tremble. A tear trickled down her cheek, creating a muddy stream of mascara.

'Come here, baby,' pleaded Fulton, holding up his arms. 'Come here. He doesn't deserve you.'

She hesitated at first before curling up on the sofa and laying her head in his lap. Fulton gently stroked her hair. He hadn't done it for years – his little girl, his love, his life.

'You're turning into a beautiful young woman,' said Fulton softly. Alana stopped sniffling and smiled as she looked up him. 'And you're bolshie as well. I like it.' She pulled her face in mock horror as if to say, who me? She sat upright on the sofa and touched one of her diamond stud earrings.

'When did you give these to Mum?'

'I gave them to her after Daniel was born – one for each of you.'

She shut her eyes. 'I miss them.'

'I do too,' said Fulton. He chewed his lip, contemplated not saying it, but when would be the right time?

'Alana, there's something I need to tell you.'

'What, Dad?'

'It's about that night.'

Alana stared at her hands. 'What about it?'

'We were arguing,' said Fulton quietly. He took a deep breath. 'I wasn't concentrating on the road . . . Your mum was saying she wanted to leave me—'

'Dad, please, just stop,' said Alana. Fulton looked at her in shock. 'I don't need to know . . . I know you loved her . . . and it's all in the past. We need to move on. It's not what Mum would have wanted for us. We need to live our lives. I think about her and Daniel every day, but you know what, Dad, I don't cry any more. I smile when I see their faces.'

Alana only stopped when her father broke down. She felt guilty. 'Come here, daftie. Don't cry,' she said as she hugged him, the tears streaming down his cheeks. At first, he was a stiff, unresponsive lump but then he loosened up and fully embraced her.

'You're the best dad I could ever have hoped for,' Alana whispered in his ear. 'I know I'm not always the easiest but I know you'll always be there for me.'

'I'm sorry, Alana. I'm just so sorry for everything.'

'It's okay, Dad. It's all going to be okay.'

Fulton didn't know how long they clung to each other. But he felt her tenderness seeping into him. Eventually, Alana pulled away and kissed him gently on the forehead.

'So, are we going to stay up and watch?' she asked.

'Watch what?'

'The results! It was the only thing we were talking about at school – your story. I was so proud of you. Now, come on, let's watch it all. Where's the remote?'

'Eh, I don't know.'

They patted the parts of the sofa closest to them. They stood up to check they weren't sitting on it. No luck. They pulled up all the sofa cushions only for Alana to spot it on the windowsill. They were both laughing as they pushed the cushions back into place. Fulton grabbed the remote and sat beside Alana. This was his domain. He hit various buttons but struggled to find the right channel.

'You're hopeless! Give it here,' said Alana, teasing her father. He handed it over. She found the BBC within seconds.

She pulled her knees up onto the sofa and leaned into her dad, her head resting just below his chin.

On the screen, a handsome, silver-haired man with a soft Borders accent was presenting the referendum coverage from a specially built studio in Edinburgh. The Scottish Parliament was lit up behind him.

'The polls have now closed,' he announced. 'Turnout was an astonishing eighty-five point six per cent, the highest on record for any Scottish vote. This is a truly historic day on which people have had their say after a tumultuous political campaign, unprecedented in our modern history. The official results are still hours away . . .'

'But based on exit polls, we can now predict that Scotland has voted to—'

Acknowledgements

The idea for this book was first planted after reading David Grann's brilliant article 'A Murder Foretold' in *The New Yorker* almost a decade ago. It was only years later that I finally started committing words to the page.

From the outset, Paul Fielder's advice kept me honest. I was also given great support by Mark Leggatt, Adam Brookes, John Sweeney, Paul Hanington and Ed O'Loughlin who all journeyed down the same road long before me.

I'd like to thank my colleagues and friends Quentin Sommerville, Michael Bristow, Chris Watson, Susie Forrest, Joanne Cayford, Patrick Hamilton, Melanie Ward, Karamagi Rujumba, John Lynch, Steven Cree and Mrs Russell who all read early drafts and whose suggestions made for a far better book. I also want to thank Nik Millard, Melanie Marshall, Cara Swift, Eloise Alanna, Firle Davies, Colm O'Molloy, Lee Durant, Wietske Burema and Dave Bull for all their support and insights over the years.

Perhaps my biggest break was landing Jon Wood as an agent – a brilliant editorial mind who kept pushing me in the best way possible. Thank you also to his assistant, Safae El-Ouahabi. I was privileged to work with Alison Rae and James Crawford who did a fabulous job in marshalling the book from manuscript to finished product. Huge thanks to the rest of the team at Polygon as well.

Most of this book was written in coffee shops across Beirut, a city that I once called home and miss every day. The only reason I ever went to live in the Middle East was because my mum and dad encouraged me to pursue my dreams. They, like my sister Susan and twin brother Stewart, have always been there for me. This thriller would never have happened without them.

Finally, this book is for my beautiful wife, Arpan, who has been at my side as we travelled the world. And, of course, Ayan, our son – and our greatest story. I love you both so much.

M.P.
January 2023